SARA WOODS

TRUSTED LIKE THE FOX

S ara Woods, the pen name of Eileen Mary Lana Hutton Bowen
Judd, was born in 1916 in Bradford, Yorkshire. She was the
daughter of Francis Burton Hutton, a garage proprietor and Sara
Roberta Woods, the daughter of a buyer for an engineering firm.

In 1946 she married electrical engineer Anthony George Bowen
Judd. Following a dozen years of farming in rural Yorkshire, the couple
moved to Halifax, Nova Scotia, Canada in 1958, where Sara began her
prolific mystery writing career. She became well-known for her detective
series featuring canny barrister Antony Maitland—a character inspired
by her beloved older brother, Antony Woods Hutton, a promising young
solicitor who was tragically killed in 1941 at the age of 33 when as a Royal
Air Force pilot in the Second World War his plane was shot down during
action in Egypt.

Sara Woods' detective novels were celebrated for their intricate
plots and the authenticity of their courtroom settings and they garnered
a longtime, loyal readership. Sara passed away at the age of 69 on
November 6, 1985, leaving behind her a rich legacy of four dozen Antony
Maitland mysteries.

ANTONY MAITLAND MYSTERIES

Bloody Instructions 196
Malice Domestic 1962
The Taste of Fears/The Third Encounter 1963
Error of the Moon 1963
Trusted Like the Fox 1964

This Little Measure 1964
The Windy Side of the Law 1965
Though I Know She Lies 1965
Enter Certain Murderers 1966
Let's Choose Executors 1966

The Case Is Altered 1967
And Shame the Devil 1967
Knives Have Edges 1968
Past Praying For 1968
Tarry and be Hanged 1969

An Improbable Fiction 1970
Serpent's Tooth 1971
The Knavish Crows 1971
They Love Not Poison 1972
Yet She Must Die 1973

Enter the Corpse 1973
Done to Death 1974
A Show of Violence 1975
My Life Is Done 1976
The Law's Delay 1977

A Thief or Two 1977
Exit Murderer 1978
This Fatal Writ 1979
Proceed to Judgement 1979
They Stay for Death 1980

Weep for Her 1980
Dearest Enemy 1981
Cry Guilty 1981
Enter a Gentlewoman 1982
Villains by Necessity 1982

SARA WOODS

TRUSTED LIKE THE FOX

With an introduction
by Curtis Evans

DEAN STREET PRESS

INTRODUCTION BY CURTIS EVANS

As the decade of the 1960s approached, the work of the quartet of English Crime Queens most associated with the between-the-wars Golden Age of Detective Fiction—Agatha Christie, Dorothy L. Sayers, Margery Allingham and Ngaio Marsh—still seemed to be going relatively strong. To be sure, one of these monarchs of murder, Dorothy L. Sayers, was now deceased, having expired in the last month of 1957 at the age of sixty-four. A week before Christmas newspapers that year reported that Sayers, like a character out of one her own detective novels, had been discovered by her gardener lying dead in the hall at the foot of her staircase at "her country home in Witham." She had just returned from a Christmas shopping excursion in London and had seemed perfectly well, according to her secretary. The cause of death, however, was neither lethal letter opener nor curare-tipped dart nor a simple sharp shove in the back, but rather—more prosaically if no less tragically—coronary thrombosis.

At her death Sayers in fact had not published a new Lord Peter Wimsey detective novel for two decades. In the 1950s one American newspaper reviewer complained that in the years after World War Two, "Sayers' books simply disappeared from bookstalls. They became practically collector's items, with your only chance of obtaining one a criminal chance, either by the use of blackmail or of theft." Two years before her death in 1955, however, American publisher Harper and Brothers began reprinting all of Sayers' Lord Peter mystery fiction in hardcover in an attractive uniform edition, a project which continued for a few years after her death. By 1958, it was being reported that Wimsey's "old friends are being joined by hosts of new ones who are refreshing themselves with a whole series of detective stories without even the mention of a half-clad femme fatale or a trenchcoated sleuth with a cigarette addiction." Sayers has not been out of print since, either in the United States or the United Kingdom.

Although Dorothy L. had left her subjects for a rather more peaceable world, Agatha Christie, Margery Allingham and Ngaio Marsh still lived on to ply the murder and mayhem trade in the material world. Allingham had slowed down, producing one of her Albert Campion mysteries only every three or four years. *Hide My Eyes* appeared in 1958, three years after *The Estate of the Beckoning Lady*, though five years elapsed before *The China Governess* made it into print in 1963. Christie and Marsh, on the other hand, were more prolific. Marsh managed a Roderick Alleyn detective novel every two or three years. *False Scent* appeared in 1959, followed by *Hand in Glove* in 1962. Old reliable herself, Agatha Christie, almost always had a new detective novel, a so-called "Christie for Christmas," ready for the enjoyment of her readers, sometimes an Hercule Poirot (*Cat among the Pigeons*, 1959), sometimes a Jane Marple (*4.50 from Paddington*, 1957), sometimes something non-series (*Ordeal by Innocence*, 1958). With Christie murder was like a box of poisoned chocolates: you never knew with her quite what you were going to get.

Yet, with upstart Time observing no deference to stately royalty, the original crime queens were undeniably going grey, as it were, like everyone else in their turn-of-the-century generation. In 1960 Christie would turn seventy, Marsh sixty-five and Allingham fifty-six. The ailing Allingham, though the youngest of the group, would follow Sayers into life's surcease in 1966, passing at the age of sixty-two. Her husband briefly continued the Campion series until his own untimely death, just two books into the continuation, in 1969. Christie lived on until 1976, but her crime writing suffered a decline in the Sixties, one which sharply accelerated in the early Seventies, with such muddled opuses as *Passenger to Frankfurt* (1970) and *Postern of Fate* (1973). Only Ngaio Marsh kept up a pretty uniform standard with her crime fiction until her own death in 1982.

Although it was evident in the Sixties that the crime queens could not go on forever, the happy news in that decade was that there were new crime queens—ladies in waiting, one might say—in the offing. All of these women wrote detective novels in the classic vein, with puzzles, precise writing and series sleuths. First off was Patricia Moyes (1923-2000), whose Inspector Henry Tibbett series was introduced with *Dead Men Don't Ski* in 1959 and ran until 1993.

PD James (1920-2014) and Ruth Rendell (1930-2015), the most lastingly famous of the second generation of British Crime Queens of what we might term the Silver Age of detective fiction (around 1960 to 2000), debuted their Adam Dalgliesh and Reginald Wexford mysteries series in 1962 and 1964 respectively with *Cover Her Face* and *From Doon with Death*. These critically lauded series respectively ran until 2008 and 2013, to much acclaim.

The series mysteries of Silver Age Crime Queens Moyes, James and Rendell have stayed in print since the authors first became well-known back in the 1960s. Surprisingly, however, the work of another praised, prolific, second-generation British crime queen, a close contemporary of the fatal female trio discussed above, was out of print for more than thirty-five years. This is Anglo-Canadian writer Sara Woods (Eileen Mary Lana Hutton Bowen Judd, May 7, 1916-November 6, 1985).

Sara Woods' forty-eight Antony Maitland detective novels appeared over a quarter century between 1962 and 1987. (The last three of them were posthumously published.) That is an average of almost two books a year for twenty-five years. Not long after moving to Canada in 1958 with Anthony George Bowen Judd, her electrical engineer husband of a dozen years, Woods—a native Yorkshirewoman and Catholic who had been educated in the early 1930s at the Convent of the Sacred Heart in Filey, a seaside town in Yorkshire—began writing the first of her Antony Maitland novels, *Bloody Instructions*.

Over the next few years, probably 1959-61, Woods followed *Bloody Instructions* with three additional titles: *Malice Domestic*, *The Third Encounter* (*The Taste of Fears* in the UK) and *Error of the Moon*. Finally satisfied with her work, Woods, then forty-five years old, in late 1961 packaged a quartet of murderous manuscripts into a deadly detective fiction parcel and posted them to prestigious English publisher Collins' Crime Club mystery imprint, the impressive stable which included both Agatha Christie and Ngaio Marsh. Collins accepted all four of Woods' manuscripts with alacrity, sending the nascent author a cablegram with the happy tidings, which Woods received while sitting at breakfast with her husband early one morning. By this time the author was writing a fifth Antony Maitland adventure, *Trusted like the Fox*, which before the end of the year she finished and sent to Collins, who promptly accepted it with the same enthusiasm as they had her previous four works.

"We've got a bonanza out there in Nova Scotia," boasted Crime Club editor George Hardinge (Lord Hardinge of Penshurst) of Woods, who was seemingly a one-woman crime fiction factory. Despite its near two-hundred-year association with the British Empire and Commonwealth, Canada for whatever reason had not proved a fertile native ground for mystery writers, with some very notable exceptions like Margaret Millar and Ross Macdonald, a criminous writing couple who had moved to the States before commencing their prominent crime fiction careers. Collins confided to newspapers that already they were thinking of their new Canadian transplant acquisition "in terms of those formidable female giants of the field, Agatha Christie and Ngaio Marsh."

George Hardinge warmly invited Woods to pay a visit to London offices, where they could discuss plans for her enticing future and introduce her to the United Kingdom's mystery reading public. On her return to her native country in February 1962, Collins feted Woods, warmly welcoming her, as the Guardian reported, "to their cosy (and very talkative) circle." Collins published *Bloody Instructions* in June 1962, thus preceding into print by six months P. D. James, who was over at Faber & Faber, with her own first detective novel. "With pride and enthusiasm" Collins heralded their new find as an injection of new, rich blood into the somewhat decayed corpus of classic crime fiction: "The Crime Club confidently introduces a new writer of whom we believe a lot will be heard.... Sara Woods is the pseudonym of a writer who has never had a book of any kind published before. We believe that *Bloody Instructions* introduces an outstanding new writer of detective fiction."

When *Bloody Instructions* appeared in England in June, Francis Iles, aka Anthony Berkeley, the self-professed Golden Age founder of that holy sanctum of classic mystery, the Detection Club, was filled with criminal delight, writing: "The Crime Club is to be congratulated on its discovery of Miss Sara Woods. Her first novel, *Bloody Instructions*, is a most accomplished piece of work: a genuine detective story along classical lines brought up to date, with very human characters, and told with a kind of amused detachment which is most engaging. Altogether, warmly recommended."

It was as if another new crime queen had been ceremoniously crowned by a past master. By this time the industrious Woods was completing a sixth Antony Maitland detective novel, *This Little Measure*. (You may cannily have already deduced that the lady had a great fondness for Shakespearean titles.) In the United States prominent editor Joan Kahn at Harper & Row accepted three of the first five Woods novels for publication in her "novels of suspense" series. Woods made a hit in the States as well, although unsurprisingly she proved most prone to appeal to Anglophile American readers, with her precise prose and pristine puzzle plots, populated by a genteel cast of series characters, complete with a knighted bachelor uncle and his imperious, elderly butler.

Wrote a Yank reviewer of *Bloody Instructions*: "Nicely styled, and enlivened with deft touches of restrained, upper-class British humor, this is a mystery tale likely to please sophisticated whodunnit fans rather than those who favour rough-and-tumble yarns." Observed another: "The characters are real and humorous and oh, so British. Even the murder is committed over a cup of tea." To these enchanted American reviewers, Woods' books seemed almost a throwback to happily remembered pre-war days across the pond, when the Golden Age Crime Queens had first crafted the gloried English detective novel of manners, in which Lord Peter and his suave company of ingenious sleuth-hounds had ruminated about murder over cups of tea and glasses of sherry and nabbed all manner of not-quite-clever-enough crooks in posh art deco flats, crumbling country mansions and quaint Tudor cottages.

*

Sara Woods derived her pseudonym from her mother, Sara Roberta Woods, who passed away the day after Christmas in 1961. She partly based her genteel series detective—attorney Antony Maitland—whom some reviewers dubbed the Perry Mason of English mystery—on a beloved elder brother who had also been named Antony. A promising young solicitor in the London firm of Sir William Charles Crocker, one of England's few genuinely celebrity solicitors, Antony Woods Hutton had tragically died in 1941 at the age of thirty-three when, as an RAF pilot in the Second World War, his plane having been shot down in Egypt. His superior Sir William Crocker likely helped inspire Antony Maitland's renowned barrister uncle, Sir Nicholas Maitland, while dare I suggest that Antony's wife Jenny shared certain aspects with the author herself?

Although Sara Woods was employed for a couple of years in London as a legal secretary in her brother's office, when her brother went off to fight in the conflict's Egyptian theatre, she left the City to work as a bank clerk in Shrewsbury. Before this she and Antony, along with an aunt, Margaret Anne Woods, had lived together at flat three, Kenilworth Lodge on Farnan Road in Streatham. Years later Eileen would derive the "Woods" in her pseudonym Sara Woods from her mother's maiden surname.

After war's end Woods in 1946 wed electrical engineer Anthony George Bowen Judd. For the next dozen years the couple rusticated, operating a series of pig farms in Yorkshire. In 1958 the pair abandoned rural English life, moving across the pond to the city of Halifax, the provincial capital of Nova Scotia, where Tony, whose parents lived in Canada, resumed engineering work and Woods became registrar of St. Mary's University. After establishing herself as a mystery writer, she left her position at St. Mary's in 1964 to devote herself full-time to her crime writing.

Despite the initial fanfare of publicity Collins gave her, Sara Woods in the long run proved a remarkably publicity-shy individual. Over the decades her press interviews came few and far between, though in 1962, when she was launching her crime writing career, she modestly told an interviewer with the Montreal Gazette, when asked about Collins comparing her to Agatha Christie and Ngaio Marsh, "I feel terribly honoured and flattered by this comparison." Another rare newspaper profile of the author marvelled of Woods in the 1980s: "She has no agent. She does not promote herself via the talk show and autograph session circuit."

Today very little is known about the author and her books have been out of print for nearly four decades. Moreover, some of the published information about her is simply incorrect. For example, Woods' birth year has long been given erroneously as 1922, which would make her two years younger than PD James, when in fact she was born in 1916, making her four years older than James, and only four years younger than Silver Age crime writing stalwarts Julian Symons and Michael Gilbert, whose criminal débuts went back to the 1940s.

Thus Sara Woods was forty-six, not forty, when her first detective novel was published. She died in 1985 at age sixty-nine (not sixty-three) and was laid to rest at Niagara-on-the-Lake (where she and her husband had been residing since 1981) in the cemetery of St. Vincent de Paul Roman Catholic Church, the oldest surviving Catholic Church still in use in the province of Ontario. Being such a prolific writer, Woods left three completed Antony Maitland mysteries behind her, which were duly published in hard-cover editions in the UK and US in 1986 and 1987, while at the same time the American paperback publisher Avon reissued over a dozen of her Maitland novels in attractive soft-cover editions with cover art by much-in-demand illustrator Dave Calver. His droll depictions of sundry knifed, strangled, shot and poisoned murder victims combined Eighties pop sensibility with an appreciation of the formal conventions of classic English crime fiction.

Around this time, mystery fiction authority Jacques Barzun declared of Sara Woods (with a backhanded slap at PD James' much-publicized desire to transform the detective story into more of a "credible" mainstream novel): "If critics really put their minds to what they say, they would call Mrs. Woods, and not some other lady, the new Agatha Christie. For here is a writer playing virtuoso variations on a formula without stepping outside a medium range of familiar and respectable existence—no nonsense about turning the tale into symbolism or psychology or 'a true novel'." Back in 1962 the author herself had allowed simply: "I write mysteries to amuse people. I like books about ordinary people in queer circumstances. I don't write detective stories because of any satisfaction from brooding over corpses."

A couple of years after Woods' death in 1985, Jacques Barzun wrote sadly of the late author that the "pleasure she has given will be much missed." Yet unaccountably the publishing world in one of mystery fiction's strangest vanishing acts soon forgot all about Sara Woods. By no means have all vintage mystery fans forgotten her, however, and hopefully with their re-issuance by Dean Street Press, new fans will join the old in enjoying Sara Woods' Antony Maitland mysteries.

*

Published in Britain in June 1962 and in the United States in March of the following year, Sara Woods' debut Anthony Maitland detective novel, *Bloody Instructions*, introduces the three main characters in the series, who would remain through the publication of its final volume, Naked Villainy (which appeared posthumously thirty-five years later in 1987). These are Anthony Maitland (of course), barrister-at-law, a tall, dark man with untidy hair and a thin, intelligent face; his steadfast, curly golden-brown-haired, grey-eyed wife Jenny; and his imposing uncle, handsome, tall and fair-haired, Sir Nicholas Harding, Queen's Counsel of the Inner Temple, London ("one of the really great counsels"). There are as well additional recurring supporting characters, like Mallory and Gibbs, Sir Nicholas' legal clerk and his po-faced butler, not to mention the Scotland Yard men Inspector Sykes and Superintendent Briggs, the latter being Anthony's overbearing police nemesis.

Antony, a Second World War veteran (intelligence) who still suffers from physical impairment to his right arm and shoulder and psychic impairment to his mind (he exhibits a stutter when he becomes angry), serves as junior barrister to his Uncle Nick. He and Jenny -whom he wed during the war in 1943 when she was serving as an ambulance driver—reside with Sir Nicholas in their own quarters at his elegant, formerly bachelor establishment at Kempenfeldt Square. Antony was born in 1921 and in the early quartet of novels he is deemed to be thirty-six or thirty-seven years old, meaning that the events take place in the late 1950s.

Bloody Instructions is a highly traditional British detective novel, with the murder taking place in the first chapter and a sketch plan of the murder premises, drawn by Uncle Nick himself, unveiled in chapter two. The victim of foul play is elderly attorney James Winter, senior partner of "that old-established firm of solicitors" Messrs. Ling, Curtis, Winter and Winter of Bread Court, not more than a five minutes' walk from the Inner

Temple. Antony himself happens to be on the scene when the solicitor is found 'done in'—stabbed in the back—at his desk in his chambers. Winter had not even had time to enjoy his tea, surely a ghastly social faux pas on the part of his murderer.

Police run their eyes over a large number of suspects, including perhaps even Antony himself, but their sights soon settle on leading Shakespearean stage actor Joseph Dowling, whose wife was being represented by Winter in her divorce suit against him. A flamboyant character currently playing Macbeth to a fresh, new Lady Macbeth, Margaret Hamilton (who will appear in the series again), it seems that Dowling even had a dagger at hand before him, as it were, which just may have been the murder weapon. Enter the Maitlands, uncle and nephew, for the defence. Will Uncle Nick's brilliant courtroom tactics and Antony's flair for investigative work and deduction save the day, in this the first recorded of their cases?

As the title implies, the second Maitland mystery, *Malice Domestic*, involves one of those good old intimate family murders, with a list of characters provided for the reader's elucidation. It is a good thing too, for there is a large cast of characters indeed in this novel, largely comprised of various members of the extended Cassell family, headed by old Ambrose Cassell, Managing Director of Cassell & Co., a prominent firm of vintners.

When Ambrose's brother William, Manager of the firm's Lisbon office and its Chief Buyer, returns home for the first time in eighteen years, he arrives just in time for a delightful afternoon tea, followed by his own late evening murder—in his brother's study, no less. Police arrest the victim's great-nephew, Paul Herron, who is found outside the study's open French window with a dazed look on his face and a smoking gun in his hands. Concluding that Paul had a whacking great motive for shooting his Grandfather Ambrose, they believe that the young man has mistaken William for the family patriarch. In the face of the determination of most of his own family, including his grandfather, to have him declared insane and put away in an institution, Paul is defended by the Maitlands— though not without grumbling from Uncle Nick about a case which is overstuffed like a fatally fruity plum pudding with sleep-walking, possible inherited insanity on the part of two different people, two sets of twins and a trio of murders in the past. Huffs Sir Nicholas sarcastically: "In the best storybook tradition, I make no doubt!"

With the next pair of Maitland detective novels, *The Third Encounter* and *Error of the Moon*, Sara Woods effectively merges detective fiction with the espionage thriller, a hugely popular mystery sub-genre in the

Fifties and Sixties, the era of Ian Fleming and John le Carre. *The Third Encounter* is thrilling indeed, as a case of murder becomes entangled with espionage. Initially, Anthony investigates the stocking strangulation of his kindly old friend Dr. Henry Martin, as he and his Uncle Nick are defending Dr. Martin's impecunious scapegrace cousin and heir, whom the police suspect of having committed the dread deed. Along the way, however, Antony gradually begins to suspect that an implacable old enemy from his wartime past has what might be termed a rude Germanic hand in the whole affair.

In this novel we learn about Antony's awful experiences in France during the Second World War and the tragedy which Jenny has suffered in London during the conflict. Reappearing are Inspector Sykes and Superintendent Briggs, the latter "one of the few people he really dislikes," Antony finds just as provoking as ever, with his heavy jaw, bulging forehead and cold blue eyes and his overbearing official manner. Antony is pressed into working surreptitiously with the Secret Intelligence Service, a position which puts him in further conflict with the Yard, which is investigating Dr. Martin's murder. "I'm afraid you may have to resign yourself to the fact that your husband is getting mixed up with that gang of thugs in Whitehall again," Antony ruefully tells Jenny, sounding like a world-weary le Carre character.

Espionage and murder are again the crimes of moment in *Error of the Moon*, Sara Woods' fourth Anthony Maitland detective novel. Moon is the first Maitland mystery which Woods sets in her own native Yorkshire from where, we learn by the by, that Inspector Sykes also hails. The novel concerns murderous goings-on and spying at the Carcroft Works of General Aircraft Limited, located on the lonely moor above the fictional town of Mardingley, about a half hours' drive from Harrogate.

Under what is dubbed the Full Moon Project, research is being conducted at the Works into a new anti-missile missile. A researcher is killed in a hit-and-run "accident" in the parking lot on a foggy, fatal November night and papers related to the missile design are believed to have been compromised. Antony, on account of his doings with Intelligence in *The Third Encounter*, is pressed by representatives from the company to investigate on the scene, in the guise of a new employee with the title of Assistant Company Secretary. Jenny comes along as his wifely "cover," marking the first time in the series where Mrs. Maitland is really in on the ground, as it were, on a case. Sir Nicholas, on the other hand, plays no part in this adventure.

Sara Woods wrote her highly-lauded fifth detective novel, the courtroom mystery *Trusted like the Fox*, in late 1962, meaning that there is a bit of a break between it and the earlier books, which were likely all to have been written in close proximity around 1959-61. In Fox, which is explicitly set in 1962, Antony Maitland has "taken silk," like his distinguished preceptor Uncle Nick, as a Queen's Counsel and performs as lead barrister on his own case. His client is Michael Godson, who stands accused of being in reality the viperous traitor Guy Harland, who two decades earlier stole papers concerning biological weaponry and fled with them to Germany, where he turned them over to the Nazi regime, which later experimented with them most diabolically on a Polish village, producing what today is clinically termed an MCI, or mass casualty event. Although Michael denies being Guy, in court he is identified as the same man by a series of witnesses, including an upright Yorkshire police sergeant by the name of Fell.

The pivotal events in the Guy Harland case took place long ago at a country house, Burnham Towers, in the village of Burnham Green on an October night in 1942. As witnesses undergoing questioning on the stand recall that night, readers might well feel that they are in a wartime Agatha Christie tale (*The Submarine Plans* say), awaiting the entrance of Hercule Poirot. However, the setting of this novel remains mostly confined to the courtroom. There Antony, a knight in silken armor, jousts with Paul Garfield, his forbidding prosecutorial opponent, and tries to temper sardonic asides from Mr. Justice Conroy, the cynical presiding judge. (Sir Nicholas, Jenny and Inspector Sykes make appearances as well.) There are many twists and turns to this teasing tale, including a major revelation a third of the way in and, near the finale, a present-day murder that has a decisive impact on the outcome of Antony's case.

Curtis Evans

"For treason is but *trusted like the fox*, Who, ne'er so tame, so cherish'd, and lock'd up, Will have a wild trick of his ancestors. Look how we can, or sad or merrily, Interpretation will misquote our looks."

KING HENRY IV, part i, v, ii.

The Case for the Prosecution

CHAPTER 1

TUESDAY, the first day of the trial

It was stuffy in the courtroom, the Judge—who had a morbid fear of draughts—having ordered some time since the closing of any window that might conceivably be guilty of encouraging a cross-current of air. The shafts of dusty sunlight that slanted into the room tantalised with the thought of a different world outside: of a mellow October day gilding St. Paul's dome and the buildings on the north side of Ludgate Hill; striking—more pertinently— an answering gleam from Justice's scales above the Old Bailey. In the shadow of the building the overflow of spectators still surged hopefully; inside, their more fortunate neighbours, who had managed to scramble into the public gallery, were for the most part congratulating themselves on their luck; though one or two had begun to wilt under the combined onslaught of the heat and the severity of the looks which the Judge directed at them from time to time.

Mr. Justice Conroy was short and inclined to stoutness; and despite the dignity of wig and robe displayed to the court a cherubic cast of countenance. In this appearances were, perhaps, misleading; more than one of the Counsel who had appeared before him since he was raised to the bench would have maintained, and heatedly, that his looks belied him. However that might be, he was not the man to be impressed by the fact that the case he was trying seemed to have turned itself into a *cause célèbre*. Certainly it could not be expected to affect his handling of the matter, and if the public wished to be present in his court, the public must realise that there were certain standards of conduct . . .

But the crowd seemed to be orderly enough, and he might turn his attention with propriety to more important matters. Counsel for the Crown was well into his opening address: a man of medium height, almost handsome in spite of a bony, enquiring, over-prominent nose. He was famous for his careful mastery of detail; but if his tones held sometimes too much of the pedagogue, it did not seem that juries found this distasteful. A formidable man, Paul Garfield . . . altogether, the Judge reflected, the trial promised to be of some interest, a sort of Tichborne case in reverse.

The prisoner now, Godson . . . Harland . . . whatever his name really was; at first glance he might be dismissed as an insignificant-looking fellow, but take a second look . . . not a nonentity, after all, definitely not a nonentity. A quiet man, slightly built, with fair, straight hair and a steady look about him. But nervous, thought the Judge, noting shrewdly the tight-clamped lips, and the quick involuntary movements he made from time to time. Which was natural enough; for Garfield, in full flight now, could not make good hearing for the man who was accused.

"The prisoner has lived for the past thirteen or fourteen years at Brightsea, and has been known by the name of Godson—Michael Godson, a photographer. This fact is undoubted, we admit it freely. But it is the Crown's contention—and I shall presently bring evidence to support it— that he is in fact Guy Harland." His pause was impressive; the jury were attentive, even in the gallery all signs of restlessness seemed to have died away.

"Now, Guy Harland, as you will hear, was arrested in the year 1942 for a cowardly and murderous attack on the distinguished biologist, Doctor Ronald Fraser, whose assistant he then was. You will hear, members of the jury, the proofs of his guilt . . . of this assault, and of the further crime of treason. How Guy Harland was heard to quarrel with his employer; how he denied that he went again to the room where Doctor Fraser was working . . . but we shall give you clear evidence that he did in fact return there; how the weapon with which Doctor Fraser was struck down was later found in his possession. That is only the beginning. You have heard the words of the indictment, 'that he did traitorously adhere and aid and give comfort to the enemies of our lord and King' . . . solemn words, an accusation not lightly to be made. And this, I must remind you—again to quote the indictment—was at a time when 'an open and public war was being prosecuted and carried on.'

"But there is more still." His voice sank impressively. "You will hear evidence of what befell as a result, a direct result, of his treachery. You will hear how four thousand civilians, of the town of Dubenocz in occupied Poland, died in their own homes. They were our allies, members of the jury; and the 'experiment' which caused their death might, in different circumstances, have been carried out here . . . our own homes might have been ravaged, as theirs were, by a dreadful disease."

Thus Garfield, for the Prosecution, a dangerous man at any time. He was talking now, to the Judge's amusement, with an eye lifting for his opponent's reactions. He was giving no grounds for an objection, though he seemed to be expecting one. Maitland was wise not to intervene at this stage, it would certainly have been an unpopular move. There was matter for interest here, too; the younger man had something of a reputation, but coming up against an adversary of Garfield's weight might teach him a thing or two. Conroy regarded the prospect without sympathy, even with a certain gentle malice; he was a man over-confident, perhaps, in his own ability, but he would arbitrate fairly when the time came, and who could ask more than that, even of one of Her Majesty's judges?

Counsel for the Defence was taking his ease, arms folded across his chest, long legs stretched out under the table. This was his first chance of gauging the real strength of the Crown's case; unfolded in Garfield's dry, precise tones it sounded even more formidable than it had appeared on paper. Even so, he was not ill pleased with the affair. Garfield was reaching the point now, and for all he sounded confident he must know it was a tricky one.

"In face of his denial, it must also be my task to prove to you that the prisoner is, in fact, Guy Harland. I do not think, members of the jury, that when you have heard the witnesses—"

Well, facts were facts, and there were two ways of looking at them. In these cases that hinged on identity it was easy enough to find witnesses, not so easy to ensure that they continued under pressure to maintain their early confidence. He had witnesses of his own, for that matter, but wasn't counting on them for more than a sort of counter-balance to the weight of the Prosecution's case. He put more faith in this instance on what could be done in cross-examination; and the prisoner himself (hard not to think of him as Harland, in view of the way that name recurred in the depositions), the prisoner should make a good witness in his own behalf. His story was credible, Counsel thought; and he doubted whether even Garfield's onslaught would shake him. Which was all to the good.

". . . and so, members of the jury, I have three sets of facts to put before you, and I shall arrange them, for your convenience, as nearly as possible each fact within its own group—logically, rather than chronologically. First, I must prove that the prisoner is, in fact, Guy

Harland. Then I must show you our reasons for believing him a traitor, which I shall do by calling witnesses to his actions in Germany. And lastly I must substantiate the claims made by the Crown as to what happened at Burnham Green in those unhappy days in 1942, when our country struggled for her very existence, and a man who was, I contend, the man now before you, planned how he could, for his own enrichment, betray her. Some of you were children at the time of which I am speaking, but even you will remember—"

Antony Maitland, who might have been supposed by a casual observer to be more than half asleep, cocked a sardonic eye in his opponent's direction. A sop for the ladies, he thought, half amused, half exasperated. But the jury were lapping it up. That dry as dust manner was effective; it added weight to Garfield's more sober pronouncements, and gave to his occasional extravagances of phrase an added bite.

Mr. Justice Conroy caught the look, and compressed his lips on a tight little smile. He would give Maitland credit for not missing much, but he lacked Garfield's experience as a leader; this must be his first big case since he took silk a few months ago. Conroy's eyes rested on him consideringly for a moment. An able-looking fellow, he would admit that; but not half the man his uncle was, either for looks or sheer personality. The defendant's solicitors, he thought, would have done better to have briefed his old friend, Sir Nicholas Harding . . . or perhaps he hadn't been available?

He continued to ruminate on the subject of the Defence Counsel, and widened the scope of his meditations to include his junior, Derek Stringer. Two out of the same stable, for all their differences in temperament; on the whole, he would put Stringer down as the older, but they were both members of the generation that grew up in the last uneasy days of peace; with seven lost years of war service of one kind or another behind them, and an outlook that was as different from that of to-day's youngsters as it was from that of the veterans of 1914. Stringer looked pale, as he generally did; for all that he had a vitality that seemed to carry him, unwearied, through the longest day. Made one wonder what he had been doing with himself during the long vacation. Maitland had acquired a tan, which had by no means worn off yet. Looked effective with wig and bands . . . the Judge's reflections were tinged with a hint of sourness; he had known the Defence Counsel for something like twenty-five years, and was inclined to see him still as a schoolboy. An unprejudiced observer might indeed have thought Maitland surprisingly youthful looking, now when his face was in repose, but could hardly have failed to be impressed by the fact that he looked intelligent.

Geoffrey Horton, the defendant's solicitor, sitting behind the two Counsel he had instructed, was conscious of irritation as he noted Maitland's relaxed attitude, and the desultory way Stringer's pen moved across the paper in front of him. He was the youngest of the trio by several years; a solidly-built young man, with red hair, a cheerful disposition, and no more simple faith than was becoming in one of his profession. During the past few years he had been associated with Antony Maitland on many occasions, both in and out of court; always before he had been the sceptic, his rather pedestrian good sense restraining, where necessary, his colleague's more erratic flights of imagination. Now he was irked to find the roles reversed. Maitland seemed confident enough, but more detached than was usual with him; while Horton, paying for once more than lip-service to his client's innocence, found himself passionately concerned with the outcome of the trial. He had been in sympathy with Godson from the first moment of their meeting; but nobody could deny these identity cases could go adrift only too easily.

Just then Maitland, as though sensing something of the turmoil behind him, turned his head and grinned at the solicitor. Geoffrey, who was secretly relieved to find the other man awake, scowled at him, and then smiled half-heartedly at Counsel's eyebrows lifted in comical enquiry. Antony winked at him, and slid down again in his seat, to resume his appearance of somnolence.

And what does that mean? thought Horton resentfully . . . except that he isn't actually asleep. He had been listening with a good deal of trepidation to Garfield's opening speech. If the Prosecution could prove one half of what he said . . . and, of course, with Garfield one could be pretty sure they could . . . the Defence had nothing to match it, even if some of the Crown's witnesses didn't come up to proof. He looked across at the prisoner, noting—as the Judge had done—the evidence of nervousness. Not to be wondered at; the man, after all, wasn't a statue, and only a fool would have been unaware of the danger in which he stood. Maitland seemed sure he would do well in the witness box, and perhaps he was right; after all, the only fact at issue was his identity. He shouldn't be easily shaken, thought Horton, relaxing a little; he is Michael Godson, not this Harland chap that everyone is talking about. But the witnesses were confident, too; could you be certain the jury would listen to even the most specious of Maitland's arguments, the most telling of cross-examination?

The prisoner, who was beginning to become accustomed to the watching eyes, and therefore to discount them, looked down at Counsel's table with a wariness he tried to conceal. Viewing things dispassionately, as he had learned to do, he was amazed at his own lack of emotion. Garfield's voice came to him as if from a distance, and the events of which he was speaking seemed equally remote; he was aware, of course, of the import of the speech . . . somewhere in the recesses of his mind a feeling of panic struggled for recognition. Counsel seemed so sure, and what had they to oppose to his assertions, after all? A string of denials, his own tale of his life before the war . . . and Maitland's wit, in which, after their one meeting, he found himself placing an unexpected confidence. But this chap for the Prosecution was effective . . . it was perhaps as well that the Defence were not concerned to clear Guy Harland's name. 'A very smiling, damned villain,' thought the prisoner. But as his eyes moved along to rest on his own Counsel's face, he was aware that there was no real peace to be found in this evasion of the issue. Sooner or later the jury would deliver their verdict; and whether it was life or death he must face after that, there wasn't much comfort to be found in either.

Garfield at last seemed to be coming to the end of what he had to say. ". . . when you have heard the evidence, when the whole dreadful truth is before you, I do not think any doubt will remain that the man who struck down Doctor Fraser was the prisoner, Guy Harland. That the purpose of his crime was to obtain possession of laboratory reports which the Doctor had in his own care, and to sell them to his country's enemies. That he aggravated his treason by proceeding abroad (we shall even indicate to you, though this is not strictly necessary to our case, the route by which he travelled). That he lived and worked in Germany for long enough to complete the unfinished portion of Doctor Fraser's research. And that, in consequence of all this, he is—more than any other person—responsible for the tragedy of Dubenocz." Counsel paused, briefly: to gauge the effect of his words? . . . perhaps to emphasise them? "My lord, members of the jury, that is the case for the Prosecution." He bowed to the court, and sat down with an air of achievement.

The Judge was nodding approval of a lucid statement. Garfield's junior, Potter, a stout man, now past middle age, was sorting among the documents on the long table with an important air; Derek Stringer wrote one last phrase with a flourish, and threw down his pen; Horton leaned forward, to whisper urgently in Maitland's ear. But Counsel, straightening himself, gave him a brief, preoccupied look. "Not now, there's a good chap," he muttered. And gave his entire attention to the little stir in the court that accompanied the calling and swearing of the first witness. Horton leaned back again, scowling; but Maitland's attention was elsewhere, and he had no time to waste just then in soothing his colleague's ill temper.

CHAPTER 2

TUESDAY, the first day (continued)

Police-Sergeant Fell, in his own idiom, was a stiffish sort of chap in his mid-forties. He had a fringe of reddish hair round a bald, pink dome, and a complexion smooth as a child's. He took the oath firmly in a broad, West Riding accent, and with no appearance of nervousness. Maitland, who had regarded his proof with some misgiving, found no comfort in his appearance. A sensible-looking man, not over imaginative; not at all a good subject for the sort of questions he had in mind.

The sergeant's name and circumstances were quickly disposed of, and his present appointment in Pontefract. "And in August of this year, Sergeant, you were staying at Brightsea, on the south coast—?"

"That's right, sir. Thought we'd give Blackpool a miss this year," Fell agreed cheerfully. But immediately assumed a more solemn expression, as the next question brought to his mind his dual role as witness and as policeman.

"Perhaps you will tell us, Sergeant, of the events of the 21st August. I am referring to the early afternoon of that day."

"Well, sir, it was like this. I was proceeding along the promenade in the direction—"

The Judge looked up, catching Counsel's eye. "Er . . . Mr. Garfield—"

"My lord?"

"The witness was on holiday, I believe you said?"

"He was, my lord."

"Then I think we can dispense with the official language. In the case of police evidence I am always most happy when we can get away from the atmosphere of the note-book."

"As your lordship pleases." Garfield turned again to the witness. "You were on holiday, and you were walking along the sea front—"

"That's right sir . . . me lord," added Fell; his quick, anxious look at the Judge was apparently to assess his chances of appeasing an angry deity. "I was on me own, sir; the missus—my wife, that is—was having a hair-do." (As he listened, Maitland was seeking a possible opening.

"You were a little bored, perhaps . . . only too ready for some diversion?" No, that wouldn't do . . . not with a man as transparently honest as the sergeant.)

". . . So, I'd nearly got to the end of the prom, the east end, that is, sir, where the lifeboat house is, when I saw a man coming along the other way."

"Walking westwards along the promenade?"

"That's right, sir."

"You had some special reason for noticing this man?"

"Well, yes, sir. Because I thought to myself, I know that chap; and I gave him a bit of a nod and a smile."

"Did he respond at all to these overtures?"

"No, sir, he did not. But after I'd walked on a pace or two it came to me . . . you know how it is . . . that I knew who he was."

"We must be quite clear about this. At first you saw a man you felt you knew, though you could not remember his name; but a few moments later you were able positively to identify him."

"That's it, sir. Exactly!"

"Then perhaps you will tell us his name." Garfield's tone was not without its note of impatience, but it was obvious that the witness was not to be rushed.

"His name was Guy Harland, sir."

"Thank you. And—to put the matter beyond doubt —do you now see this same man in court?"

"Why, yes, sir . . . the prisoner—"

Garfield let the pause lengthen; Maitland, not looking now at his client, was aware that every other eye in the courtroom must be upon the man in the dock. Damn Garfield! He was a master of these tactics . . . the pause that underlined a point he wished to stress . . . the brief, significant silence which he could make effective either for conviction or disbelief. Intangibles whose effect no objection could soften. When at last the Prosecuting Counsel spoke it was with an air almost completely casual.

"You identify the prisoner, then, both as the man you saw at Brightsea, and as Guy Harland?"

"Yes, sir, I do."

"And after you had reached this decision, what did you do then?"

"Well, sir, knowing what I did—"

"Your knowledge does not at this moment concern us, Sergeant."

"No, sir. What I did, I turned back, and followed the man. He wasn't hurrying, just taking a stroll, same as the rest of us. Farther along, you know, there's a fun-fair, and then a row of shops facing the front. He crossed when we got opposite the first of them, and walked on a little way farther, and then let himself into one of the shops with a latch-key—"

"Which shop was that?"

"A photographer's, sir. There was the name, right across: 'Michael Godson, Photographer.' He went inside, and propped the door open. It was just two o'clock, I suppose his lunch hour was over."

"Yes, Sergeant, we don't need your suppositions. Just tell us what you did next."

"Well, I had a bit of a think, like. And then I thought, better be sure than sorry. So I went round to the police station, and had a chat with the sergeant there."

Garfield hesitated, this time without any devious motive. He would have been glad enough to rest his questioning there; the trouble was, you couldn't rely on Maitland . . . he might even waive his right to cross-examine. Better make sure, better ask the further questions himself, even though the information would have been more effective if revealed in replies made to the prisoner's own Counsel.

"Now I must ask you, Sergeant, when last you saw Guy Harland?"

"Back in 1942. At Burnham Green, in Yorkshire. I was a constable then, and stationed there."

"But the circumstances under which you knew him were such as to impress themselves upon you?"

"I don't think, my lord," said Counsel for the Defence gently, "that I care for the phrasing of that question." The Judge inclined his head, and fixed Counsel for the Crown with an eye which was suddenly steely.

"Perhaps, Mr. Garfield—"

"Certainly, my lord. There can be no harm, I am sure, in my asking the witness to tell us the circumstances in which he knew the prisoner—"

"In which he knew Guy Harland," Maitland corrected him, and not at all gently now.

"You mustn't make unwarranted assumptions, Mr. Garfield."

"That would indeed be unforgivable, my lord." The Judge eyed him suspiciously, but waved a hand after a moment as a signal to proceed. Garfield added, carefully: "We should like you to tell us, Sergeant, how you came to know Guy Harland."

Fell's smooth, pink face was grave. He looked like an unhappy child.

"He was under arrest," he said, "for attacking Doctor Fraser. Attempted murder, actually; we still thought that he would die."

Maitland might have been observed to raise his eyebrows at this; Garfield said smoothly, without any effect of haste: "You did not make the arrest yourself, I believe?"

"Oh, no, sir. That was the Inspector. But I was present, and afterwards Harland was in my custody when he went to pack his things."

"I see. And did anything else of an—er—memorable nature occur while Guy Harland was in your charge?"

"To be sure it did." Fell's glance flickered momentarily to the impassive face of the prisoner. "Packed a case, he did, and couldn't get it shut. Well, sir, it was only natural to ask me to help: seeing he was a slim sort of chap, and I was a good two stone heavier, even then."

"So you helped him?"

"That was the idea, sir. I went across and knelt on the case, like." Twenty years after the event, Fell's voice rose a little as he recalled the outrage. "Knocked me out, he did, clean as a whistle; which he couldn't have done if I'd had my wits about me. But I was young then, and suspecting nothing, like I said."

"Thank you, Sergeant," said Garfield again, this time with a note of finality in his voice. Maitland thought, a little viciously, that he might well be grateful. But he was beginning to have his own ideas about the witness. He came to his feet as his opponent seated himself, and gave the sergeant his most winning smile.

"Nineteen-forty-two. That's a long time ago, isn't it?"

"Twenty years, sir," said Fell helpfully. Maitland's grin was genuine now, and appreciative.

"Yes . . . precisely. And, twenty years ago, you saw Guy Harland . . . how often?"

"Well . . . at the time Doctor Fraser was hurt, of course, sir; but before that, I'd been seeing him round the village for the best part of a year . . . to pass the time of day, or for an occasional chat."

Maitland's air of courteous enquiry did not alter; too early yet to be rattled, but he could have done without that last remark. He turned his course slightly, and perhaps only Stringer was conscious of the faint hesitation before he spoke again. "After all this time, just how sure are you of this identification, Sergeant?"

"Sure enough, sir. I'm sorry to say it, but . . . sure enough."

"You use that expression, I expect, as the rest of us do: a little carelessly, to denote something less than certainty?"

"My lord," said Garfield, coming to his feet, "if my learned friend is to put words into the mouth of the witness—"

"I should rather have thought, Mr. Garfield, that this was in the nature of taking words out of his mouth." Mr. Justice Conroy, eyeing Counsel with his head on one side, sounded deceptively mild. "The court has a right to know how much weight should be given to any statement," he added. "I find the question in order, Mr. Maitland."

"Then, perhaps, Sergeant—"

"Begging your pardon, sir, I don't think I rightly got your meaning."

"You said you were 'sure' the prisoner is Guy Harland. I asked you whether you did not on occasion use that phrase casually."

"Well, sir, perhaps I do." The witness had a naturally careful manner, but now his anxiety to say the right, the accurate thing became only too obvious.

"If you said, for instance, 'I am quite certain this man is Guy Harland'—would not that have an even more positive meaning?"

"Perhaps it would, sir, but—"

"Are you sure, Sergeant?"

"Yes, sir." But he sounded cautious, even as he made the assertion.

"And on that day in August, the 21st, when you were walking along the sea front at Brightsea and thinking, no doubt, of your own affairs: were you equally sure?"

"Not straight away. Well, I knew it was someone I ought to remember, but like I said it wasn't till I was past that I put a name to him. Then I turned back, and followed him—"

"We are not disputing that the man you saw was Michael Godson."

"No, sir." Fell tugged at his collar. Maitland, who hoped he had a pretty fair idea of the good sergeant's feelings—a conscientious man, with an almost morbid fear of giving a wrong impression in his evidence— began to feel he might be getting somewhere.

"The point at issue," he said, "is more simple than that. It is your recognition of the man you saw that I am querying; at that moment—at two o'clock on the afternoon of the 21st August—when you first set eyes on him."

"Well, sir, that's why I turned and followed," Fell pointed out. "Because I remembered who it was."

"You did not recognise him immediately, however?"

"Only as someone I knew."

"And after twenty years, that is not to be wondered at. But to come back to the present: how many times, during the last two months, have you seen Michael Godson?"

"Not at all, sir. Well, it was out of my hands once I'd talked to the sergeant at Brightsea."

"The 21st August was a Tuesday, was it not? How much of your holiday remained?"

"Just to the end of the week."

"And you did not see Godson during that period?"

"No, sir." But he added (again giving evidence of the trait in his character which the Defence Counsel found so admirable): "I did walk by the shop once or twice, with the missus, but I didn't see him either time."

"Still, you were sure then, and you are sure to-day, that the man you saw, the prisoner in this trial, is Guy Harland?"

"I am, sir."

"Quite certain?"

"Yes, sir."

"Positive, Sergeant? No doubt? No doubt at all?" He had quickened his pace now, and the questions came swiftly, with barely time for the witness's agreement. And at the final reiteration Police-Sergeant Fell, despairing apparently of ever making his own position clear, hammered with one fist on the broad ledge of the witness box and said in a rush:

"For God's sake, sir, ain't you never 'eard of Adolf Beck? How can I be sure when there's things like that happen, and no question of malice, or owt of that?"

Maitland drew a deep breath, and straightened himself. Better than he had expected, but he couldn't relax yet. He kept his eyes carefully from the Prosecuting Counsel, who was on his feet again, and trying to catch the Judge's eye.

"Certainly I have, Sergeant. A classic example of a miscarriage of justice through wrongful identification." And let Garfield object now if he wanted! It would only serve to underline the point, not that it needed any emphasis.

"My lord!" said Garfield; and stopped abruptly, as though he had suddenly seen the pitfalls ahead of him. "This is not relevant," he added, and the words came with a sense of anticlimax. Maitland assumed a look of bewilderment.

"My learned friend," said he, "has strange ideas as to relevance."

"Has he, Mr. Maitland?" The Judge's tone was dry.

"I only wished to establish, my lord," said Counsel meekly, "whether the witness was *sure*."

"And have you done so, Mr. Maitland?"

"To my own satisfaction, my lord."

"I am relieved to hear it. I must admit some agreement with Mr. Garfield, this line of questioning has gone far enough. And the witness has been allowed a good deal of latitude."

"Oh, yes, my lord, I have thought the same thing myself." Maitland permitted himself (perhaps unwisely) a reproachful look at his opponent. "I have no further questions," he added. And sat down again.

"Do you wish to re-examine, Mr. Garfield?"

Counsel for the Crown was, of course, already on his feet.

"I only wish to clarify a little the point my friend has tried so earnestly to obscure." (Stringer turned an enquiring look on his leader, who grinned at him and shook his head.) "So I must ask you, Sergeant, when you spoke of being sure you meant—did you not?—sure for all reasonable and practical purposes . . . sure as a reasonable man is sure?" ("The man on the Clapham omnibus," Maitland muttered to himself, and began to draw on the back of his brief.)

"Why, yes, sir; only, you see—"

"No real doubt?"

"Oh, no, sir. I mean, I know the prisoner is Harland, only when—"

"Thank you, Sergeant. That is all, unless . . . Mr. Maitland—?"

The Defence Counsel, who seemed once again to have lost interest in the proceedings, disclaimed any desire to take over the witness again. He leaned back to admire his sketch, and then asked his junior in an audible aside whether he happened to have a red pencil on him. Sergeant Fell, fumbling, produced a white handkerchief of enormous dimensions, and departed, mopping his brow.

*

The Foreman of the Jury was conscious of—or, more precisely, felt without being conscious of—a pleasant thrill of complacency. It wasn't everyone, he reflected, who would have got the allusion, and it would give him great pleasure to explain the matter, when the time came, to his fellow jurors. "Adolf Beck," he would say, "was a chap who was convicted—not once, mind you, but twice—of another man's crimes. And all because he was identified wrongly by a whole string of witnesses who were obviously honest, and appeared reliable." And not everyone, he thought, who could have summed it up so neatly; let alone that only a reading man would have known what the sergeant was talking about. Made you think, a thing like that . . . not that he'd made up his mind yet, either way. Up to all sorts of tricks, these lawyers, make you believe black was white if you didn't look out. He sat back in his place again: a stout, respectable figure with a heavy gold albert gleaming across the navy-blue expanse of his waistcoat. Here came the next witness, and must be given due attention: a solemn business this, and up to him to keep pace with what was happening. Need putting straight, these others, he wouldn't wonder.

Derek Stringer caught the look of self-satisfaction, and made a mental note to advise his leader that the shaft had gone home. Maitland's luck again, he thought (and if the reflection was very faintly coloured with envy, who shall blame him?). Or was it, after all, a matter of chance? He was comfortably aware that his own mind was as quick as the other man's . . . quicker, perhaps, if one were being exact for once . . . his wit sharper. But one must also admit some added quality in Maitland's case, a perception where people were concerned (yes, that was it); a perception that paid, from time to time, a dividend beyond all possible expectation. So that now the foreman (what was he, anyway, small businessman, shop-keeper?) would explain to his fellow jurors just what was bothering Sergeant Fell, and make the point much more effectively than any amount of elaboration from Counsel.

The next witness might have been chosen with a deliberate eye for effect, to form a contrast to his predecessor. He was a professor for the faculty of Science at Guy Harland's university; a small, grey man who looked, at first glance, defenceless without his academicals; but who tugged at an invisible gown and prepared with obvious enjoyment to do battle when his recollection was called—be it never so mildly—to question.

His identification of the prisoner was positive enough. Garfield seemed to have decided on the line to follow . . . the "reasonable man." who had appealed to the sergeant might expect sympathetic consideration from the jury, too; but he got summary treatment when he ventured a query.

"Sure?" snapped Professor Dobson. "Of course I'm sure! Not a fool, you know." Counsel for the Prosecution decided to leave well alone, and sat down in the uncharitable hope that the Defence, by some incautious move, would bring down upon themselves the full fury of academic anger.

Maitland was perfectly aware of Garfield's strategy, and not unamused by it. He eyed the professor warily. No use trying to change his certainty, a stubborn old party if ever there was one.

"When did you last see Guy Harland, Professor?"

"Last month, when the police—"

"Leaving aside the question of identification, which is—forgive me—not yet proved."

"Very well then! In the spring of 1941. That was a year after he graduated, and just before he took up his appointment with Fairfield Chemicals."

"Was that a casual encounter?"

"No. He wanted my advice—or said he did—about the job. Whether to stay where he was, and join the forces when his call-up came; or whether to accept this new position, which would mean he was 'reserved'."

"That might, perhaps, have been felt to be an advantage?"

"Might have been . . . wouldn't expect him to have had so much sense . . . dreamy young idiot," said Dobson, with a glance at the man in the dock that was almost vindictive.

"But you gave him an opinion?"

The professor gave a sudden bark of laughter. "Told him to make his own mind up . . . please himself. I expect he did."

"But there was this indecision?"

"The point seemed to be worrying him. Said Fraser was being pressing. Thought it might be his duty." He paused, and met Counsel's eye with something approaching belligerence. "Nothing wrong with my memory," he said.

"No, indeed." Maitland's tone was mild. "And you remember Harland's appearance as well as you remember what passed between you?"

"Certainly I do. Not just that . . . way he talked, mannerisms, everything."

"But in making this identification you have had to rely solely on your memory of Harland's appearance, have you not, Professor? And the years, unfortunately, bring changes to us all."

"I have had no opportunity of conversation with the prisoner," Dobson admitted.

"Thank you." Maitland had seated himself again almost before the witness had finished his reply. Let Garfield make what he liked out of that . . . at least they had got away without open warfare.

"One moment, Professor." Garfield's tone was at its smoothest. Maitland glanced at him quickly, and away again; he distrusted this blandness. "Tell us a little of Guy Harland, as you remember him."

"He was . . . of medium height and build. Fair hair, fairer than it is now, and not so well-controlled." (Stringer made a hasty movement as the witness began to speak, and turned now to his leader with an air of eagerness. But Maitland, who had turned his head quietly and seen the professor, eyes tightly shut in an effort of unprejudiced recollection, made no sign that he had noticed the other's interest.) Dobson opened his eyes again, and went on with less hesitation; "Well enough turned out, clothes a bit shabby, but neat in his appearance."

"And as a scholar?"

"Satisfactory." He drew the word out grudgingly, and added with remembered impatience: "Always had his nose in some book or other—poetry, literature, not the stuff he should have been reading. Told him a hundred times he should have been on the Arts side, but he just laughed and came out with one of his damned quotations; and went on to get a good first," he added, with what was obviously still a sense of grievance.

A close observer might have noticed Maitland's lips tighten during this last exchange. Garfield's round, he thought a little grimly; but perhaps he didn't realise it, and with any luck . . .

He wasn't sorry to see the witness step down.

*

There was little more of interest that first day. A string of Prosecution witnesses whom the two Defence Counsel divided impartially between them: the butcher, the baker, from the country town where Harland had grown up (the candlestick-maker would be giving evidence for the Defence); an elderly man, who claimed to be his only living relation, and who spoke with the bitterness which, perhaps, only the blood tie can engender; a careful selection of students who had been his contemporaries, a strangely mixed bunch after so many years' separation to varied occupations; a tall man who looked like a stockbroker and turned out to be the Chief Research Chemist of a well-known firm—a former colleague of Harland, and in close association with him for some time before his arrest. All of them sure ("reasonably sure," said Maitland, twisting his opponent's repeated phrase into a less definite, less damaging form); all of them with the clearest remembrance of their former friend, or acquaintance, or relation, though some of them were less positive than others, a little diffident in asserting the infallibility of memory over so long a span. Taken altogether, thought Maitland, thrusting books and documents into his clerk's keeping after the Court rose, not a bad day's work. He said as much to Geoffrey Horton, who had come round to join them, but the solicitor was not yet to be placated.

"I thought you were asleep half the time," he grumbled. "I admit you had some luck." "What about to-morrow, Derek?"

"Might have been worse," said Maitland placidly.

"I don't much like the sound of Doctor Fraser," said Stringer. They began to move in a group towards the entrance. "His proof is discouragingly precise; he won't play your game for you."

"Anything," said Maitland, still unmoved, "is better than cross-examining a jellyfish. Don't scowl at me so, Geoffrey. If you hadn't lost your sense of proportion over this business, you'd see for yourself we're not doing badly."

"If you say so." Horton was still ungracious. Maitland gave him an enquiring, sidelong look, and said persuasively:

"Jenny wants to see the film at Marble Arch. Why not forget your worries and come with us?" But there wasn't much sympathy in his laughter when Horton repudiated the suggestion with every appearance of disgust, and went off with the declared intention of "going over things again."

CHAPTER 3

TUESDAY, the first day (continued)

Outside, in the bustle of home-going London, the Foreman of the Jury was waiting, patiently enough, for the bus that would take him on the first part of his way to Tooting Bec. His thoughts were comfortable companions, and he was not even worried by the reflection that, for the time being at least, they must be kept to himself. He was a self-sufficient man, and quite content in the unshared knowledge of his own importance.

An interesting day, he thought, watching indulgently the surge of prospective passengers towards a number 11 bus. The Prosecution had a formidable array of witnesses, and so far as he could see the whole thing was going to hinge on this question of identity. Maitland was quick enough off the mark when any assumption was made that the prisoner was, in fact, Harland; the allegations of treason, and all the rest of it, would come in for examination later on, he supposed. And a nasty business that had been, as he remembered . . . the "Dubenocz experiment." the papers had called it when first the facts came to light . . . a shock to all decent people, even among the many revelations with which the war ended. Not that there seemed to be much doubt that Harland was guilty. And in spite of the doubts the Defence had raised, it didn't seem reasonable that so many people should be mistaken . . .

There were three women on the jury. The youngest of them, a blonde in her early thirties, had already found a taxi and was on her way westwards. She was the sort any driver would stop for, good-looking, beautifully turned out; the fair curls and ridiculous little hat gave her an appealing look of helplessness which was altogether misleading. In fact, she was a shrewd woman, and had been living on her wits (among other, more obvious attributes) since she was seventeen years old. It would have been surprising if a certain air of calculation had not coloured her

attitude upon occasion. Now, as the taxi moved its slow way towards
Charing Cross, she was considering what she had just heard, and
wondering . . .

She was inclined to favour the Defence, because she had taken a
dislike to Counsel for the Prosecution, and rather fancied the looks of
his opponent. Something about him—a humorous look about the eyes,
perhaps— made her think he'd be good company. Not dull! (Her thoughts
went for a moment to the evening ahead of her, and she grimaced a little
at the prospect.) Pity the prisoner wasn't more interesting; a wishy-washy
sort of chap she thought him. But as the taxi jerked into motion again her
thoughts turned, reluctantly, to Paul Garfield. Gave her the shivers . . .
everything so carefully worked out, every word another nail in that poor
chap's coffin. And come to think of it, what did they do to you if you were
convicted of High Treason? The death penalty, she supposed, but did they
shoot you, or what?

She shivered now in earnest, and fumbled in her handbag for lipstick
and mirror. The familiar, flawless reflection steadied her. Mustn't take
this graveyard atmosphere to her meeting with Denis. But her lips
quivered into a smile as she tucked away the mirror. Cold as ice, Paul
Garfield, not her type really, and no doubt about it, the Defence chap
would be more amusing. But she couldn't help regretting that there was
no chance of personal contact. A difficult conquest was always more fun,
and these self-righteous people . . .

*

Counsel for the Prosecution was unconscious of the emotions he had
aroused; which was fortunate, because they would have shocked him
profoundly. He stopped for a moment to speak to the representative of
the Director of Public Prosecutions, who surprised and affronted him by
asking bluntly: "What about it, Garfield? Is the prisoner Harland?"

"I should have thought it quite clear—" He spoke huffily, but did not
point out (as Maitland certainly would have done) that he was speaking
of the man who had instructed him.

"Oh, yes, of course. But I'd watch the Defence if I were you. Maitland's
been known to have a few surprises—" He laughed, not without malice,
as his companion's lips tightened to a thin line. "Don't like him, eh? Well,
you're not the only one. But don't underrate him, that's all I ask."

"I'm not likely to do so," said Garfield; and made his farewells stiffly.
His wife would be nervous if he was much later; they were entertaining

that evening—one of her perfectly arranged dinner parties—and she was never at ease on these occasions until he was back from court and no last-minute consultation or late sitting could be expected to interfere with her plans.

*

The thin man who sat all day inconspicuously in the corner of the back row of the jury-box had already succeeded in effecting his transfer to the Edgware-Morden line, and was making good speed towards his destination. He was, none the less, nervous and fidgety, and the stout woman with the multitude of parcels thought a little resentfully that if he couldn't make himself comfortable he might just as well have given her his seat. He was far away from the court already, for him its dream held no fascination, the opposing Counsel made their points in vain; twenty minutes from now he would be fitting his latch-key into his own front door, and once inside . . . there would be Doris to greet him. No longer would he be the shabby, underpaid shipping clerk, but a bridegroom of three months' standing . . . Prince Charming reflected in her admiring eyes. He smiled to himself at the thought, and the stout woman, shifting her weight from one foot to the other, sniffed her discontent and turned her mesmerising gaze on the youngish man farther down the carriage, who might, perhaps, be a better prospect.

*

Mr. Justice Conroy was home already; or at least had reached the set of chambers he still retained in Middle Temple Court. He had kept the rooms largely out of sentiment; a convenient *pied-à-terre*, he would have said had anyone questioned his decision. But now, since Marian died, he made increasing use of them. The journey to Haslemere was not worth the making without her comforting welcome. His mind turned momentarily, and without much affection, to the daughter who kept his house there with such earnest attention to his wishes. But that gave him no pleasure; if only she had a little spirit, some life of her own instead of this endless preoccupation with his well-being. So he turned deliberately to the events of the day, and criticised instead the conduct of both Defence and Prosecution; things had been better done in his time, he'd have revelled in Garfield's place now, none of this caution, a bold attack. As for the Defence, he admitted a trifle grudgingly, Maitland had done well enough. But his old friend, Sir Nicholas Harding, would have been (he thought) so much more effective. Maitland had a look of his uncle at times, an expression that reminded Conroy briefly of the older man. And, as sometimes happened when he thought of Sir Nicholas, the Judge's thoughts were at once self-satisfied and envious. A distinguished career in the criminal courts was a satisfying achievement; his own practice had been built along less spectacular lines, and he found his present eminence a lonely affair. He enjoyed the position, but was genuinely convinced that when his other distinguished contemporaries had achieved a similar dignity the great days of the bar would be over. And hard on the thought came the memory of a similar remark . . . Fletcher, had it been? . . . the leader of the chambers he had joined soon after his call. But that older generation had had no idea of all the talent that was coming on.

Strangely enough, that evening, his thoughts did not occupy themselves with the prisoner, who was—after all —the cause of all the fuss. No doubt when the man came to give evidence he would emerge as a character in his own right . . . and in a case like this Maitland could hardly keep him out of the witness box. Meanwhile, there he was, neatly docketed as the *casus belli*, the bone of contention over which Counsel could wrangle according to their ability and inclination.

Mr. Justice Conroy sighed a little—for his lost youth? . . . for his own days in the arena?—and turned his mind resolutely to thoughts of his dinner. Perhaps the past would seem less remote, the present more friendly, after an hour or two at the more genial of his clubs.

*

The man who denied he was Guy Harland was waiting in the cells below the court for the car that would take him back to one more night at Brixton Prison. They were waiting, he supposed, for the crowds to disperse; so he sat on the edge of his chair, hands between his knees, and let his mind range idly. Nothing he could do now, it was all in Counsel's hands. Just drift with the tide, perhaps that was for ever his destiny; and did it matter very much after all? The quiet years at Brightsea, how much had they really meant to him? There was pleasure in a job well done, in catching (when it was possible) the fleeting look that was the expression of character . . . the child's sidelong glance that spelled mischief . . . the unexpectedly proud tilt of the head that was the only beauty of the drab little girl who had collected her photographs on the morning of his arrest, and had exclaimed in delight and wonder when she saw her likeness. Yes, there was pleasure there, but did it outweigh the dark hours? Looking back dispassionately he had, he discovered, a certain affection for the town, for the strange mixture of dignity and vulgarity that he now knew so well. But was all that living . . . a job to do, a walk in the evening . . . sun on the water, the bright path of the moon across the sea? A drink in the pub round the corner, a friendly atmosphere, a babble of talk; but . . . friends? And he had had the truth of it, a moment ago . . . what did it all matter?

So now, the tide must take him where it would. He had no energy to fight the current, no real will to survive. He looked down at his hands, and saw them—almost with surprise—locked tightly together. Nothing mattered . . . nothing mattered . . . wasn't that something to hold on to? So why was he so frightened of what lay ahead?

*

Counsel for the Defence went home to supper, and afterwards took his wife to the pictures. The film was soothing: an epic in glorious Technicolor, which was for all that morally black-and-white. Antony, meditating a little sadly as they walked away from the cinema on the comparative simplicity of a life whose values were clear-cut, unarguable, felt his wife's hand on his arm.

"This case of yours," said Jenny Maitland. "It seems to be making a stir."

The placard on the corner asked only: HARLAND—OR GODSON? Antony said indifferently, "Nothing interesting, really. Run of the mill stuff."

"Will you win?" asked Jenny. Her grey eyes were clear and candid; she looked up at him with the innocent serenity that was all her own. "I hope you do," she added. "You know, darling, I don't really like Mr. Garfield."

"Good lord!" Maitland stopped, and looked down at her, his attention caught at last by this drastically out-of-character remark. Jenny ignored his startled look, and elaborated a little.

"I don't think he's always . . . kind," she said. Her husband grinned at her.

"Which of us is, come to that? Don't be too hard on us, love."

"Well, do you think—"

"If all goes well to-morrow . . . well, one can't be sure."

Illogically, this seemed to surprise her. "But, Antony, all those people—"

"You," said her husband, looking down at her affectionately, "are obviously the sort of person for whose benefit judges explain everything three times . . . and end up in trouble in the Court of Appeal, poor devils."

Jenny tilted her chin, and said with dignity: "Uncle Nick says I have a very logical mind."

"Don't you believe it. To go back to your question, I admit Garfield has plenty of evidence; but we're not hunting the snark, you know—what I tell you three times isn't necessarily true."

"No," said Jenny, doubtfully.

"Wait till you've heard our witnesses," her husband urged. He felt her hand tighten on his forearm. "Some of them may even be telling the truth," he added. And watched with pleasure the frown disappear from between her eyes, so that her whole expression lightened; and presently she began to laugh.

CHAPTER 4

WEDNESDAY, the second day

The following clay was Wednesday, and again the sun shone, and again the court was stuffy and the Judge concerned to exclude any possible breath of air. And again Garfield summoned his procession of witnesses, so that the look of strain deepened a little on the prisoner's face, and Maitland, bored by a reiteration of evidence which gave little opportunity to vary the attack, snapped at his clerk and showed every evidence of being out of temper when at last the court rose. Geoffrey Horton walked with him back to chambers.

"There are one or two points—" he remarked; and though his tone was faintly apologetic, there was a stubbornness in his manner that Maitland knew only too well. He resigned himself to the inevitable, therefore, with no more than a passing regret for the delay the other man's insistence would cause him.

"Though I wish to goodness," he said, fretfully, "that Joan would hurry back. As a grass widower, you're quite impossible."

Geoffrey ignored this. "How did you think it went, to-day?" he asked.

"Well . . . I defy anyone at this stage to be sure our client is Harland. The awkward part will come tomorrow, Doctor Fraser's evidence is bound to carry weight, but if we get over that hurdle—"

"What then?" The elaborate unconcern in the solicitor's voice did not deceive his companion for an instant. Maitland, whose ill temper was never of a very durable nature, grinned at him.

"I shall submit there's no case to answer . . . or rather that there's no reason to suppose our client is the man who should be answering it." He glanced at his companion, and added bluntly: "And you may pray we get away with it, Geoffrey. I suppose you realise we've shot our bolt over this question of identity?"

"Yes, of course, it couldn't be otherwise," said Horton seriously. Maitland's expression was momentarily compounded of sympathy and irritation.

"If they make us go on," he said, with the slightly exaggerated patience one might use to a child—or to an idiot— "if they make us go on, our case may not look so good. We've our own identity witnesses, I admit . . . people who knew Harland; but Garfield will shake them, as Derek and I have shaken his lot. We can show that our client said his name was Godson when he turned up in Switzerland during the war, and that he has been known as Godson ever since. His story of how he came here is circumstantial, and I think he will tell it well . . . but we can't prove it, however plausible he is in the witness box."

"I suppose not," said Geoffrey. "A damnable business," he added angrily.

"But not hopeless," said Maitland, suddenly brisk. It was getting dark now, and the shadows were thick as they passed into Inner Temple Court. It was cooler, too, and the thought of a fire suddenly attractive. He could have done without Horton's company, and any further discussion of the case that evening, but that just couldn't be helped. Sir Nicholas Harding's chambers lay up a steep flight of stairs, in one of the buildings on the right of the court. Antony went up with the thoughtlessness of long familiarity; his uncle was out of town, but there was a light in his room. Maitland pushed the door open, and found his clerk on his knees in front of the fire. It was typical of Willett that, although he had left the court only just ahead of the other men, he had already stacked books and papers neatly on the big desk, and coaxed the fire to a friendly blaze. He had also taken time to find out what had been going on in his absence.

"Mr. Maitland, sir," he announced impressively as he scrambled to his feet, "there's a lady waiting—"

"Not to-night," said Maitland. He walked across to the desk, moving now a little stiffly, and sounded suddenly weary. "Get rid of her, there's a good chap. Tell her—"

"Which I would have done, sir . . . naturally. Only it seems it's urgent, Mr. Maitland. About The Case." Horton was hovering, ready to make a tactful withdrawal, but the clerk's gesture invited his attention also. "It's Mrs. Guy Harland!" he said. And stood back with a pleased expression to watch the effect of his announcement.

It was not precisely as he expected.

"It only needed that," groaned Maitland, and sat down at the desk with his head in his hands. Horton threw an exasperated glance in his direction; Willett's jaw had dropped so that he looked for a moment, absurdly, like a dog whose offer of a dead rat has been rejected.

"Ask her to come in," said Geoffrey eagerly.

Maitland raised his head at that and met his clerk's enquiring look. "I suppose you think you know what you're doing, Geoffrey," he said grimly. "All right, Willett, we'll see her."

Mary Harland, coming in from the comparative austerity of the waiting-room, was shaken unexpectedly by nostalgia and a confused sense of familiarity. Because she was nervous, she had no more than a vague impression of the room; of firelight reflected from well-polished mahogany; of an array of books, battered and not-too-orderly, with a look of constant use; of a carpet, old fashioned, no doubt, in design, but whose colours were warm and mellow. It needed no more than this to take her back to the tranquil days before her marriage when someone else—surely, not herself—had lived as happily as the atmosphere of her parents' home invited.

It was Horton who went forward to greet the newcomer, and who fussed gently over her until she was seated near the fire. She took stock of them both then, quite frankly: the younger of the pair had a friendly look, she thought; it wouldn't be too difficult, perhaps, to explain to him why she had come. The other man came round now from behind the desk to lean one shoulder against the high mantel and look down at her; she thought he looked aloof, perhaps even disdainful, though he had greeted her politely enough. Characteristically, it was to him she addressed herself.

"Mr. Maitland, you're the barrister in this case . . . my husband's trial?"

Geoffrey Horton, looking at the visitor, saw a slightly- built woman in her late thirties, with fair, straight hair and a composed manner. Not a pretty woman, but pleasant-looking. Her tweed suit was shabby, and had never been elegant; she might be hard up, or she might be careless of appearances. It seemed to him completely natural that she should have come, and it never occurred to him that she might be feeling any embarrassment.

Antony Maitland, his interest aroused by the choice of phrase, saw her pallor and the taut way she held herself. Someone, he thought, who has come almost to the limit of endurance, and to whom the thought of this present interview seems unbearable. Her face was too thin for beauty, but her eyes were lovely: brown eyes, unusual with her colouring, and they were fixed on him steadily enough, but he couldn't mistake the fact that she was afraid. He was conscious of a feeling of sympathy, which was the last sentiment he wished to indulge; and because this irritated him he spoke abruptly.

"The case is in the lists as 'Regina versus Harland'. My client, however—"

"Oh, yes, I know that. I've read the papers. That's why I came." Strangely enough, she did not seem disturbed by his tone; rather, she relaxed, as though by infecting him with her previous tension her own burden had been eased.

"Have you seen the prisoner?" His look was intent. She glanced up at him briefly, and then down at the fire again.

"No. No, I haven't." She leaned back in her chair now, and rubbed her hand along the arm as though the feel of the leather pleased her. Antony said, still roughly: "The police were looking for you, you know that don't you? With all the publicity it seems strange they didn't get word of you."

"Not so odd, really. It's more than fifteen years since I started using my maiden name again. Mary Garrick. So no one knew."

"Except yourself, Mrs. Harland."

"Yes, of course. But I didn't know what would be best to do; only then . . . well, I had to know if it really is Guy . . . and if it isn't, perhaps I can help. So I thought if I came to you—"

"I see." He spoke slowly. Not a fool, this woman. Her directness pleased him, even though the fact that she had engaged his sympathies was still an irritation. She had made a mistake, of course, in coming forward at all, but perhaps that could be remedied . . . always supposing she wanted to help her husband, which was a thing it wouldn't do to take for granted. Meanwhile, no harm perhaps in satisfying curiosity. "When did you last see your husband?" he said; and for the first time he smiled at her.

Geoffrey had pulled up a chair; he looked intent and eager. He said, "I'm sure you can help us, Mrs. Harland," and ignored Antony's sour look in his direction as he spoke.

Mary Harland's glance flickered from one to other of the two men. They were friends, she thought, but so very different, and so much at odds over this matter. She did not understand the attitude of either of them; but because it was not in her to take the easy way she smiled briefly at the solicitor, and spoke again directly to the other man, in whom she sensed hostility.

"I last saw Guy the day he was arrested. They said he tried to kill Doctor Fraser . . . well, you know that, of course." She paused, and looked again, a little doubtfully, at each of them in turn. As neither of the men made any comment she went on after a moment. She spoke hesitantly, picking her words. Antony couldn't decide whether this was because she found her story distasteful, or because she was trying for some definite effect. "He went upstairs to pack a case; I was upset, of course . . . they wouldn't let me go with him; so Lady Torrington made me go into the drawing-room with her. The next thing I heard, he was gone. He knocked out a policeman, you know; he was a very quiet sort of person, so I expect he took the poor man by surprise. I never saw him again . . . none of us ever saw him again."

"He was seen in Germany." The words dropped into another silence. Mary Harland looked at the speaker, and the fear was back in her eyes again.

"I knew that, of course . . . they told me. I think they thought he might have got in touch with me. Only I didn't want to believe it . . . I think I pretended, even after I knew it must be true."

"That's very natural."

"Well, perhaps. But not very sensible. I didn't mean to mislead you."

"Never mind. You were living at Burnham Towers then, with your husband?"

"Yes, we were lucky . . . we thought we were lucky. You know how hard it was to find somewhere to live, so when we were married we thought it was wonderful to be able to stay there. It was wonderful, the Torringtons were so very kind . . . even afterwards, they were so very kind to me." She broke off, and flushed a little as she met Maitland's enquiring look. "I'm talking too much," she said. "About things that don't matter."

"Don't they matter, Mrs. Harland? It's a long time—isn't it?—since you spoke of all this." His tone was gentle now. Horton noted with annoyance, and some amusement too, how the visitor relaxed at his words and smiled at him, for the first time, in a friendly way.

"A very long time," she agreed. "Afterwards, when there was no news of Guy, I went home. My father was ill, he died three years later. They weren't nice years, those. But, of course, they passed."

"And what then?"

"That was when I started using my maiden name again. It wasn't difficult, I just said I'd lost my identity card; you see, when they were first issued I was still unmarried. I didn't know whether they'd check up or not, and find the change, but apparently they didn't. And I hadn't been working, so when I got a job I just started from the beginning with income tax, and insurance."

"Did you come to London?"

"Yes. It seemed the best place to . . . to get lost in. I didn't quite know what to do. My father had been living on an annuity, so I hadn't any money. And I wasn't trained for anything. While we were at Burnham Green I was working at the hospital in Fairfield, but I wasn't trained for nursing, and I didn't like it really. I found a job with a wholesale dress firm in the West End . . . not one of the best firms. I did book-keeping, and anything else that came along. After a while I was able to change to my present job, with a travel agency. I still do book-keeping, not reception work, of course . . . I couldn't compete with the posters." She smiled again, with real humour this time, so that Geoffrey thought 'she's not bad-looking, after all'; and Antony found his own part in the affair suddenly distasteful. But for that there was no remedy; the mischief had been done when she married Guy Harland. He shifted his position a little, away from the direct line of the fire.

"And at this firm they know you as Mary Garrick?"

"Yes. I've never told anyone who I am."

"I see." He had a trick, which she found disconcerting, of looking away as he asked her questions; but then, a moment later, she would find his eyes fixed on her again, with the intent look she had noticed when first she came in. "You said, Mrs. Harland, 'they' thought your husband might have got in touch with you. Did he, in fact, do so?"

The question seemed to confuse her. "No. No, he didn't. I don't know whether they believed me, or not; but there was never a word . . . all these years!"

"Did you want to hear from him?"

"I . . . don't know." She was silent for a while, looking down at her ring-less hands; and then she looked up at him again, and said in her forthright way, "That wasn't true, Mr. Maitland. At first, I just didn't believe that Guy could have done what they said. Afterwards, when there didn't seem to be any doubt left, I think I got past caring any more. I suppose I ought to be ashamed to tell you that; but I just wanted . . . desperately . . . to have some word of him."

"Yes, I see. Well, now, Mrs. Harland—" Something in his tone puzzled her, and seeing her enquiring look he added, with a return of irritation: "Why have you come here?"

Geoffrey intervened at this point. "I don't think that's material, you know," he protested.

"It's the whole point at issue," said Maitland, angrily. "She sees that, if you don't." He shifted his position, to look down at her more directly. "Don't you, Mrs. Harland?" he asked.

"At least, I'll try to answer you. I don't really think it's Guy . . . but I have to know."

"And what then? If you're wrong, and your husband is alive, what then? So easy to testify to his identity . . . almost a duty, in a case involving treason." Horton said something in a protesting voice, but he ignored the interruption and went on relentlessly: "A chance of your being a widow pretty soon . . . free, after all these years. Is *that* what is in your mind?"

There was a moment of complete silence. She did not look away, and after a while she answered him with no more than a tremor in her voice. "If that's what I wanted, I'd have gone to the police." As she spoke, her eyes filled with tears; but she did not seem to notice. "I don't know how I can convince you," she said, helplessly.

"Twenty years, Mrs. Harland," he reminded her. "No other man?"

"No . . . at least . . . only Philip." The tears were on her cheeks now, but still she disregarded them.

"Tell me," said Maitland, "about Philip."

"There's nothing to tell. He's a junior partner in the firm I work for. He wanted . . . he wants to marry me."

"And your own feelings in the matter?"

"I thought . . . for a while I thought that was what I wanted, too. Only when it came to the point, I couldn't tell him about Guy. I suppose that meant," she added, desolately, "that I didn't care enough."

Maitland made a sudden movement. He pulled a clean handkerchief out of his breast pocket, and offered it to her; his smile was persuasive, completely at variance with his previous manner. "Forgive me, Mrs. Harland. I had to be sure."

She took the handkerchief without protest, blew her nose, and looked up at him with a touch of defiance in her manner. "I could lie to you," she said, "easily enough, if I wanted to."

"I'm sure you could," he agreed. "But I don't think you have, you know."

"I don't see," said Geoffrey, interrupting again with a mixture of aggressiveness and bewilderment, "what all this is about."

"Don't you?" said Antony, cryptically.

"No, I don't. It's obvious her evidence will help us. You were saying our witnesses would no more than balance Garfield's . . . but Harland's wife—"

"And who is to say, my dear Geoffrey, that when she has seen the prisoner she will be *our* witness?"

Horton got to his feet, and stood looking at the other man in an unbelieving way. "You're telling me you think our client's Harland," he said. "I've been so sure—"

"I know." He looked again at Mary Harland, who was sitting very still now in the big arm-chair. "That's why I wasn't too pleased when you arrived," he explained. "You see, it's fairly simple for you. If you recognise the prisoner you can go away and keep your mouth shut . . . that's what you thought, isn't it? But for me, it's different. Once I *know* my client is Guy Harland, I can have no further connection with the case. Not so long as my instructions are to deny the fact." He added, with an edge to his voice: "I'm pretty damned sure now, as a matter of fact . . . unlike Horton here. But I'm entitled to give him the benefit of the doubt."

"I didn't understand." She had put away the handkerchief now, and seemed to be grappling with this new aspect of the situation. "If it is Guy, he's been living all these years in Brightsea . . . just a few miles away." She looked up again at Maitland, questioningly. "You mean, you want me to go away without seeing him; and never know—"

"If you value your husband's life, I think that is what you must do. But I'm not infallible."

Geoffrey said, suddenly energetic.

"Of course he's Godson. Not a doubt of it. We'd be fools to throw away—" He stopped as Mary Harland came to her feet, and put out a hand to silence him.

"I gave my address to your . . . your clerk. If you want to argue, I think I'd rather go home now. I won't get in touch with you again, but I'll be there if you want me." She gave a hand to each in turn, and had reached the door almost before Willett, summoned by the bell, had got it open. She went out without a backward glance, leaving the two men looking at one another with an odd sense of anticlimax.

"Whew-w," said Geoffrey, at last. His amiability seemed to have been miraculously restored. "You can say what you like, Antony—"

"I know what our client would say," replied Maitland, with the glimmer of a smile. "I pray you, be not dainty of leave-taking. That's a very brave woman, Geoffrey," he added, sombrely. "I suppose you realise I've told her to go back to her own little hell, and not even try to get out of it."

CHAPTER 5

THURSDAY, the third day

Maitland was not in the sunniest of tempers when he arrived in court next morning. He greeted his colleagues in a preoccupied way, and settled himself down to a perusal of one of the documents Willett had brought with him. Horton and Stringer, recognising the signs, exchanged glances; the solicitor's was frankly alarmed, but Derek's look was one of amused resignation. If his leader was in fighting mood there should be no harm in that; he could be trusted to keep his temper within the bounds of expediency. Though Geoffrey, obviously, from his worried look, was by no means so sure of that.

Perhaps it was fortunate that the first Prosecution witness to be called that day was Sir Gervase Torrington, the owner of Burnham Towers— and of most of the village of Burnham Green—where all the trouble had started. He was an old man of considerable charm, and Antony, who had been puzzled when he read his proof, realised now that its bald, rather abrupt tone was the result of drastic pruning on the part of the person who had prepared it. Certainly, it had not reflected his own natural style; and the Defence Counsel found now some small satisfaction in noting that his opponent seemed decidedly ruffled by his witness's gentle garrulity. Garfield fumed visibly as the answers to his questions flowed unchecked, but it was no use trying to dam or divert the stream. The old man was a little deaf now, and took no heed of interruptions. Most probably, Maitland decided, he was a lip reader, for he seemed to find no difficulty with a direct question, when he was facing the man who put it and giving him his full attention.

Sir Gervase was tall, and thinner now than he had been when a master craftsman cut his suit for him. His hair was silver and rather scanty; but his eyes were clear and grey, and his complexion fresh and rosy. As Maitland already knew, it was at this point that Garfield would deviate for the first time from the direct line of evidence as to identity, and begin to display the full weight of the charge; and he was not surprised that the Prosecuting Counsel wasted little time over the preliminaries.

"I should like you to tell the court, Sir Gervase, something about the household at Burnham Towers in October, 1942."

"You mean, I suppose, our guests. And, of course, my dear wife was alive at that time." He paused, and smiled confidingly at Garfield. "Well, I must be precise, must I not? And perhaps the word 'guests' was a euphemism. 'Lodgers' would be better, you know; though we felt they were our friends . . . we were fortunate, I think you will agree, to be able to do so. But I was, perhaps, guilty of a little evasion when talking the matter over with Lady Torrington." (The Judge said "Harrumph!" at this point, but the witness did not hear him, and went on happily.) "I used to speak of our 'war work' . . . half in jest, half in earnest, you know. Because it was indeed very difficult to find accommodation, with so many new people moved into the neighbourhood to work at the plant; but I cannot deny that the money was useful to me as well."

"A matter of mutual convenience," said Garfield, with a rather strained smile. Antony met Derek Stringer's eye, but maintained his solemnity. "But you were going to tell us—"

"Yes, indeed. I'm afraid it is a bad habit of mine, to stray from the subject. But I should not like to leave you under a misapprehension—" His smile invited Garfield's sympathy, and Counsel responded as smoothly as he could.

"I think we all understand the position, sir."

The old man seemed a little taken aback at this, and looked round in a bewildered way. Perhaps the use of the plural confused him, he seemed to be treating his evidence as a private conversation between himself and the leader for the Prosecution. He said, vaguely: "I'm afraid I forget—"

"Your guests, Sir Gervase." Garfield's patience might be tried, but he concealed the fact admirably.

"Of course, of course!" This was familiar ground, it seemed, and he was relieved to find himself upon it. "There was Doctor Fraser, first of all. He was the first arrival, and the first in importance too, I suppose, though I must admit I never understood fully—however, it all came about quite naturally when he first came to Burnham Green. An old friend of mine telephoned—William Welland, he's dead now, poor fellow—and asked me to put Fraser up for the week-end. After that, I was only too happy to ask him to stay on, when he seemed to be in difficulties over accommodation."

"But Doctor Fraser was not the only one of your guests?"

"For a short time only. Then there was his secretary—Miss Marne, she was then—and obviously it was convenient for her to be there. Their work was important, you know, Mr. Garfield, and nobody kept office hours in wartime."

"I understand that, Sir Gervase."

"Of course you do! You must forgive me, when I leave the course of my narrative. Young Conrad was the next arrival . . . Charles Conrad. I should not speak of him so familiarly, he is an important man in the world of business, I believe. But then he was—oh, thirty, perhaps —just at the beginning of his career. A charming fellow, and it was he who asked me whether we could take the Harlands, at the time they were married."

"And you found no difficulty in agreeing to that?"

"Oh, no, indeed! I could not plead lack of room, we were singularly well placed in that respect. And I was glad of the company for my wife, she became very fond of Mary Harland; and at that time, you know, I was out a good deal at nights, because of my Home Guard duties." He paused, and it was obvious that he was lost in his memories. Maitland, who had found this picture of a wartime world so different from his own strangely evocative of the atmosphere of those far off days, watched with a half smile (in which there was now nothing malicious) Garfield's obvious struggle between sympathy and impatience. But before the issue was decided Sir Gervase shook himself out of his reverie, and went on in a determinedly businesslike tone. "Those were all the permanent members of the household. But during the period you are interested in—"

"The second week in October, Sir Gervase," Garfield reminded him.

"My son, Hugh, was on leave. Embarkation leave, as we found later; but he didn't tell us that. And he brought a friend with him, Harry Wilmot—a young man in the same regiment. They arrived just two days before . . . before the attack on Doctor Fraser, you know. And they were staying until the Sunday. Just at the end of the previous week I had found that some friends of Charles Conrad were staying nearly twenty miles away, in rather uncomfortable lodgings in Shipford; perhaps if I had known Hugh was coming I might not have been so ready to suggest they came to us. But that, I am sure, would have been selfish—and they really were a delightful pair, and most appreciative of what little we could do for their entertainment—so perhaps it was just as well I didn't know exactly when Hugh's leave would be."

"You have not told us the names of these last two guests, Sir Gervase."

"Have I not? Robin Thurlow and his wife; poor fellow, he wasn't fit enough for the services. He used to make a joke of it, but I believe he felt it very much. His wife is Marjorie Manningham, the singer; she was touring with E.N.S.A. at that time, and he was with the Ministry of Information. I gathered from what he told me it wasn't often they could arrange to have leave together."

"Thank you, Sir Gervase. That is a very clear account. Now I must ask you—" Maitland's attention wandered at this point. It was unlikely that Garfield, having come so far with an unpromising witness, would actually lose control of the situation, or of himself; and failing such a diversion there was little to interest him in this part of the evidence. Even if he had been concerned with the facts of the case (and in the circumstances they were of academic interest only), Sir Gervase's evidence would not have been the place to look for help. He glanced across at the man in the dock, who maintained the now familiar air of composure, almost of aloofness, and he came back to the question, as he had done each day since the trial began: was the man Harland?

Somehow the assumption was not quite so easy to make to-day as it had been before Mary Harland's visit to chambers. Could a man be so indifferent? The answer was, of course, that he could . . . very easily. That many men had disappeared before, and many would in the future; and the wives might say (or infer) in good faith that there was no reason, no trouble between them . . . but it didn't follow that they were telling the truth.

Stringer pushed a note in front of him, "pity we're not defending Harland . . . there's a point there." He hadn't heard the point, but it roused him to temporary interest in the course of the examination. Garfield didn't seem to be making much headway, the witness appeared to have had a positive genius for being elsewhere when anything of importance was going on; but the old man was showing definite signs of distress. Probably, Maitland reflected, turning over his colleague's note and beginning to scribble on the back of it, probably he was one of those rare people to whom it is genuinely painful to have to speak or think ill of their fellows. And, not a doubt of it, the case against Guy Harland was black indeed; even before they got to the "Dubenocz experiment." which was going to cause a stir.

Counsel sat back and admired the sketch he had made: a stout man in mandarin's robes . . . Poo Bah, of course . . . "I wasn't there." He hadn't made the association consciously, and it was tenuous enough in all conscience. In a spirit of mischief he pushed the paper along the table in front of his junior; it would give him something to puzzle over, anyway. There was a certain tedium about a case whose conduct was so circumscribed; there would have been more amusement in really defending the prisoner than in this Harland-Godson quibble. And that was an unprofitable thought, because if the brief had been offered on those terms he wouldn't have touched it. Jenny would say *that* wasn't logical; he grinned a little to himself at the thought of her indignation if he ever tried to explain an attitude which depended on the difference between moral certainty and legal proof.

Now Garfield would make the most of the treason angle, and good luck to him; but his arguments could not but lose force by being unopposed. More illogicality? But true, he was sure of that. And here they were, back to identity again. He laid down his pencil, and glanced quickly round the court before giving his full attention to Garfield and his witness. The Judge had a look of bored indifference, but he wasn't asleep . . . no such luck! (Counsel's memories of Mr. Justice Conroy went back over a good many years, and were both vivid and unwillingly respectful; he wasn't likely to underrate the older man's ability.) As for the jury, they looked stuffed, but what jury didn't? Garfield was urbane as ever; he didn't like the chap, too cold a fish by a long way, but you had to admire his technique. His manner was affability itself as he came to the end of his examination.

"One last question, Sir Gervase. We have been speaking of Guy Harland, who lived under your roof for over six months. Do you now see him in court?"

The old man turned a little, and the man in the dock met his gaze squarely; and again Maitland was surprised by a feeling of doubt. There was anxiety, of course, behind the look of blank incomprehension on the prisoner's face, but no more than was natural. Even when Sir Gervase turned back to the leader for the Prosecution and said regretfully, "The prisoner—" and gestured towards him, there was no sign of recognition. Garfield thanked his witness smoothly, and sat down. As Maitland rose,

Stringer pushed the sketch along the table again in front of him; he had added the words "How Hi is a Chinaman?" and a row of question marks. Antony mentally chalked up a score to his own credit (though, to be fair, even a psychologist might have been puzzled to explain his train of thought); he stooped, and picked up the note, and crumpled it. And by that time he had the witness's attention.

"I do not think I need trouble you for long, sir. A few months' acquaintance, so many years ago—"

"I must object, my lord." As Garfield came to his feet again his tone was perhaps unnecessarily sharp, but after all his unexpressed irritation with the witness had to be worked off somehow. "If my friend wishes to make a speech, he will have opportunity later."

"I withdraw my remarks. They were most ill-advised," said Maitland, with half an eye on his lordship's reactions. "It is only too natural that my learned friend finds the subject a little . . . touchy."

Garfield opened his mouth, but the Judge's question forestalled him. "Do you intend to cross-examine the witness, Mr. Maitland?" he asked gently.

"Indeed I do, my lord."

"Then please proceed with your questions. Unless, of course, you would like me to put them for you. I seem to have detected a certain sameness in your approach—"

Garfield allowed himself a smile. Maitland, who felt this judicial interference was a little unfair, said with an air of cheerful agreement. "There has been—er—a 'sameness' in the evidence offered to the court. But I should be grateful for your lordship's help."

Conroy gave him a disagreeable look, and waved a hand as an invitation to proceed. He turned back to the witness, who was standing with his mouth a little open, obviously bewildered by the delay and the exchange of comments which he could not hear. The confident manner with which he had first given evidence had gone now; Sir Gervase looked old, and tired, and his shoulders sagged with weariness. Maitland, looking at him, was suddenly angry again; angry, this time, at the mischance that had brought them both into this stuffy courtroom, that had ordained that a kindly old man should now be badgered and distressed because once he had known a villain. He said, again:

"I won't keep you, sir." And then, "Just how sure are you of this identification?"

Sympathy between strangers can be as swift and inexplicable as antagonism. The witness looked at Counsel and saw (by his reckoning) a young man, who seemed for some unexplained reason ill at ease. He smiled at him and shook his head a little sadly, and said,

"As sure as a man may be." But the weariness in his voice robbed the words of any effect of certainty, and Maitland, with the rest of his questions still unasked ("how good is your eyesight, Sir Gervase? . . . did you see a photograph before you attended the identification parade? . . . what points of resemblance—?"), startled the court by saying, "Thank you, sir," and sitting down in his place again.

Garfield, unprepared for what seemed like a capitulation, was aware of an uneasy feeling that a point had been made by his adversary, but he shrugged it away angrily; his job was facts, not the nebulous sort of conviction that depends on a tone of voice, or the tired droop of a shoulder.

He did not offer to re-examine.

CHAPTER 6

THURSDAY, the third day (continued)

I t is a commonplace that a witness in a criminal trial, unless emotionally involved, will tend to identify himself with the side which has called his evidence. It soon became apparent that Ronald Fraser (PhD, *Exeter*) might well have been cited as a text-book example of this attitude. Even the careful suggestions put to him on direct examination seemed to be resented as in some way belittling his testimony. Listening, Maitland was conscious that Horton was moving uneasily behind him, and hunched an impatient shoulder. He was in no mood to sympathise with the other man's worries.

Fraser was a big man, with a shock of sandy hair above a massive forehead, and a strong, bony face. His voice was harsh and rasping, and he showed no signs whatever of self-consciousness; he did not exactly ignore the court officials and the spectators in the public gallery . . . he simply wasn't aware of their presence. But the man in the dock endured a close, inimical scrutiny, and the identification, when it was called for, was vehement and uncompromising; so much so that Garfield, it was obvious, felt the need of some qualification of what had been said.

"To get the matter quite clear, Doctor Fraser: before the identification parade at which you picked out the prisoner had your memory been refreshed in any way . . . for instance, had you seen a picture of him in the Press?"

"There was a photograph in the *Tribune*," Fraser admitted. "A damn' bad one, as a matter of fact, quite unrecognisable."

"That will, I am sure," said Garfield, with a glance at his opponent that was not altogether devoid of malice, "set my learned friend's mind at rest." Not to be outdone in courtesy, Maitland made him a slight bow. The witness's eyes moved appraisingly from one man to the other; from Garfield, pale, erect, unsmiling, a puritanical figure, immaculately neat; to Maitland, lounging in his place, his gown crumpled across the shoulders, his eyes bright and amused. Two clever men, Doctor Fraser thought them, but rated his own intelligence sufficiently highly not to resent the fact. But indignation mounted as he turned his considering look on the prisoner again; there was that feller Harland, pretending not to recognise his former chief. And a deliberate lie, mind you, didn't even claim to have lost his memory. Well, he'd have a thing or two to say if anyone tried to cast doubts on the matter.

Garfield, shrugging slightly, turned from his opponent (whose amusement he did not relish), to meet again the witness's belligerent stare. "Having asked the court on this point, Doctor, I must ask you to turn your mind—"

"But, has he?" said Maitland, getting up suddenly. He turned an enquiring look in the direction of the Judge.

"You have some comment you wish to make, Mr. Maitland?" Mr. Justice Conroy leaned forward and peered at Counsel in a short-sighted way that didn't deceive the younger man in the least. The old blighter could see perfectly well, and only assumed this attitude when he was looking for a chance to annihilate you. His answer came with a smoothness that rivalled, and even mimicked to some degree, the Prosecutor's manner.

"I object to my friend's assumption, my lord."

"And with good reason," said the Judge, shifting his ground suddenly. Maitland gave him a suspicious look, and Garfield said quickly:

"If your lordship pleases, I will re-frame the question." He turned again to Fraser. "Please tell the court where you were living, and how you were occupied in October, 1942."

"I was living at Burnham Towers, Burnham Green, Yorkshire; and I was working at the laboratory of the Fairfield Chemical Company. More precisely, I was occupied on a government research project of a classified nature."

"And—without going into too much detail—you would, perhaps, describe this project as being of importance to the war effort?"

Maitland was on his feet again. "We are willing to grant the vital nature of Doctor Fraser's work, but is it really necessary to lead him?" he asked apologetically.

Garfield looked up at the Judge. "In the interests of brevity, my lord . . . in the question about which there is admittedly no dispute—"

"I can see no harm, Mr. Maitland. Do you wish to persist in the objection?"

"Certainly not against your lordship's wishes," said Maitland, unfairly. Conroy, who prided himself on his impartiality, greeted this misleading deference with a grim look. But Counsel for the Defence was looking again at the witness. Doctor Fraser, as he had hoped, did not relish the interruptions. He was angry and disturbed, and with any luck . . . but that damned, smooth-spoken fellow, Garfield, would be sure to get him calmed down again.

"Can you remember the question, Doctor Fraser?"

"You were asking me about the importance of the work I was doing in 1942. As I understood the matter, the enemy were known to be carrying out advanced experiments in the large-scale contamination of water-supplies. I think I may say it was of importance that our own knowledge should match theirs." Fraser's tone was harsh, but he was much less inclined to impatience when speaking of his own subject. "That was why the interruption might have been disastrous; the work was not quite complete when I was injured, and I was unable to take it up again for almost a year. But it was even more important that it should not fall into enemy hands."

Garfield, only too conscious that he had lost control of his witness, if only for a moment, glanced sidelong at his opponent. But Maitland had subsided again; all this, his expression seemed to say, was not his concern.

"At least," said the Judge, dividing an acid smile between Defence and Prosecution, "you cannot on this point be accused of 'leading,' Mr. Garfield."

Counsel took this thrust each in his own way. Maitland looked up and grinned appreciatively; Garfield pursed his lips primly, while nodding his acknowledgement of his lordship's right to say what he pleased. He turned back to his witness.

"Now, on the evening of October 16th, Doctor Fraser, you dined, I believe, at Burnham Towers."

"That is correct."

"The company was rather numerous, was it not?"

"Eleven persons, including myself. Lady Torrington had been kind enough to take in three other employees of Fairfield Chemicals besides myself; and the wife of one of them, of course, Mary Harland. In addition, there were four guests . . . temporary members of the household."

"Please tell us what happened after dinner on the evening we have referred to."

"I went directly from the dining-room to the study, which had been given over to my use. The butler brought me coffee, and I settled down to work. Guy Harland came in for a short time, and went away again. Later that evening I was attacked, and rendered unconscious."

"You have no knowledge of the identity of your assailant?"

"Direct knowledge . . . no. From the police enquiry, however—"

"Thank you, Doctor. We must let the evidence speak for itself. But perhaps you will tell us what motive you attributed to this attack." Maitland opened his eyes at this point, though he did not bestir himself; and Counsel for the Prosecution said almost pettishly: "Oh, very well, very well. We will go the long way round. Tell me, Doctor Fraser, had you to your knowledge any enemies among the residents at Burnham Towers?"

"Certainly not," said Fraser. He spoke, perhaps, too forcefully, and Maitland turned his head to look up at him, frowning. Another point there . . . if it had been his job to look for them. And it might be worth a little probing, if only to annoy. Enmity was a strong word, of course, and the best of witnesses not above a quibble if they could square it with their conscience. He'd be willing to bet there was someone Fraser disliked in that party . . . someone he still disliked, even after the time that had passed.

Garfield was proceeding to his point.

"Was there anyone who would at that time have benefited from your death, Doctor? Say, financially?"

"My nephew, who was in the Far East with his regiment."

"Were you robbed while you were unconscious?"

"Not of any personal belongings. But my papers . . . laboratory reports . . . the notes of the project of which I spoke . . . they were missing." Even now, the memory disturbed him; Garfield pressed home his point.

"These were important documents, were they not?"

"Extremely so." Again, as he spoke of his work, the harsh voice took on a quality of humanity. "Five years' work . . . complete almost to the last detail. The final adjustments to be made—" He stopped, shaking his head, and suddenly one remembered that he had already been an eminent man twenty years ago; and not young then. "It was a great loss," he said.

"Then let me be assured I have the facts correctly, Doctor. You were working in the study on the papers connected with your invention; you were attacked and rendered unconscious by some person you did not see. Later, upon enquiry, you found that the documents were missing."

"That is quite correct; though the word invention should hardly be applied to a research project of that nature."

"Thank you, Doctor. Now I should like you to cast your mind back to a time just after the war ended when you visited the headquarters of Military Intelligence in London." Fraser nodded his agreement. "You were then shown certain documents . . . my lord, I should like to put this file into evidence."

"Something of interest, Mr. Garfield?"

"Of melancholy interest, my lord. It is the account, as it appeared in the German war records, of an experiment conducted in the late summer of 1943 in occupied Poland." He turned back to the witness. "Do you identify the file as being the one you then saw, Doctor Fraser?"

"Yes, I—"

"We are particularly interested in the pages I have marked. Will you tell us what they say? A paraphrase will be sufficient of all but the most important parts; there are copies here for the jury's use."

"They refer, as you have said, to an experiment made in 1943; there is the translation of a report of the *S.S. Oberfuehrer*, who himself took charge of the *Einsatz-kommando* who were ordered to initiate the experiment and observe its results." He paused, and Garfield said with bland insistence:

"Please read from the files, Doctor."

Fraser cleared his throat and sounded self-conscious as he obeyed. "He says: 'The canisters were taken at midnight to the bank of the town reservoir . . . we wore protective clothing, as instructed . . . the canisters contained a jelly-like substance which was introduced into the water of the reservoir . . . it started to break up immediately

His voice faltered.

"What else does the report say?" Garfield demanded.

"The troops of the *Wehrmacht* had been ordered to leave the area served by the reservoir. Within two weeks a violent epidemic broke out among the townspeople, the symptoms of which resembled those of *cholera sicca*. Under the direction of *S.S. Oberst Professor Doktor* Fritz Schmidthuber, the local doctors' requests for assistance were fully complied with." He looked up, and added, by way of explanation:

"The report becomes extremely technical at this point. Perhaps it will be better if I say that all known measures for fighting the disease were used, but in spite of wholesale inoculations, and everything that could be done, the outbreak went on unchecked for nearly five months." Again he paused, and this time Garfield made no attempt to break the silence. It was uncanny, Maitland thought, how still a crowded room could be. His glance flickered to the prisoner's face; there was an expression he couldn't quite place . . . surprise . . . shock? Or just plain incredulity? Unfortunately, the tale was by no means unbelievable . . .

"When a final accounting was made," said Fraser, in an expressionless voice, "the records showed that at least four thousand people . . . over forty per cent of the population . . . had died. There was also on the file," he added, "a note which recorded the townspeople's gratitude for the help they had been given."

"Thank you, Doctor; now, perhaps you will tell us the reason you were called into consultation upon this matter."

"There were reports on the file." He began to turn the pages. "It doesn't seem—"

"They have been removed. I must ask you to accept this evidence as it stands, my lord, without documentary corroboration. The matter is still classified as Top Secret."

"In the circumstances, Mr. Garfield, I shall be pleased to hear Doctor Fraser's statement of what he saw on the file in 1946." Conroy turned to the witness. "You will understand, Doctor, how much detail you can properly give."

"Yes, my lord. Perhaps it will be sufficient if I say that the reports were of a long series of experiments carried out under my supervision in Fairfield. In addition, there were the reports of the further work which had been done to complete the project . . . to produce the culture we were seeking."

"In your opinion, could the first experiments have been carried out independently in a German laboratory?"

"Not in precisely the same way. Such a duplication would have been quite impossible."

"I see. Now, there is just one further point, Doctor. Allowing them to be your reports, is it possible that they were stolen at a later date, after you had recovered from your illness and yourself completed the work?"

Fraser frowned. "Quite impossible," he said, again.

"If you will explain to us—"

"The final experiment took place in August 1943. There is no doubt that the reports on the file related directly to what was done at Dubenocz. But no further work was done on my project until November 1943, when I returned to my laboratory. In fact, in my absence—and Harland's—no work *could* have been done. It is true that there were duplicates of most of the documents on file, but my notes of the work I had done that day . . . the day I was attacked . . . were missing. They recorded, as it happened, an important breakthrough."

"So we must conclude that the information which led to this inhuman experiment was contained in the papers which were stolen on October 16th, 1942."

"I think that must be admitted."

"And that the notes you had made had been supplemented by the later work of some other person?"

"That, too, is obvious."

"Then I think I need not trouble you further, Doctor Fraser. Thank you for your help." His gesture invited his opponent to proceed.

Maitland got up slowly, he hadn't quite made up his mind yet as to the line of attack. There had been something odd there, something that had disturbed him, but he wasn't quite sure . . . go back, then, to the old question of identity; and try, above all, to lower a little the emotional temperature of the court.

"This picture that you said was unrecognisable, Doctor Fraser. You studied it, I have no doubt."

"I looked at it carefully."

"It had a caption, I suppose. Ah, yes—" Stringer pushed a folded newspaper in front of him, and he picked it up and read: 'Michael Godson, Brightsea photographer, who is assisting the police—'"

"Are you putting this newspaper in as evidence, Mr. Maitland?"

"Yes, my lord. But I should first like to know if it is the one the witness saw."

The paper went the rounds. To the witness, who nodded and said "that's the one."; to the Judge, who scrutinised it from several angles, and then peered suspiciously at the prisoner over the top of his spectacles; and finally to the jury box, where it went from hand to hand.

"The date of the newspaper," said Maitland, "is September 7th. Did you know at that time that this man was suspected of being Guy Harland?"

"The police had told me that an identification had been made."

"And so you looked at the picture very carefully?"

"I did."

"But saw no resemblance to the man you had known."

"None whatever." His tone was firm. That, he seemed to be saying, should settle the matter.

"The picture is admittedly of my client, Michael Godson. But you say there is no resemblance to Guy Harland?"

"I say you couldn't recognise anyone from that photograph."

"Look again, Doctor." (The newspaper was retrieved from the jury, and handed back to the witness.) "Discounting the swarthiness. The shape of the head, now . . . the hairline—"

"Harland's hair was thicker when I knew him than it is now."

"You will forgive me, sir, that is an extremely contentious remark. Look at the picture, please. The shape of the head—"

"It isn't clear . . . too blurred . . . no telling from that what the feller's really like."

"Very well. We will go back to your recollection of Guy Harland. You have already told us one point of difference—"

"If you mean his hair, that's natural, isn't it? After all this time."

"Oh, I agree, Doctor," said Counsel quickly. "After all this time!"

"If you mean he's changed in other ways too," said Fraser grudgingly, "I suppose he has. But that doesn't mean I don't recognise him."

"Well, tell me the points of resemblance then," Maitland invited. "His eyes wouldn't change, would they?"

"No, of course." Fraser studied the prisoner as he spoke with a bland unconcern for his feelings. "Blue," he added, and turned back to Counsel with a grin, as though somehow he had scored a point there.

"Not uncommon in fair men. You have blue eyes yourself, Doctor Fraser."

"Well, that's not the only thing, you know. He's thinner, I'd say, but he always was a dab of a fellow. No presence," he explained.

"But capable, I suppose, so far as his work was concerned."

"He was my assistant, wasn't he? I wouldn't employ a fool."

"And he worked for you . . . for how long?"

"Eighteen months. And for six months after he married, I must remind you, we lived under the same roof."

"I wonder if you have ever noticed, Doctor, how little one really observes about the people one sees every day."

"That's true enough. But it's not to say you wouldn't know them again."

"Even after twenty years, Doctor?"

"Yes," said Fraser. He spoke with something of a snap, and Derek scribbled a few words, and pushed the paper in front of his leader.

"You were ill for a year, I believe, after your injury," said Maitland. He looked down, and read Stringer's agitated scrawl: "Better leave it . . . more harm than good . . ." Well, there was something in that. He was thrusting in the dark for an opening, and getting nowhere fast. Fraser was keeping his head, if not his temper; but there was something odd, if only he could put his finger on it . . . something he had noticed . . .

He looked up at the witness again, and caught the end of the doctor's reply. ". . . longer than expected. It was another six months before I got back to work." And he remembered suddenly the completely unrelated fact that had previously struck him.

"What did you talk to Guy Harland about, Doctor, the evening you were attacked?"

The question seemed to confuse the witness. There was an appreciable pause, while he scowled at Counsel, and then he said slowly: "Does it matter? Is it important?" Maitland spread his hands in a consciously extravagant gesture.

"How can I know . . . unless you tell me?"

"My lord—"said Garfield, coming urgently to his feet. The Judge turned to the Defence Counsel.

"You seem to be shifting your ground, Mr. Maitland. Are you now querying Guy Harland's guilt?"

"That, my lord, is no affair of mine. I am querying the witness's recollection of events nearly twenty years ago; and that, I believe, *is* my concern."

There was a pause while Conroy reflected; with his underlip thrust out he looked more than ever cherubic . . . a sulky cherub, perhaps. "I believe you are right, Mr. Maitland," he said at last. "You may proceed." He turned a quelling glance on the Prosecution, in case they were inclined to protest this decision; Garfield was already seated again, but his eyes were watchful. If this was one of Maitland's tricks . . .

"The question, Doctor, concerned the subject of your conversation with Guy Harland—"

"We talked about the work we were doing . . . I suppose."

"You suppose, Doctor?"

"Yes, I . . . he was a much younger man, we had very little to say to each other, outside the laboratory."

"You deduce it, then. You don't remember?"

"Not precisely. But that would have been it . . . something about our work."

"How long was he with you, Doctor?"

"For ten minutes."

"And you had been together at the laboratory all day."

"Oh, yes."

"Then what remained to discuss, in so short a time as ten minutes, with this man with whom you had so little in common?"

"Our work." Fraser sounded dogged now.

"But you don't remember that, Doctor." Maitland's tone was insistent. "You only deduce it. Isn't that right?" The witness did not reply immediately, and he went on: "Do you know of your own knowledge, Doctor, how long Guy Harland was with you that evening?"

"Ten minutes . . . I was told."

"And when you say: the butler brought you coffee . . . you were working in the study . . . you were attacked—you are telling us what you were told, are you not? Not what you remember?"

Garfield took one look at the Judge's face, and thought better of a half-framed protest. Doctor Fraser kept his eyes fixed on the Defence Counsel and said gruffly: "It was all true!"

"Oh, yes, Doctor, I'll grant you that. The truth, as it was *told* you." He was pressing the witness frankly now, his whole attention absorbed in what he was doing. No time to note the expression on the prisoner's face (doubt, bewilderment?); no time to look down and see Stringer's hand suddenly still on the note-pad, or to hear the quick intake of breath with which he greeted an approaching crisis. No time to notice the sudden alertness in the jury-box, or to watch Garfield's expression grow colder and more disdainful. No time to see the Judge leaning forward, frowning. "But how much do you remember about the events that evening?"

"I remember going to the study." If Fraser was ill-at-ease, it was obvious he was also puzzled. "The rest . . . well, it's not uncommon to be forgetful after a blow on the head."

"Very natural," said Counsel; and the note of satisfaction was evident in his voice. "You were ill for a long time, weren't you? And now tell me, Doctor . . . how much do you *really* remember about Guy Harland?"

*

"Who'd have thought it?" said Derek Stringer. The Judge and his glory had departed; the prisoner had disappeared from the dock; the public were dispersing in a cloud of speculation. At the other side of the courtroom the jury were filing out, self-conscious still, and on their dignity. "But—did you see their faces?" asked Derek, exultantly.

Maitland was piling his papers together, but he looked up at his colleague with a gleam in his eye.

"If Conroy had sat for another five minutes—" he said. But the other man swept aside the tentative objection.

"It doesn't matter," he maintained. "Tell the court to-morrow there's no case for *Godson* to answer. They'll believe you!" He jerked his head in the direction of the leader for the Prosecution, who was standing near the door in stiff and apparently acrimonious converse with the representative of the Director of Public Prosecutions. "Take a look at Garfield," Derek invited. "He knows!"

Maitland took a quick glance across the court, returned to his task for a moment, and then abandoned it unfinished to Willett's eager hands. He leaned back with his hands clasped on the table in front of him.

"Mad as fire . . . *and* I don't blame him," he remarked. "If ever a witness didn't come up to proof . . . and after all the trouble he took bringing out the details of that filthy 'experiment.'" He turned to look up at his clerk. "I'm going straight home, Willett, when I've had a word with Mr. Horton; so don't wait for me."

"Yes, where is Geoffrey?" Stringer looked around as the clerk departed.

"He went to have a word with our client. I don't suppose he'll be long." And almost as he spoke the solicitor rejoined them. It would be too much to say that his air of jubilation had left him, but he was frowning to himself in a puzzled way.

"Can you spare a minute, Antony?" he asked. "Godson wants a word with you."

Maitland got up.

"Can't it wait?" He sounded reluctant. "After all—"

"I told him we'd make application to-morrow for the case to be dismissed, and that we'd every hope of being successful," said Geoffrey. He sounded aggrieved as he went on. "He didn't seem interested."

"Oh, well! Five minutes," conceded Maitland. "Are you off, Derek?"

"Unless you want me? It can't be all that important at this stage," said Stringer. "I'm due at the Hardakers."

"See you to-morrow, then. And I hope," he added, over his shoulder, as he turned to follow the solicitor, "I only hope your estimate of our chances is correct."

Their client was waiting in one of the narrow, cheerless rooms which are provided below the court for such interviews. Maitland thought as he went in that the light from the unshaded bulb was unkind to him, etching more deeply the lines of strain which by now were become habitual. The accused man got up, and stood with his hands in his pockets, waiting for Geoffrey to shut the door. Then he looked at his Counsel, and said with a faint smile:

"I thought before we go any further I'd better tell you I lied to you. I really am Guy Harland, you know."

CHAPTER 7

THURSDAY the third day (continued)

I n the room the silence lengthened. Horton gave a sharp exclamation of protest, but quickly thought better of what he had been about to say. Maitland was standing very still, his attention fixed on the man who had spoken. The prisoner's statement had not been without an undertone of apology, but still there was about him that disconcerting air of amusement. Antony said at last:

"So I have always s-supposed." His voice was quiet, but Geoffrey, hearing the slight stammer which he knew spelled trouble, came up quickly to his colleague's side. He was hurt and disappointed, and his voice was sharp with both these emotions.

"What the devil do you mean," he demanded, "by telling us that at this stage?"

Harland spared him a quick glance. "*Magna est Veritas,*" he remarked, as though absently; and turned again to Counsel. "Please don't think I don't appreciate all you've done," he added formally.

Maitland's smile held no amusement. "Finish the *quotation.*" he suggested. "You will forgive me for reminding you that in this instance the prevalence of truth is unlikely to be healthy for you."

"I hoped to persuade you," said Harland, still with diffidence, "that perhaps with your help—"

"D-damn you!" said Maitland. His own feelings were quite simple . . . he was furiously angry, and no longer tried to hide it. "You've made a f-fool of me—isn't that enough?—and now you have the impudence—"

"Do all your clients tell you the truth?" asked Harland. His tone was mildly curious.

"I'm not complaining that you l-lied to me," Maitland pointed out. "But why did you wait till now to tell me the truth?"

Guy Harland seemed to be growing cooler as the other man became more heated.

"You see, I didn't really know much about you," he explained gently.

Something in the simplicity of this statement caught Maitland's attention. His angry retort remained un-uttered, and he stood looking frowningly at the prisoner.

"If I'd told you the truth at the beginning—"said Harland.

"I wouldn't have taken the brief."

"Because I'm accused of treason?" For the first time he flushed, a faint tinge of colour only, but startling by contrast with the pallor he had acquired in prison. "I don't see the logic of that, I'm afraid."

"Don't worry, there isn't any. I nearly refused—"

"I wonder why you didn't?"

"Because . . . oh, Horton was pressing. (I'm not blaming you, Geoffrey—it was my own damn' silly fault —but you were keen on the case, weren't you?) And, after all, you were entitled to the benefit of the doubt." He paused, and looked at Harland in a puzzled way before harking back to his grievance. "Why did you tell me . . . now?" he asked, again.

The other man took his time about replying. He said, at last:

"I have realised for the past few days that for me this trial is the point of no return. I've drifted long enough; whatever happens, that's over now. But I've been watching you in court . . . you're a fighter."

"It's my trade," said Maitland. His interest was caught, and his anger was dying. "Words, words, words," he added, in a tone of discontent. Harland laughed suddenly.

"I can cap that for you," he said. "'Words and deeds are quite indifferent modes of the divine energy. Words are also actions—"

"Are they now?" Maitland eyed him consideringly. "I suppose you realise," he added, with gloomy satisfaction, "you'd have given yourself away within five seconds of opening your mouth in the witness box."

"I don't see . . . you mean, after Professor Dobson's evidence? I used to look up apposite quotations to annoy him, so I suppose you may say it's a judgment on me."

"I might even say," remarked the other bitterly, "'be sure your sins will find you out.' If I felt in the mood for badinage . . . which I don't."

"Anything," said Harland, "so long as you don't drag in the engineers. But I'm sorry . . . I seem to be managing this very badly." He paused, and added tentatively: "Couldn't we sit down while I tell you—"

"It isn't any use." Maitland's anger had been replaced by a sort of weary patience. "I can't act for you now."

"I don't think you understand. I'm not asking you to lie for me—"

Maitland took a step forward, and gripped the wooden back of the nearest chair.

"You must get another Counsel," he said. "Even if you've decided to change your plea—"

"I haven't. I . . . look here, you said before I was entitled to the benefit of the doubt—" For the first time he spoke with energy, even with desperation. "Doesn't that still hold? Won't you even listen to me?"

"What are you trying to tell me?" His voice was quiet, disbelieving. "You say you are Guy Harland. You say you don't wish to change your plea—"

"I'm trying to tell you: I didn't slug Fraser, I didn't pinch the lab reports. I was in Germany, yes, as a prisoner. There wasn't any treason about it."

Listening, Maitland was for a moment vividly aware of the man as he had been twenty years ago. Was the thought too fanciful . . . that it was Michael Godson who had lived through those years, while Harland (as witness the schoolboy phrases he had just produced) had remained unaltered?

"But the time for all this," he said implacably, "was sixteen years ago, when the war ended."

"I told you, I'm not a fighter." The animation left him again; he pulled out a chair, and sat down heavily, his elbows on the dusty table. "But it's gone on long enough. If this is the end . . . I'm still glad I told you."

"You're free to get another Counsel—"

Harland shook his head. "If you won't listen to me—" And as Antony looked at him the last shreds of his anger vanished. This was not the man described in the indictment . . . schemer, traitor, murderer. Or rather, he might be all these things, but still a man who had made his appeal for justice; and was he to be condemned unheard?

"All right—" he said, and pulled out the chair he was holding. As he seated himself, he looked round at Horton with a faint smile. "Without prejudice, Geoffrey," he said.

Horton was standing at the foot of the table. He looked confused and upset, very unlike himself.

"If I hadn't believed him innocent, I'd never have asked *you* to take the case," he said. And saw Maitland's expression harden as he spoke, so that he looked older, suddenly, and unfamiliar. Harland, watching, knew in that moment that his instinct had been a sound one: words were not Maitland's only weapon, or they had not always been. "In any case," Geoffrey added urgently, "you can't go on with it now."

"That's what I must find out. Don't you see?" He sounded tired. Horton shrugged angrily, and set his lips in a thin, stubborn line.

"I suppose we must listen," he said, grudgingly.

Harland was leaning back in the hard chair. His eyes were alert to take in what passed between his companions. Otherwise, he seemed the most relaxed of the three; and as the others turned their eyes on him— Horton angry and resentful; Maitland obviously reluctant—he met their scrutiny steadily enough.

"You know a good deal about me already," he began. Maitland laughed, and oddly his amusement seemed genuine.

"So we do," he agreed. "But you realise, I imagine, that there are things that need explaining."

Harland took his time to consider this. "I can tell you what happened," he said cautiously.

"You know, I suppose, the strength of the police case against you for the attack on Fraser?"

"Pretty well. I don't think I can answer it," he admitted. "I mean, I can tell you what I did, but—"

"We'll come back to it. An equally important point is the attack on the police officer, and your subsequent escape. Are you going to deny responsibility for that, too?"

"No, I . . . no. It seemed the only thing to do at the time. But I'm going to have to go back a bit if I'm to make you understand—"

"I suppose so," Maitland agreed. He glanced briefly at Horton, and then back again at the prisoner. "Well, tell it your own way," he said.

Harland did not respond immediately to this invitation.

"What Professor Dobson said was true enough," he said at last. "I didn't know whether to take the job with Fraser. The work I was doing was nominally reserved, but I didn't consider it vital, and I'd made up my mind to chuck it when my call-up came. But Fraser's project really did seem important, so that was that." He paused again, and again his glance from one to other of his companions was deprecating. "You'll think I'm telling you this, of course," he said, "to impress you—"

"Of course," Maitland agreed. "If you could just forget how it sounds, and give me a straightforward narrative—"

"Very well. But it isn't easy—"

"I don't suppose it is," said the other, unsympathetically. "Go on."

"I took the job, and went into digs in Fairfield. When I was getting married, about a year later, Lady Torrington said we could go to the Towers—"

"Just a minute. How did that come about?"

"That was Charlie . . . Charlie Conrad. He was at Fairfield Chemicals too, in the works. Production Engineer, or something. Efficient sort of chap, and by way of being a pal of mine. He was at Burnham Towers already, and as it was almost impossible to find anywhere to live . . . well, we'd had to put off the wedding once, so the chance to go there was a godsend. It was a funny household, I suppose, though it seemed natural enough at the time. I was thinking about it to-day when Sir Gervase was giving his evidence. He's aged a lot, of course, and I got quite a shock to hear the old lady was dead."

"It was in the depositions," said Maitland.

"Yes, but I couldn't let you know I had any interest in them . . . remember? Anyway, there we all were. You saw Sir Gervase; Lady Torrington was very like him, I don't mean in looks, but without an unkind thought in her head, I should say. Fraser . . . well, you've seen him too. He wasn't best pleased at our going there. A clever chap, mind you, but not exactly a sympathetic character. And there was his secretary, Esther Marne—"

"She's one of the Prosecution witnesses. But her name's Conrad now."

"So old Charlie finally made it." He shook his head over the thought. Up to a point he seemed to be enjoying this excursion into the past, but it was unlikely, Antony considered, that he would be able to maintain his detachment. "He was pretty deeply in love with her," Harland went on, "but she never seemed able to see him. Her fancy was a chap called Wilmot—Harry Wilmot— a friend of Hugh Torrington who used to come on leave with him fairly regularly. I couldn't see that, either, he was a quiet sort, not much personality." He caught Maitland's eye, and for the first time his smile was completely natural. "I say, aren't we having a lovely, vulgar gossip!"

Maitland grinned at that.

"Go on," he repeated. "You haven't told me what you thought about Mrs. Conrad."

"A hell-cat," said Harland promptly. "Handsome enough . . . you couldn't say pretty; dark, a little hard-looking. About twenty-eight then, a little younger than Charlie, a little older than Wilmot, I imagine. Tongue like an adder."

"You don't seem to like the lady."

"No." He seemed about to add some further comment, but thought better of it and bit the word off with a snap. Maitland stored up a question in his mind, but did not press it then.

"And the other visitors?" he prompted.

"I've mentioned Wilmot. I didn't get to know him really well, although he was there a good deal. Hugh I was friendly with, a thoroughly good chap. Not one of the world's great brains . . . a little conventional, perhaps. I liked him."

"And Mrs. Harland? Did she share your sentiments?" (Yes, that was the point round which Harland had been skirting so deftly. He kept his relaxed pose, but his right hand clenched momentarily.)

"Mary?" His voice at least held no emotion. "As far as I remember, she shared my views. That only leaves the Thurlows—Robin Thurlow and his wife. They hadn't been there before."

"A full house," Maitland commented. His tone was light, but his eyes were watchful. "And so, at last, we may come, perhaps, to the facts?"

"So far as I know them," Harland amended. "The first thing, anyway, wasn't a fact at all, it was a feeling, an impression. I've thought about it since, of course, I've had all the time in the world to think about it. But still I can't be definite, I can only say there was something wrong at the lab. It was as if some unauthorised person were prowling about, reading one's notes, moving things from where they had been left. But there was nobody there but the four of us . . . Fraser, and Montague whom you saw in court the first day), and Esther Marne, and myself. Well, I put it down to imagination, but still I felt jittery."

"Take your time," said Maitland. "We are coming now, I suppose, to the day Fraser was attacked—"

"Yes, well . . . the trouble was, you see, Fraser was damnably careless. He'd got into the habit of bringing stuff home to work on, and that night I had a feeling . . . there was a sort of excitement about him, most unusual. I'd done my best to persuade him, tactfully, that it wasn't a good idea; and that was why I went into the study after dinner, to try to find out if he'd brought home anything he shouldn't."

"The other members of the household—"

"Sir Gervase went out. The others were in the drawing-room then, I think. Later . . . I don't know."

"Well, tell me about your talk with Doctor Fraser."

"He was writing a letter when I went in. I hinted around the subject for a bit, and then asked him point blank if he'd brought his notes home. He told me it was none of my business . . . well, he put it rather more forcibly than that. And when I saw I wasn't getting anywhere, I came away."

"After about ten minutes?"

"Yes. At least, I don't remember exactly, but that was pretty well established when the police started checking up on times, and so on."

"I see. We can leave the details for the moment; what else must you tell me before you explain your attack on the unfortunate Sergeant Fell?"

"I don't suppose I can explain it," said Harland. "Even to me, at this distance of time . . . well, you know that, for one reason and another, the police suspected me of trying to kill Fraser. But they hadn't any ideas about motive. On the other hand, I was worried to death about what might have happened; but you must remember I didn't *know* whether he'd had the reports with him, I only thought it was possible. If he'd brought them home, they had gone now . . . that was certain. The local inspector told me that; at least, he told me there was only some personal correspondence in Fraser's brief-case."

"I don't see why you didn't ask somebody straight—"

"Of course, it's obvious now," said Harland, sounding for the first time a little impatient, "what I should have done. Then, my only desire was not to start anything. With the security people, you know. They'd have raised hell, and it wasn't as if I knew—and Fraser was my chief, after all."

"You could have found out, I suppose, at the laboratory."

"The police weren't exactly encouraging; besides, there was very little time. The balloon went up on Friday night. On Saturday morning they were busy interviewing us all; and in the afternoon they found the gun in my suitcase. When they had satisfied themselves it had been used as a blunt instrument and was what they were looking for, they arrested me without any further ado."

"Whereupon you made doubt certainty by knocking out one of them and decamping?"

For the first time since the beginning of this strange interview, Harland seemed ill at ease. He tugged at his collar, and the look he gave his Counsel was almost furtive.

"It isn't easy to explain," he said.

Maitland's smile was mocking, and to mimic the other man's habit of quotation was as natural to him as breathing.

"'He either fears his fate too much,'" he remarked. "But you can't do yourself any harm by telling me."

The other man took the point.

"I suppose not," he said gloomily. "Well, I had managed to phone Montague; he wasn't much impressed by my alarms, but he said he'd go over to the lab a bit later on. He had a date for lunch, so it was afternoon before he got there. When he did he phoned back. 'I can't find the file of reports,' he said, 'or Fraser's working papers. You'd better come over right away.' So I went to find the police superintendent, but he was already looking for me, and I never got a chance to ask him if I could go over to the lab."

"Montague was called by the prosecution. There was none of this," said Geoffrey, "in the depositions."

"There wouldn't be." Maitland answered the objection absently. "Nobody asked him, of course. Why should they? But if we do ask him, and he confirms what happened, it still doesn't help us at all."

"I thought perhaps you'd understand that bit," said Harland. He sounded depressed. "I got the wind up badly . . . strangely enough, it was quite a disinterested emotion at that stage. So I thought I'd better go and look, and decide—with Montague—what had better be done. It sounds foolish now, but I didn't really take the police accusation very seriously."

"Well, you admit *this* attack. We'll go on from there. You left Fell unconscious, and left Burnham Towers without being seen?"

"Without being seen by the police," Harland corrected him. "I saw Harry Wilmot as I crossed the hall, but I don't suppose he knew what had happened."

"So what did you do?"

"I set off for the lab, going cross country, not by the lanes. The track came out on a hill, with the works at the other side of the valley. You had to go down through a churchyard—the village was about a quarter of a mile away—and across a couple more fields, and through a farmyard. But the last thing I remember is climbing the stile into the churchyard."

"Don't tell me!" said Maitland sceptically. "You were knocked out, too!"

"I know it doesn't sound likely, but I was," said Harland. He looked at the other man helplessly. "I don't see how I can convince you," he added.

"Well, do your best." His tone was not encouraging. "For a start, you might try explaining—"

"If you mean, how anyone knew I'd be there, I can only suppose I was followed. Whoever took the reports must have been backed by some outside organisation. I think they kept me under drugs after that, because I only remember a very little about the journey." Harland spoke doggedly. He seemed to have lost all expectation of being believed, and Maitland interrupted him with a return of his former anger.

"Like a dream, I suppose? And you woke up in Germany? And somebody else—not you, of course!—became a collaborator. I don't think I like this story, Harland."

"I don't care for it much, myself. Is it worth my going on, do you suppose?"

"Having got so far," said Maitland. Harland stared at him for a moment, as though trying to find in his expression an encouragement his words did not give. Then he shrugged.

"'Things past redress are now, with me, past care,'" he remarked. The affectation of his student days had become, with the passage of time, a habit so strong that he no longer noticed its indulgence. "As you guessed, I came fully to myself in Germany . . . a big, old house in the country; a place called Litzen, not too far from Berlin, I was told. And I wasn't left long in any doubt as to the position. The police at home were looking for me still, they told me, and for Fraser's papers, too, now that they were known to be missing."

"Did they tell you why they had gone to so much trouble—?"

"The theft of the papers had taken place before the time it was planned for, I was never quite clear why. They seemed to know the work wasn't quite completed, and I got the impression that taking me along was more or less of an afterthought. I suppose the main idea was to make use of me, but there's no doubt my disappearance lent a certain amount of verisimilitude to an otherwise bald and unconvincing narrative."

Maitland was looking up at the window, where a small patch of darkening sky was visible beyond the dusty panes.

"I see," he said, drawing out the words doubtfully, so that the claim seemed to have no substance. Then he said, "And so, you agreed to help them?" and his eyes were on Guy Harland again, and they were intent.

"But that's just it, I didn't!" the other man protested. His voice (light, anyway, in contrast to his companion's) rose as he went on. "I strung them along for a while . . . that wasn't just self-interest, though I don't mind admitting I was scared stiff; but it seemed better than letting one of their own top brains get at it."

"And meanwhile, you were comfortable?" The words were softly spoken, but cutting in their very quietness. Harland leaned forward suddenly, and banged both his fists on the heavy table.

"Dammit, no!" he exclaimed. "Can't you see, it was the best thing I could think of? But it wasn't easy, fooling them; they didn't trust me, you know, I couldn't relax a minute."

"You needn't labour the point," said Maitland. "My imagination will carry me that far."

"Well, if you don't believe me—"said Harland, answering the other's tone rather than his words. "But there is one thing—and you can check on this, even if those depositions you're always talking about don't mention it. That 'experiment' they were describing to-day . . . I was already in Switzerland—"

"What difference would that make," Antony demanded, "if you'd finished your work before you went?"

"But I didn't . . . that's what I'm telling you." His voice rose on the assertion.

"Who, then?"

"I don't know . . . oh, God, I don't know."

Maitland's eyes were fixed on his face. "That lab assistant," he suggested. "What's his name, Geoffrey? Gunther? Could he—?"

"Well, to be honest," said Harland, reluctantly, "I doubt if he'd have had the intelligence. I mean, he was spying on me, I suppose, under guise of helping me; I used to hear him in the lab at night. And a fine game of round-the-mulberry-bush we played with each other. But 'lab assistant' isn't really the right description."

"It's how he describes himself in his proof."

"Well, he had a degree, I'm pretty sure I heard that from someone or other. But I don't think he was particularly bright. In six months he never seemed to realise I was doing a Penelope on him, and we weren't getting anywhere."

"That," said Maitland, "doesn't comfort me at all." Horton looked at him frowningly; but the prisoner was intent on his story, and went on without apparently noticing the interruption.

"I kept up the pretence for as long as I could—nearly seven months, in fact. Then they were getting a bit too suspicious for comfort, I knew it meant they'd hand the thing over to one of their own chaps. I suppose I'd been hoping some chance of escape would present itself. So when there was nothing else to do, I destroyed the whole thing . . . the file of reports and all Fraser's notes." He looked at Maitland, trying to read his expression, and then added urgently. "I should have done that in the first place, as soon as they trusted me enough to give me an opportunity. But it isn't an easy decision . . . to choose death deliberately. I kept on hoping—"

"But you didn't die?" The words were a question, gently spoken; but Harland seemed to sense some implied reproach. He looked down at his hands, clenched on the table in front of him, and said:

"I don't suppose you'll believe me—"

"You may as well try," Maitland suggested. "You've said that before, you know," he added, "and it doesn't really help."

"You won't," said Harland, "find it at all easy to digest. Especially as the work got itself completed, anyway. Orders came through that we were to move, I don't know to this day where we were heading for. I stuffed a brief-case with scrap paper, left instructions about packing the equipment, and set off in the back of a car with two guards. We seemed to be going in a south-westerly direction, and we travelled for an hour or two. Then we had an accident."

"A fortunate coincidence," said Maitland politely.

"Yes, wasn't it?" His dry tone matched the other man's. "We skidded off the road and hit a tree . . . my impression was, the driver was taken ill, a heart attack, perhaps, but I could be wrong about that. The guard on my right was . . . injured . . . dead . . . I don't know. The other chap forced the door open, and we scrambled out. It was the queerest thing, I never remember thinking about it at all, but I'd grabbed the other man's revolver, and I let him have it, in the back. After that, I made myself scarce." He stopped, and looked carefully at his two companions in turn. Maitland's expression he found enigmatic, but the younger man was obviously hostile, it seemed a pity now he had espoused his cause so heartily in the beginning. Maitland had been angry when he admitted his identity, but not disillusioned. "That's it, really," he said, and the diffident note was back in his voice again. "Unless you want an account of my travels."

"You'd better tell us," said Maitland, "where Godson came into the picture. You had his story off pretty smoothly . . . or was it just invention?"

"No. I fell in with him when I was making for the Swiss border. We nearly got caught, and had to double back and hide up for a day or two. That's when I found out so much about him . . . all the things I told you were true enough. His parents had lived in Germany since about 1930; he'd been to school in England, but spent the rest of his time with them. Now they were dead there were no other relations, and precious few acquaintances, as far as I could make out. He'd been interned, and was trying to get away . . . as I was. They shot him when we were crossing the border."

"Why did you use his name?"

"It seemed the easiest thing to do." He sounded tired now, as though it was no longer worth the effort to try to force their belief. "I was very conscious of being 'wanted' in England, and I didn't see any chance of clearing myself. But I could start afresh as Godson, when at last I got home."

"Yes, of course. But you haven't explained," said Maitland, leaning forward, "what place your wife had in these plans."

Harland's weariness seemed to have taken him beyond resentment, but he did not meet the other man's eye.

"I wouldn't have helped her much by coming out into the open to face a charge of treason," he said. And added, with an odd mixture of shame and diffidence: "You see, I thought most likely she believed it too."

And that, thought Maitland, is probably as near the truth of it as we can get . . . as near as he knows himself. He looked at the prisoner, trying to view him dispassionately: a man who, if his story were true, could move on occasion with courage and energy, but who wasn't a fighter by nature . . . who took the easy road, when stimulus was lacking . . . who was asking him now for help. But there had been a ring of truth in the story about shooting the German guard, the mood of its telling was one he could understand. He turned to look at Geoffrey, and found the solicitor eyeing him enquiringly.

"I hope you're not going to walk out on us, Horton," he said. "I've decided to keep the brief."

Geoffrey went on looking at him, and what he saw gave him no confidence in his own ability to dissuade his friend from a course of action he saw as foolhardy.

"I have no cause to withdraw," he said.

"Precisely." Maitland gave his sudden smile. (But there was a question of loyalty here, which both of them recognised, though neither would have mentioned it.) "Then, we'd better get down to cases, hadn't we?"

Guy Harland was leaning back in his chair. Again he seemed to have resigned responsibility for what was going on; he was watching his companions with detached interest. Now he looked at Counsel and asked,

"If you believe me, is there any more to be said?" (As though it were all perfectly simple, thought Antony, his irritation back in full measure.)

"A good deal, I'm afraid," he said. "First, I want some details, and then we'll go over them, and over them, and over them again." He watched Harland's expression change from apathy to consternation, and laughed shortly. "Did you really think it was going to be easy?" he asked.

The prisoner looked down again, not meeting his eye.

"I've been drifting for so long," he explained. "I'm beginning to wish—" He broke off and looked up, and smiled, surprisingly, with what seemed genuine amusement. "I'm very brave generally," he apologised, "only to-day I happen to have a headache."

*

When Antony made his way home at last, it was with his friend's warning loud in his ears.

"You're going to make a fool of yourself," Horton had stated bluntly, and his own reply had been almost petulant.

"Well, I know that, don't I?" But the alternative . . . to pass by on the other side . . . was not in his nature. The appeal had been made, and his mind had reluctantly accepted its validity. That he should respond was, therefore, inevitable; he might not like the consequences, but that couldn't be helped.

"But I only wish," he said disconsolately to Jenny—much later, when the light was out and the darkness friendly, "I only wish it was anyone but Garfield. He's such a sarcastic brute," he complained, "and if I lose my temper—" Jenny gave a consoling grunt, and he rolled over and pulled her towards him, so that his next words were muffled in her hair. "Not to mention old Conroy," he said. "Oh, lord!"

CHAPTER 8

FRIDAY, the fourth day

Mr. Justice Conroy leaned forward. His air of patient courtesy had never been more marked, or more deceptive.

"I think perhaps I did not hear you correctly, Mr. Maitland. Would you mind repeating—?"

"I said, my lord, that I must advise the court of a change in the Defence which we are putting forward." His voice was strained, with the effort of repeating himself without sounding impatient.

"So much I had gathered," said the Judge, drily.

"Yes, my lord." He glanced down at the notes he had made, which were scattered untidily on the table in front of him. Indecipherable, anyway . . . it was lucky he didn't need them. "As your lordship knows, my instructions were to contest the case, not on the grounds of Guy Harland's innocence, but on the grounds of mistaken identity. The prisoner was, in fact, Michael Godson, a photographer from Brightsea, and a victim—as Adolf Beck was a victim—of a chance resemblance and the fallibility of human recollection. To-day I know that this contention was untrue. Last night he admitted to me that he is, in fact, the man named in the indictment . . . that he is Guy Harland."

Counsel's words fell into a silence as cold and uncanny as only the absolute hush in a crowded room can be. Maitland was not looking his best this morning; as he had been up half the night with Stringer, that was hardly surprising. To his further discomfort, the Judge seemed in no hurry to comment on what he had said. Conroy was looking round the court, and noted as he did so the prisoner's aloof air; Geoffrey Horton's anxiety; Stringer's tense look, so very uncharacteristic; Garfield's sudden eagerness, and the rather cruel smile with which he listened to his opponent's words.

"Well, Mr. Maitland," he said at last, "that is not what I expected to hear from you this morning. I should like to know, if I am not unduly curious, what moved your client to make this admission?"

"My lord, when the time comes for him to give evidence, he will explain the matter himself. But in the circumstances, I think you will agree, his action was certainly not prompted by self-interest."

Conroy ignored this. "I should like to have your own position clear, Mr. Maitland. Do you wish to retire from the case?"

"No, my lord."

"But you say your client has confessed—"

"With respect, my lord, he has *admitted* his identity—"

"A distinction, in this case, in which it is hard to detect a difference."

Maitland, protesting, noted from his eye corner that Stringer's pen had begun to move across the fresh sheet of paper in front of him.

"My lord, in the circumstances which have arisen I must, of course, retire from the case if I believed my client guilty—"

Counsel for the Prosecution was on his feet.

"My lord—"

"Yes, Mr. Garfield?"

"My friend's position is a strange one, when for the past three days he has tried so earnestly to convince the court that the prisoner was nothing but an innocent bystander."

"In the circumstances—"Maitland began.

"The circumstances seem to be that the prisoner lied to you, as he has lied to the authorities." Garfield's tone was sharp. Maitland, who was not enjoying the interlude, hung on to his temper with both hands and turned again to address the Judge.

"My client, my lord, can best explain his evasion—"

"We are to proceed, then?" Garfield's inflection of sarcasm was no balm for wounded feelings.

"Certainly we will proceed. Guy Harland has pleaded 'not guilty,' and we are prepared to substantiate that claim." His glance flickered to the impassive face of the Judge. "When my friend has had his fill of an amusing situation—"

"If you feel it proper to continue to act, Mr. Maitland, I shall not question your decision. Mr. Stringer?"

"I shall follow my leader, m'lord," said Derek, looking up and smiling with one of his rare flashes of humour.

"And now, I suppose," said Garfield, still heavily sarcastic, "after this affecting display of unanimity, the Defence will ask time to prepare their case." As he spoke Maitland realised, with a sense of shock, that his opponent was genuinely antagonistic . . . that he felt some trick was involved, something against which his stern ideas rebelled. That was worse than he expected; also, it was . . . annoying. He said sharply:

"Would you dispute our right?"

"No indeed. I think if you are to defend Guy Harland you will need all the assistance you can get—"

"We shall ask for no indulgence."

"Very well!" said Garfield. And the words sounded like a threat. The Judge leaned forward again.

"If you are satisfied with the position, Mr. Maitland, it is not for me to cavil," he said. "Shall we proceed?" he enquired of Garfield.

"As your lordship pleases. But may I first say that I envy my learned friend. I hope the years will not rob him of his simple faith—"

Maitland sat down, fuming.

"Simple faith," indeed! Then the humour of the situation struck him, and he looked up at Garfield and gave one of his sudden smiles. The other man frowned back at him suspiciously; and Mr. Justice Conroy, catching the exchange of glances, for once in his life owned himself puzzled.

"You may call your next witness, Mr. Garfield," he said. And as he waited he looked for the first time with real interest at the man in the dock. Now his identity was admitted, he was more of an enigma than ever; Maitland was no fool, there must be something to be said for the Defence . . . but Maitland, outwardly unruffled, saw only too clearly the difficulties which lay ahead. His own belief in Guy Harland was an intangible thing, and his reasons for holding it could not be adduced as evidence. And even if he was right . . . where now to look for proof?

*

Jenny Maitland sat back on her heels, and looked down at the sheets of newspaper which were spread around her on the floor with something like despair. She had been prepared, of course, for a mild sensation; the question "Harland, or Godson?" had caught the public fancy, and the abrupt answer her husband had given in court that morning could hardly be expected to go unremarked.

But now, with the headlines screaming at her dramatically, she was appalled by the extent of the turmoil. It would have been so easy just to have withdrawn from the case, as anyone else would have clone. ("So easy, love, and so damnably impossible," Antony had said to her; and when he felt like that there was nothing to be done about it.) And now, Uncle Nick had come home unexpectedly, and she didn't know whether to be glad or sorry . . .

Sir Nicholas Harding had taken his favourite chair, and was leaning back watching her with a half smile that Jenny found anything but reassuring. She ran her fingers through her hair again, leaving her brown curls in an even wilder disorder, and looked up at him with her head a little on one side.

"You mustn't be cross, Uncle Nick," she said.

"Cross!" said Sir Nicholas, stung by this inadequate description of his emotions. "I am not cross. Outraged, if you like . . . infuriated—"

"I don't like," said Jenny firmly. "And I think it's a pity you came home at all, if you're going to be disagreeable."

"They settled out of court," explained Sir Nicholas patiently. "Unexpectedly," he added.

"Yes, I know. You know I'm glad to see you. But I don't see why you need to be so horrid about all this." Her gesture embraced the scattered sheets of newsprint. Sir Nicholas looked down at them briefly, and his eyes came back to her face again.

"Because it's insane!" he protested. "Last night the case was as good as over—"

"But he didn't want Harland to tell him! I explained that, Uncle Nick."

"You've been 'explaining' ever since I came in," said Sir Nicholas, with sudden tartness. "I just don't understand. Antony went into this case with a properly cynical attitude, no illusions at all. And now—"

"Now he believes what Harland has told him. I don't know if he's right, Uncle Nick, but—"

"But no one has ever suggested Harland might be innocent . . . it just hasn't arisen. And if he is, how can it be proved at this stage? Look at the papers: 'Harland confesses . . . Counsel clash' (whatever that means). And as for Conroy—"

"He has to do what he thinks is right," said Jenny stubbornly. Sir Nicholas looked at her—curls ruffled, cheeks flushed, eyes bright and indignant—and his expression softened.

"Of course," he agreed. Jenny looked at him suspiciously: an indolent figure, whose sudden capitulation did not deceive her for a moment.

"You weren't always so concerned with what's sensible," she said, accusingly; and he laughed.

"Put those rags out of sight before Antony gets home," he advised. "And come and sit down and be comfortable. I'll reserve my strictures, at least until I've heard what he has to say."

Half an hour later, Maitland found them conversing amiably in the firelight. He showed no surprise at his uncle's presence, but turned on the lamp behind his chair and handed him an evening paper folded open at the account of the morning's proceedings.

"You've seen that, I suppose," he said.

Sir Nicholas took the paper without looking at it, and tucked it down the side of his chair.

"I've seen it," he admitted. His nephew looked at him quickly.

"You must be wondering—"

"Not at all," said the older man, blandly. "Jenny has been explaining—"

Antony looked doubtfully from one to the other. He had the greatest possible affection for his wife, and no faith at all in her ability for lucid exposition. Sir Nicholas smiled at him.

"She wasn't very clear," he confessed. "But I think I understand matters. Your principles are rampant again."

"I suppose that's fair comment," Maitland admitted. He looked down at the fire, approved it, and took up his stand with his back to the hearth. "I never wanted a brief less than I want this one . . . now," he said.

"But you feel you must continue?"

"Yes . . . unfortunately." Jenny had been pouring sherry, and he took a glass from her with rather an absent smile, and turned to put it down carefully on the mantelpiece. "'Stay me with flagons,'" he remarked. "But I could do with something more substantial than apples, love, if you really want to comfort me."

"Supper's nearly ready," said Jenny. "Though, of course, with Uncle Nick here—"she added, doubtfully.

Sir Nicholas looked alarmed. "My dear child, it's bad enough that I arrived home unexpectedly. I cannot . . . I simply cannot ask Mrs. Stokes to give me a meal at a moment's notice," he said. Jenny showed no signs of relenting.

"I expect I'll find you something," she said severely, and went out to the kitchen. Her husband looked after her with amusement.

"A dry crust and a piece of salt cod, I shouldn't wonder," he remarked. But his expression was serious when he turned again to his uncle. "I'd like to tell you, sir," he said. "If you won't be bored."

Sir Nicholas listened without comment to the account of the interview with Harland the previous evening. He was frowning when his nephew had finished.

"I don't need telling you think he's innocent," he said. "I wish I felt equally convinced. He sounds a strange sort of fellow."

Maitland turned to retrieve his glass, and moved across to the chair opposite his uncle's.

"No stranger than the rest of us, I suppose," he said, thoughtfully. "I'm inclined to like him. And there's a sort of . . . of consistency about his actions; he says himself he isn't a fighter, but when matters reach the stage when there's nothing else to be done, he acts. His decision to admit his identity yesterday was all of a piece with killing the German guard and knocking out the constable. He couldn't face life again as Godson, and so he made his announcement—"

"And left you to pick up the pieces. Which brings us," said Sir Nicholas, "to what happened in court to-day."

"Substantially what you saw in the papers. Garfield's out for blood now . . . he can't see where the trick lies, but he feels there must be one somewhere."

"Well, I suppose there is this much in your favour," said Sir Nicholas, thoughtfully, "that Harland's belated candour is more easily explained on the assumption of his innocence than of his guilt."

"Do you think so?" He did not sound wholly convinced, and the older man looked at him questioningly. "After we'd finished wrangling, the case continued. First we had a couple who saw a boat put out to sea from the Suffolk coast that Sunday night—the 18th October, 1942. Three men were in it, and they were 'acting suspicious.'" He turned, and looked down moodily into the fire. "Well, you know, Uncle Nick, it didn't even help the Prosecution much; it certainly didn't help us."

"If Harland was genuinely incapacitated at the time—"

"They wouldn't remember. All they *do* recall is an impression that something was wrong. And a vague idea that one of the men was older than the others. Derek did his best with that, but they just wouldn't be pinned down."

"How did the Prosecution get in touch with them?"

"That was quite easy. The man was a gunner at the time—A.A.—and when he got back to camp he put in a report. Well, that got passed on 'through channels,' and eventually finished up in the Intelligence files. They weren't sure at the time it meant anything, but when the reports came in that Harland had been seen in Germany—"

"Yes, I see. And that, I suppose, is how this extremely vague couple happen to be able to swear to a date nearly twenty years ago?"

"*She* remembered it, anyway," said Antony. He grinned almost cheerfully. "It was the evening they 'fixed to get married'; and 'six months to the day before young Tom was born.'" His uncle scowled at him.

"Not at all funny," he agreed apologetically. "But Garfield's face as he tried to head her off was the one bright spot to-day."

"I envy your light-heartedness," said Sir Nicholas coldly. "If we could return—"

"Yes, well, we got through all the witnesses who knew Harland in Germany. Except the lab assistant, Hans Gunther—I got his evidence postponed. Conroy pointed out—of course—that I'd said I didn't need any favours. But he gave me what I wanted, so I suppose I shouldn't grumble that he had his fun first." His voice took on a note of apology as he continued. "I know my limitations, Uncle Nick. I ought to leave Gunther to Derek."

"Your own feelings," said Sir Nicholas, "have no place in court, as you very well know." He spoke with his usual authority, but absently. "As things stand at present—"

"I know, I'm going to swot up on cholera and tackle him myself."

"That," said his uncle, coldly, "should enliven the proceedings considerably. And the other witnesses?" he added sharply.

"An inconclusive lot, sir. There were some R.A.F. types who were taken to the house at Litzen at one time or another for questioning. In particular a chap called Myles—a squadron-leader at that time—who saw Harland on several occasions. They had all heard that he was 'assisting' the Germans; they knew nothing to prove the assertion, but neither had anything come up which tended to disprove it, and he was apparently moving about freely. A security chap was next (name not given). He was more dangerous. He'd been working in the neighbourhood, knew all about Harland from the Nazi point of view, wasn't to be shaken in his belief that he was collaborating up to the hilt."

"Yes," said Sir Nicholas, drawing out his words in a meditative way, "I see your difficulty."

"I thought you might. They were all obviously in good faith, it was delicate work, a violent attack would only have antagonised the jury."

"At least, there was nothing that couldn't be rebutted . . . nothing completely and finally damning."

"Nothing like that."

"And if your precious client is telling the truth—"

"I know," said Maitland. "It means he was framed by someone living (or staying) at Burnham Towers. So it is there we must look for the traitor; and for the evidence—if any—of his guilt."

"Exactly. And how do you propose—you will forgive the question, I know!—how do you propose to set about it? You've got the whole weekend before you," he added, helpfully. His nephew laughed.

"Do you think I'm mad, sir? But at least, I can try."

"Of course you can," said Sir Nicholas. The note of cordiality in his voice did not deceive his nephew for an instant. "But—failing a miracle— what have you got, now, at this moment, to oppose to Garfield's case?"

"Harland's own story." Again, Maitland sounded apologetic.

"You *are* mad!" said the other man, positively. "I admit I haven't given the matter much thought yet, but I cannot feel that the tale he told you is going to sound convincing."

There was a gentle bumping on the door, and Antony, opening it, found Jenny outside with a tray. As he helped her, he found that his spirits were rising. He had come home depressed and over-tired; but already, under the stimulus of his uncle's disapproval, his mind was beginning to grapple with the problems ahead. He lifted the lid from a casserole, and sniffed absent-mindedly; and then picked up a spoon and began to stir the contents.

"It smells good," he said. "Couldn't we begin? I'm famished."

Jenny put down the pile of hot plates she was holding, and took the spoon from him firmly.

"That's the general idea," she said. "Come along, Uncle Nick. Have you finished complaining yet?"

Sir Nicholas accepted a plate, and said meekly: "I was just getting into my stride. However, I'm prepared to postpone hostilities. Er—what is this you're giving us, my dear?"

"It's . . . well, it's a sort of a mixture," said Jenny, who hated to be pinned down to details. "It tastes all right, doesn't it?" she added, suspiciously.

"Excellent," Sir Nicholas assured her. Antony prodded with his fork and said hollowly:

"Salt cod . . . I told you so."

"It's nothing of the kind," said Jenny, rising to the bait as he had known she would. "There is some lobster in it, but—" Antony gave a shout of laughter.

"I was wondering," said Sir Nicholas, a few minutes later, "what my old friend Conroy thinks about all this."

"It was pretty bad luck we got him," said Antony. He looked at his wife for sympathy, and added sadly, "He thinks I'm frivolous."

"And with reason," said his uncle. "Did he never tell you," he asked Jenny, "what happened the first time they met?"

"When I was about thirteen," said Antony, indignantly. "He came to dinner, and of all the—"

"He was telling me a most interesting anecdote," the other interrupted firmly. "A trifle protracted, perhaps, but that is by the way. The point of the story concerned a question of champerty—which is a serious matter, child, no cause for amusement." (Jenny was looking unnaturally solemn.) "Well, just as we thought he was really coming to the point at last, your husband—who was certainly old enough to have known better—asked his neighbour in a far-too-audible whisper if champerty wasn't 'drinking out of an actress's slipper'?"

"Well, I really wanted to know," the younger man pointed out reasonably.

"I might have found it amusing," Sir Nicholas reflected, "if you hadn't gone on, in the midst of one of the most ghastly silences I remember, to confide in that same neighbour—Bird, wasn't it? Yes, I'm sure it was Bird—that I, being a bachelor, would be able to tell them all about that."

"It doesn't really matter what your emotions were," said Antony, passing his plate hopefully to his wife, "but Conroy is still apt to eye me thoughtfully, as though wondering what I might be going to say next. It seems rather unjust, after all this time."

"You didn't tell me, however—"

"To-day? Well, I think he was puzzled. He's a chap who never misses a chance of taking a rise out of one, Uncle Nick; so I suppose he enjoyed himself, really."

"Will you reach the core of the Prosecution's case on Monday?"

"Yes, I forgot to tell you. We had the police inspector from Burnham Green to-day; and the medical evidence about Fraser's injuries."

"What did the police evidence amount to?"

"Too much," said Antony. He sounded rueful. "Harland went to the study and 'had words' with Doctor Fraser. His cigarette case was put into evidence; he was seen with it after he left the study, but later it was found on the floor there, between the desk and the window."

"Does he admit that he went back?"

"No." He paused a moment, in expectation of comment; and then added, defensively, just as if his uncle had spoken: "As a matter of fact, I think he's telling the truth."

"So you have already indicated."

"Well—"With no grounds for starting an argument, he seemed at a loss. Sir Nicholas said impatiently:

"What else?"

"We didn't cross-examine." The older man looked at him sharply. "Well, I thought," he added, "there was just a chance—" The sentence trailed into silence; but, strangely, Sir Nicholas did not seem dissatisfied with the reply.

"Is that the whole of the police case?" he asked.

"Not precisely. The main point is the weapon. A gun was found in Harland's luggage; Inspector Cummings testified to that. Then there was another witness, from the police laboratory at Wakefield, who proved pretty conclusively that this same gun had been used to hit Fraser over the head—"

"It seems an unlikely sort of weapon," said Sir Nicholas.

"Well, it would have made too much noise to shoot him; and, after all, how many blunt instruments do you find lying about in the average room?" Antony enquired. "A gun's quite handy, if you hold the barrel." He gestured with his left hand.

"I must take your word for it." His tone was polite, too polite; the storm-signals were hoisted again.

"You may. It's going to be a busy week-end, Jenny, I'm afraid. You'll sit in on our discussions, won't you, Uncle Nick? I hope you will."

"Nothing," said Sir Nicholas, with a sudden reversal of mood, "would keep me away." But he added, with a sting in his tone that made his nephew grimace at his empty plate: "It will be interesting to watch you dealing with an impossible situation. Interesting and —I am sure, my dear boy!—instructive."

CHAPTER 9

FRIDAY, the fourth day (continued)

"I don't understand it," said Mary Harland. "I don't understand it at all!" Her voice rose on the assertion. She was agitated, as well as bewildered, and retained only a trace of her former self-possession.

She had arrived at the Kempenfeldt Square house just before nine o'clock, with the inevitable evening paper tucked under her arm. She was apologetic, but quite firm about her desire to see Mr. Maitland.

"And, after all," he remarked ruefully, "as well now as later."

"I put the young lady in your study, Sir Nicholas," said Gibbs, frigidly. Gibbs was Sir Nicholas's butler, a disagreeable old man who refused to be retired, but most unfairly made a martyr of himself over his continued service. He had been disapproving of things as long as Antony could remember: of his own entrance into the household, so many years ago when his father died; still more of Jenny's joining the establishment upon their wartime marriage; and with a final crescendo of disparagement when the tall, old house was divided, soon after his demobilisation, to provide an upstairs flat. That the new arrangement decreased Gibbs's work was, unreasonably, an added grievance. That it was, as his employer had assured him, purely temporary, he took leave to doubt; and as events had turned out, in this at least he had proved correct. It was far too comfortable an arrangement for any of them to wish to change it; and the dividing line between the two households, at first rigidly observed, had tended to disappear as time went on. So now it was natural that a visitor for the younger man, who was not a personal friend, should be shown into the study on the ground floor. Gibbs, of course, could quite well have announced the fact by the house-phone; if he preferred to stump up two flights of stairs there was nothing anybody could do about it. But Sir Nicholas followed his nephew down with a guilty, harassed air.

Mary Harland was sitting stiffly on the edge of the deep wing chair that was reserved for visitors. Gibbs had put a match to the fire, which meant that, in his fashion, he had given "the young lady" the seal of his approval. Unapproved guests had been left to freeze before now. Antony made the introduction, and noted with amusement the clear-eyed look of appraisal she directed at his uncle, and the deceptive casualness of Sir Nicholas's greeting. Sitting back at ease in his favourite chair, the older man was not an alarming figure; but Maitland did not realise that his own attitude, lounging in front of the fire with one shoulder against the mantel, was in its own way equally deceptive. Or that Mary Harland, eyeing them both warily, was no longer simple enough to be taken in by a veneer of tranquillity.

"I don't have to ask you, Mrs. Harland, if you've seen the evening paper. Obviously, that's why you're here."

"Yes, of course. But I don't understand it . . . I thought things were going so well."

"I didn't invite his confidence, Mrs. Harland. Once it was given—"

But she was not interested in his problems.

"Why?" she said. "*Why?*"

It was Sir Nicholas who replied, or rather, who interrupted with a question of his own. "You were not surprised to learn the identity of the accused man?" he asked.

She turned to him quickly, and again her look was appraising, almost calculating.

"If Mr. Maitland told you what passed at his chambers," she said, after a pause, "you'll know I wasn't exactly unprepared for the idea it was Guy." But then she looked away, stared down into the fire, and said sadly: "I thought if I knew it would make everything simple. But now . . . there are so many questions." She broke off, with a helpless gesture, and looked up again at Maitland. But again it was Sir Nicholas who spoke.

"What questions, Mrs. Harland?" he asked quietly.

"Well . . . why he said he was Godson? Not now, I mean, but when he came home . . . all those years ago.

"That's very simple; as Harland, he would have been arrested." Maitland's tone was unemotional. Sir Nicholas, sitting back again, wondered a little (as he had often wondered before) at the delicacy of his nephew's touch. A less sensitive man would have embarked before now on explanations, which Mary Harland was not yet ready to hear. For the moment she was interested only in the personal aspect; and even as the thought crossed his mind she confirmed the diagnosis, hitting her hand against the arm of the chair and saying impulsively:

"But if he never saw me again . . . didn't he care?"

"You'd changed your name, he'd no means of tracing you without admitting his identity. He said he didn't think it would do you any good to have him stand trial for treason; but he added—and perhaps this was most important—that he was afraid you wouldn't believe in his innocence."

"I . . . see." She raised her head, and looked up at him defiantly. "Well, I didn't believe in him, it all seemed so sure, but I told you I didn't care." And again this question, this all-important question of her husband's guilt was pushed aside. "What did he *say*," she demanded, "when you told him you'd seen me?"

"I didn't tell him, Mrs. Harland. I felt I had no right, without your permission—"

"But of course you must tell him. I want to know . . . I've got to know . . . you must see that." She paused, and then added with difficult candour: "I want to know . . . whether he cares at all. Will you tell him what I said . . . tell him I don't mind." Her voice rose dangerously, and Maitland interrupted her, saying flatly:

"He's sticking to his plea of 'not guilty,' Mrs. Harland. I believe him."

It was ironical, perhaps, that his expression (which, if it reflected his mood, would have been one of self- derision) should have seemed to her sardonic. But at least the threatened hysteria was checked. She looked at him blankly, and after a moment spoke calmly.

"I'm glad of that," she said; "I'm glad you'll still be acting for him. But I still don't see why he told you."

Antony closed his eyes in an effort of recollection.

"He said 'I've drifted long enough; whatever happens, I can't go back.'" And as he opened his eyes again he caught the oddest expression on her face; a half-smile, denoting, he thought, some secret satisfaction.

"It doesn't really explain, does it?" she said.

"Perhaps he doesn't altogether understand his reasons himself," Antony suggested. And added, with apparent in-consequence, "We shan't be calling you for the Defence."

"But I could help him, I know I could! I could tell them he never had a gun—"

"If we call you, Mrs. Harland, you will be cross-examined."

"I don't see . . . do you mean it would harm him, if they knew I didn't always believe him?"

"No . . . no, I didn't mean that." He spoke slowly, and added with reluctance, "there are certain questions it's as well you shouldn't have to answer."

"What questions?"

He looked from her to Sir Nicholas with an uncertainty that was completely out of character.

"I am right about that, aren't I, Uncle Nick?"

"Quite right. You would be asked, madam, when first you knew the prisoner was your husband."

"Yes . . . well . . . I should say, when I saw him in court."

Sir Nicholas smiled. He looked both amused and appreciative.

"That's very acute of you, Mrs. Harland. But the matter wouldn't be allowed to rest there. Would you tell the truth when you were asked upon which day you saw him? Would you admit that—in a very natural desire to know if the accused man were your husband—you went into court yesterday?"

"I . . . well, it is true," she said. "And I don't see what harm—"

"If your husband saw you, that may have prompted him to a course of candour which otherwise seems incomprehensible. But there are still two constructions that can be put on his decision."

"Two—?"

"Yes, Mrs. Harland. One, which I believe you have already thought of for yourself, that the sight of you made his life worth fighting for: not only his life, of course, but the way of life you had together. That is understandable. But his Counsel cannot suggest it without laying the way open to a much less commendable interpretation by the Crown." He paused, as though to invite comment, but she only shook her head in a bewildered way. "It is a simpler interpretation, really," said Sir Nicholas. "He may merely have been afraid you would betray him."

A woman of less spirit might have sought refuge in tears. Mary Harland sat up very straight in her chair, and gave back look for look.

"Is that what you think?" she demanded.

"It isn't what I think that matters," Sir Nicholas pointed out (and Maitland noted with a slight sinking of spirit the avoidance of a direct reply). "It's what your husband's Counsel can make the jury believe. And he is bound to take into consideration the fact that, once it is known his client may have seen you in court, both sides of the coin will be presented to them."

"I couldn't bear it," said Mary Harland, "if Guy thought . . . that." Her meaning was clear enough. The two men exchanged glances, recognising in her what they thought a typically feminine failure to grasp essentials. And Sir Nicholas, realising for the first time that he had taken the conduct of the interview into his own hands, coughed apologetically and waved a hand as though to disclaim any further part in the affair. Antony had a private grin for that; he had worked with his uncle too long to resent what in another man he would certainly have condemned as interference.

"There are some questions I should like to ask you, Mrs. Harland," he said.

"If you don't want me to give evidence—" The words might have sounded childishly petulant, but her expression was merely bewildered. Maitland gave her his sudden, persuasive smile.

"It may help, just the same; please take my word for that." His tone was matter-of-fact, and she relaxed a little. "Think back to the night Doctor Fraser was attacked. I take it that was the beginning, so far as you were concerned?"

"Yes . . . yes, it was."

"I need the truth, Mrs. Harland, if I am to help your husband." (And as he spoke the echo of Garfield's gibe about "simple faith" rose to mock him; he was asking for the truth, but how could he be sure—?)

Mary Harland, it seemed, had for the moment forgotten her own doubts.

"Guy had been preoccupied—it wasn't any more than that, Mr. Maitland—for about a week; perhaps a little more. Of course, I wondered afterwards; but at the time I only thought it was something difficult he was working on . . . something like that."

"He didn't tell you—?"

"No. But he wouldn't, if it was anything technical I didn't understand—"

"Yes, I see. But the people who were there—"

The question brought another of her appraising looks. Maitland added, with a hint of impatience in his voice:

"If your husband isn't guilty, Mrs. Harland, somebody else is."

"I was wondering . . . you really believe him, don't you?"

He straightened from his lounging attitude.

"It would save time if you would take that for granted." But seeing her still doubtful he added, more gently: "Don't you trust me?"

She met his look with what he was beginning to feel was characteristic courage.

"It isn't that, exactly. Only nobody even suggested he might be innocent after all. And you're a stranger."

"Nobody had heard his story, until he told it to me last night."

"Well, if it was so convincing, won't the jury believe it?"

"Without corroboration . . . I doubt it." Hands in his pockets, he turned to look down at the fire, and spoke without looking at her. "You make your points well. What exactly is in your mind?"

"Just that I don't think you can help Guy unless you really believe what he told you. So I want to be sure—" (It was the removal of her own doubts she was seeking, but it was only much later that he realised that.)

The silence lengthened. Antony said at last, speaking slowly:

"Will it satisfy you if I say that under no circumstances would I act for a man I knew had committed treason?" Sir Nicholas, ignoring the woman now, saw his nephew's expression in the light from the fire and knew from its bitterness that memory had taken hold of him. "Particularly," said Maitland, still with deliberation, "one whose collaboration had had such terrible results."

"But you said—"

"I gave him the benefit of the doubt on the question of identity, I admit that. Partly at Horton's instance, because he believed in him so wholeheartedly; partly . . . a sense of fair play? . . . an unwilling liking for the man, so that I doubted, unconsciously, what my reason told me must be the truth?" He stood a moment longer, and then turned a little stiffly to face her again. "Does that answer your questions, Mrs. Harland?"

"Yes; yes, I think it does." But she looked at Sir Nicholas doubtfully as she spoke. His eyes were fixed still on the younger man, and his expression gave her no reassurance.

"Then, if you will accept for a moment my own belief in your husband's innocence . . . who would you put in his place?"

"I don't know . . . I don't, really. Someone who knew what they were doing in the laboratory, I suppose."

"Was any of your husband's colleagues a frequent visitor at Burnham Towers?"

"No. No, I can't remember any one of them coming. Just those who lived there."

"Doctor Fraser himself—"

"But that wouldn't make sense!"

"No . . . precisely. Your husband, then . . . and for the moment we are presuming his innocence. Mr. Charles Conrad—" (he was watching her, and she shook her head doubtfully) "—or the lady who is now his wife, Miss Esther Marne?"

"Did he marry Esther? I didn't think he would. But I'm sorry. I just can't see any one of them—"

"Who else might have had the knowledge—?"

"Nobody . . . nobody!"

"Did you like Esther Conrad?"

"Yes, I think . . . I didn't know her very well. But Guy couldn't stand her. I expect it was something to do with work—"

"You mentioned the gun."

"Someone must have planted it on Guy. It certainly wasn't his."

"It was found in his suitcase, and you had never seen it before?"

"That's right."

"And the cigarette case. He says he didn't go back to the study a second time, and we are—remember?— assuming for the moment that he is telling the truth."

This evidently needed some consideration. She said at last, hesitantly,

"I should think he put it down when he came back to the drawing-room, and somebody picked it up."

"But you don't remember seeing it at that time?"

"I'm afraid not."

"Very well, Mrs. Harland, I need not bother you any more for the moment." He spoke abruptly, and his uncle looked at him enquiringly.

Mary Harland got up. She said, as she pulled on her gloves,

"When you see Guy, you'll tell him—?"

"If that is what you wish . . . certainly."

"Yes, I . . . well, I'm sure you understand, so I won't say any more. Good night, Sir Nicholas. Good night, Mr. Maitland. I should thank you, I think, for your patience."

When he came back from the front door, Antony found his uncle still on his feet, pottering round the room in a rather aimless way.

"I don't know," Sir Nicholas remarked fretfully, "why people can never leave things where they find them."

"If you're looking for cigars, you know they're always in the same place." He went to the desk, produced a box out of the bottom left-hand drawer, and came back to the fire again. Sir Nicholas sat down, opened the box, and eyed the contents suspiciously.

"What do you think of her, Uncle Nick?"

"A brave woman, as you told me." The older man was occupied with the difficult question of selection, but spared a moment to look up at his nephew in an amused way. "Very feminine, and quite unscrupulous, I should say."

Maitland frowned.

"Do you think she was lying, then?"

"I didn't say that. But you'd better bear in mind that she would not hesitate to do so, if she thought it would help that precious husband of hers." He paused, and sniffed at the cigar he held, and—seeming satisfied with the result—looked up again at the younger man. "Don't misunderstand me, I like her. I think her quite an admirable person. But don't trust her an inch, if at any time her husband's interests conflict with your own."

"He's my client . . . remember?"

"Certainly I remember. And, talking of that—"

"Yes, sir?" Maitland's patience was not quite equal to the delay while his uncle went on with his preparations. He found a box of Swan Vestas on the mantelpiece, and stooped to put them on the table at Sir Nicholas's elbow. The older man smiled placidly, and produced his cigar-cutter.

"This question of filling in the background?"

"We've got to look at it all again, of course, from a different angle—"

"Do you think that will help you?"

"It may." He sounded despondent. "Any ideas, sir?"

"It occurred to me," said Sir Nicholas, "that Inspector Sykes might be willing to help you. Something in the background of one of those people led him—or her—to commit an act of treason; whatever it was, it won't appear in the depositions—"

"That's right. The police would have been on to it if it did."

"Well, then."

"You think Sykes might help with the spade-work?"

"I think he might be induced to co-operate," said Sir Nicholas, picking up the matches at last, "if we put it to him . . . tactfully." Antony grinned.

"We might also be able to ask him," he said, "for the answers to the questions I didn't put to Inspector Cummings."

"Exactly," agreed his uncle. "I am glad to see," he added repressively, "that you have some small grasp of the situation."

CHAPTER 10

SATURDAY, the weekend recess

I n the event, it was Sir Nicholas who made the first approach to Inspector Sykes, while Maitland and Horton spent a difficult morning with their client; an interview from which each man emerged with his own reasons for exasperation. Geoffrey thought, simply, that his friend was being made a fool of; while Antony was driven almost to distraction by the accused man's attitude of dependence, his shelving of responsibility. That this was consistent with what he had come to believe of the other man's character should, perhaps, have comforted him, but completely failed to do so. Geoffrey's presence, silently reproachful, was an added irritant, and his temper had almost reached boiling point by the time he got back to chambers.

Derek Stringer took off his glasses, and pushed aside the pile of documents which had accompanied the brief. He ignored his colleague's scowl, and said placidly:

"There are points, you know." He looked down at the sheet of foolscap, covered now with his own, neat handwriting. "Here a little, and there a little," he said.

"I suppose that's as much as we have a right to expect." Antony came across the room as he spoke. "It's cold," he said. "I shouldn't be surprised at rain." He kicked the fire, which retaliated by puffing smoke into his face.

Derek, who hated to see anything badly done, got up and laid hold of the poker.

"Those tactics are all very well for a wood fire," he said crossly. "You can't bully coal." And added, as he bent down to try the effect of persuasion: "Sir Nicholas phoned."

"What did he want?"

"If you got here before twelve you were to call Sykes at Scotland Yard. It's only a quarter to."

Maitland gave the fire a look of dislike, and went across to seat himself on the corner of the desk.

"I suppose you know you're making it worse," he said encouragingly. And added, as he reached out a hand for the telephone, "If only the fellow wasn't so damnably trusting, Derek. I'm no hand at pulling rabbits out of hats."

Stringer refrained from pointing out that the situation was, at least in part, of his companion's making. He completed his task to his own satisfaction, and came back to the desk again. Maitland, waiting for his call to be put through, watched a small flame which flickered hopefully out of the pile of slack coal, and grinned apologetically.

Hearing Sykes's voice a moment later brought the man vividly before him. Comfortable, square-built . . . a farmer on market-day, you might have thought him—a prosperous farmer, to judge from his cheerful demeanour —and his pleasant, north-country voice would have done nothing to dispel the illusion.

"Well, now, Mr. Maitland—"

Antony forced himself to utter the appropriate greetings. Sykes had a strong sense of what was seemly, and must be reassured of his own well-being, and Jenny's, before they could think of proceeding to business. At last he could ask:

"Did my uncle explain—?"

"Ah, yes—the Harland case."

"Can you help me, do you think? It's a question of time."

"Well, now, let's see." Antony grimaced at the telephone; it was no use trying to hurry Sykes, who took his time as a good Yorkshireman should—and if you didn't wait for him, who would be the loser? "You're not saying you haven't had the proper documents from the Prosecution?"

"I'd be complaining fast enough if I hadn't, but not to you." As well as if he could see him, he was aware that Sykes's expression was one of bland amusement. "It's the witnesses themselves I'm concerned with, the ones from Burnham Green. Their background, man!" he added, with sudden impatience. "That wasn't in the proofs."

"No, I see." Sykes's tone was soothing, without any effect of conciliation. "What exactly is it you want, Mr. Maitland?"

"Anything . . . everything! And there isn't any time—"

"You could have asked for an adjournment, sir. Why didn't you do that?"

"On what grounds? Can I say in court, I want time to incriminate someone else?"

Sykes's voice was startled now.

"You think there's something there, Mr. Maitland. It isn't just—?"

"No deception, Inspector. Nothing up my sleeve." His impatience vanished as he realised that he had caught the other man's interest. They knew each other well enough, these two, and though they had met, generally, as adversaries, there had sprung up between them a steady, if reluctant, friendship. So now, in these lightly spoken words, Sykes found the justification of what might have seemed a preposterous request. He had, besides, some cause to respect Maitland's judgment.

"The Burnham Green witnesses," he said, slowly.

"You know what I want. Not just name and address and occupation and where were you on the night of the 16th October?"

"And in return—?"

"I'll play fair, Inspector. But I could get an acquittal with a good deal less ammunition than you'd need to make another arrest; you know that, so I needn't scruple to admit it."

"Do you really expect the jury to find your client 'not guilty'?" His tone was sceptical, and Maitland's own doubts returned in full force.

"No . . . not really. But do what you can for us, there's a good chap. There's one other thing, if you could talk to Inspector Cummings . . . if there are any details that don't happen to have been mentioned in the Press, or in court—"And again, in this casual-seeming request, Sykes sensed urgency.

"I'll do what I can." It would be too much to say he sounded hopeful, but Antony was grateful enough not to have been snubbed. "There's one thing may help . . . it happens I went to school with Inspector Cummings. In Bradford, that was." He was smiling as he replaced the receiver, but the smile did not linger. It was replaced by a look of bewilderment, and he picked up a pencil from the desk and bit it meditatively.

*

"But what did he *say*." said Jenny, impatient of a conversation which was turning exclusively on technicalities, "when you told him his wife had been to see you?"

Antony was not too sorry to turn away from an unprofitable discussion, which had persisted throughout luncheon.

"He didn't say anything at first," he replied, carefully. "Then he said: 'she's out of this, isn't she? You'll not call her?'"

"Were we right?" asked Sir Nicholas. "Had he seen her?"

"Oh, I think so. Not that he admitted it. You might have thought he'd no interest in the matter at all, but I couldn't quite believe that."

"But didn't you tell him?" Jenny insisted. Her husband looked at her enquiringly. "Well, she asked you to explain—"

"If you're feeling romantic, my love . . . they haven't seen each other for twenty years. And for all that time she thought—"

"She said it didn't matter," Jenny pointed out. "Did you tell him that?" Seeing her serious look, Antony relented.

"I did my best," he admitted. "I told you, he didn't seem interested. Well, you couldn't expect—"

"Men!" said Jenny. And began to clear the table with an unnecessary clatter.

*

Flat on his back on the cot in his cell at Brixton Prison, Guy Harland contemplated the ceiling and tried to keep his mind from running on the future. It wasn't so easy, after all, to maintain a detached outlook. He had thought it possible, or he would never have spoken; now, he wondered at his own simplicity, but it was ironical, he supposed, that the one positive action he had taken in the matter should have brought him, not peace, but an even greater perturbation of spirit. He had thought, there's nothing I can do about it. Now, after a morning with his Counsel, he felt mentally and physically battered: and this, Maitland assured him, was only the beginning. There was the court to face again, and that fellow Garfield. And beyond all this, there was the question of Mary . . . something he must deal with himself, with no more evasions, no half-truths . . . no help anywhere, and a bitter realisation of his own inadequacy.

He rolled over on the hard bed, burying his face in the crook of his arm. If he hadn't spoken, he might be a free man now. But that wouldn't have resolved the real dilemma . . . he must go to her safe, or not at all. If she wanted him . . . for all her protestations, he felt no confidence in that. She had always been . . . kind; and who wanted kindness? As for safety . . . to be thus is nothing, but to be safely thus . . . well, that was fair enough, but where was it going to lead him?

*

Mr. Justice Conroy had walked as far as the Round Pond, and was eyeing the ducks with disfavour. It was grey and chilly, no afternoon for walking—and if he wanted exercise, why, in heaven's name, hadn't he gone down to Haslemere? The thing was, the affair made no sense. There was Maitland . . . case all wrapped up . . . off his head, apparently. My client has pleaded "not guilty," indeed! But even as he mentally characterised the declaration as impudent, he had to admit to himself a grudging admiration for the way a difficult situation had been carried off. And Harland still unmoved, calm, almost supercilious. Question was, had the Defence got something? Open and shut case, from what that policeman had said yesterday . . . hear both sides, of course . . . but what had possessed the prisoner to confide in his Counsel at that stage? Unless his solicitor hadn't made the position clear to him, but that wasn't very likely. Pleased as Punch they'd been—everybody concerned in the Defence—by the time Fraser had finished his evidence. Neat bit of work, that, and wasted now . . . all wasted . . .

He felt the first spot of rain on his hand, and turned grumpily to retrace his steps. No sense, these young fellows . . . no sense of responsibility . . . no sense of the fitness of things . . .

Thus Mr. Justice Conroy, stumping towards the Alexandra Gate. He would be soothed presently; by his own fireside, the latest *Hornblower*, a large pot of Darjeeling tea, perhaps even muffins. But he would still be puzzled, he realised resentfully; and whatever the outcome of the case, there were certain questions destined, he felt, to remain for all time unanswered.

*

Paul Garfield, also, was driven indoors by the rain. This to his annoyance, because the garden was looking untidy, a state of affairs he found quite intolerable. He had made a real effort to come down this weekend and dedicate himself to the reclamation of his flower-beds, and now to be stopped by a shower! He went in by the side door, to the little stone-flagged room that was reserved for overcoats and boots. Even if his own nature had not forbidden it, it would have been unthinkable to track mud all over Eleanor's rugs.

As Mrs. Garfield poured tea a little later (even here in the country she had an elaborate silver service, and delicate cups of Minton china) she asked idly:

"How much longer will the Harland case keep you in court?" Her husband smiled as he answered her; curiosity was vulgar, and that was the nearest she would come to indulging it, he knew.

"That depends, my dear, on what surprises the Defence have for us."

"Do you think . . . you know, Paul, I didn't really understand—"

"How should you?" He frowned as he spoke, the feeling of toleration for his fellows which physical exertion had induced was wearing off rapidly. There was something behind Maitland's attitude, that stood to reason. "I would explain the matter to you gladly, my dear," he said, "if I understood myself what is going on."

But he was still expounding his views on the affair when the maid collected the tea-tray; and later still, he had to interrupt himself to find the matches and light the lamps. Eleanor was a good audience, and her sympathy was comforting. He had no doubts, of course, of his own ability to handle any situation that might arise, but he'd give something to know what Maitland was up to.

CHAPTER 11

SUNDAY, the weekend recess

At about the same hour on Sunday afternoon that Antony Maitland was eyeing with hatred and despair the growing pile of papers on his writing-desk, Mr. and Mrs. Charles Conrad were awaiting guests in the sitting-room of their flat, which faced south across the park.

Three days later, when he saw him in court, Guy Harland would find his friend Charlie much changed in the years that had passed. He had put on weight since the war ended, had acquired a presence at once sleek and prosperous. But still, he was a quick-moving man, with an eager outlook on life. That he had gained assurance was natural; he had also met with considerable success.

The years had dealt even more kindly with Esther Conrad. Now past her middle forties, she had lost nothing of her good looks; and had gained an added charm from the poise that a comfortable background and the consciousness of perfect grooming bring. She was restless this afternoon, standing by the window and looking down impatiently at the rain-washed street.

"Robin said they'd be here in good time," she remarked.

"Missed the bus, I expect," said her husband lazily. They'll be here, don't worry."

"I can't think why they don't get a car." She left the window and came back to her favourite chair. Charlie followed her with his eyes: a graceful woman, well worth looking at, he would have told you, with his boisterous laugh. But there was more than admiration in the look he gave her.

"A matter of hard cash, m'dear," he said now. And watched with amusement his wife's impatient shrug. As though she were somehow affronted by this evidence of comparative penury. "They manage very well," he added. And, as though to prove his statement, the bell rang as he spoke.

The newcomers might have looked out of place against the opulent background of the Conrads' possessions if either of them had been in the least degree self-conscious. Robin Thurlow, at the beginning of the war a young writer with one successful novel to his credit, had continued his career since he left the Ministry of Information with no very spectacular results. In a quiet way, he was popular; there was a steady demand for his books. But the early fire was lacking. He was a lightly built man, with a lined face and a wide, ugly, humorous mouth. His tweed jacket was shabby, and his flannels a disgrace.

Marjorie Thurlow was more neatly dressed, but almost as shabby. There had been a time when her inability to compete with Esther's elegance had troubled her, but she was honest enough to admit to herself that all the money in the world would not have given her the other woman's air of distinction. She might have comforted herself— if the thought had occurred to her—with the reflection that she looked younger than her years. There was an air of gaiety about her that made light of the passage of time. But she was never at her best when visiting the Conrads. The two men were friends of long standing, and she had grown very fond of Charlie: but Esther's company made her uneasy—a thing she would never have admitted, as she considered it due to some defect in her own disposition . . . jealousy, perhaps.

"I thought it might be instructive to get together," said Charlie, busying himself about his guests' comfort when they were finally settled, and the tea had been made. "It's a queer business this . . . about Guy Harland."

Robin Thurlow put down his cup, and helped himself generously to wafer-thin bread and butter. He went, as was his custom, directly to the point.

"I don't see why *you* should be worried," he said. And laughed.

"Of course he isn't worried!" For all her air of languor, there was a sharpness in Esther's voice.

"Of course not," said Robin. His tone was smooth. "Are the Defence calling you, Charlie?"

"They are. And I don't quite see . . . well, what defence can they put up, Robin?"

"I suppose," said Thurlow, still amused, "they can try to prove that someone else is the guilty party."

"Precisely. And I've been talking to Hetherington. He handles most of our firm's stuff; well, his line's company law, of course, but he knows Maitland well. It wouldn't be the first time he's brought off a forlorn hope; he was in the background of several of Sir Nicholas Harding's big cases, Hetherington says."

Robin Thurlow's eyes had narrowed as he listened. He said now, softly:

"The question is, I suppose, who has been elected scapegoat? It seems to me, old boy, I've more cause for alarm than you have." He turned and met Esther's eyes, which were fixed on him speculatively. "Don't you agree?" he said.

"You mean, that old business between you and Fraser?" asked Charlie, before his wife could speak. "That must be forgotten long since."

"Not by me," said Robin. "Not by Fraser, either . . . at least, I doubt it. And—if I may remind you—anyone would have thought what happened at Burnham Green dead and buried long ago—"

"But, after all," said Marjorie, "this is a trial for treason. Just because you disliked Doctor Fraser—"

"I hated his guts," said Thurlow; he spoke viciously, so that the well-worn phrase seemed for the moment to have acquired a new meaning.

"Just as you like, dear," said Marjorie, and smiled at him. Charlie, seeing the look they exchanged, said quickly:

"I still think, if you are going to assume Harland's innocence, that I'm the obvious suspect. I worked at the same place, and had a fair idea of what was going on in the lab, even though it was so hush-hush."

"I think you're making a great deal out of nothing," said Esther. "Of course, the Defence will say Guy didn't do anything wrong . . . that's what they're there for. They'll raise a fog, if they can, and try to confuse everybody. But nobody really thinks he's innocent, it won't do any harm."

"Well, you may be right." Charlie was doubtful, but his worry, though genuine, did not go very deep.

"I don't like the idea of having to give evidence," said Marjorie. "You were being called anyway, Esther. Don't you hate it?"

The other woman shrugged. "Not particularly," she said. And added, without conviction, "It isn't nice to feel one is incriminating someone, of course. But then, treason—"

Marjorie shuddered. "I don't know how he could," she said. "I liked them both so much . . . Guy and Mary. I wonder what happened to her." But none of them knew the answer to that question.

"His solicitor came to see us," said Thurlow, after a moment. "Chap called Horton. Seemed pleasant enough."

"He came to see me, too," said Charlie. "Not Esther, of course, she's the Prosecution's witness. Queer sort of questions he asked." And again he sounded uneasy.

"What sort of questions?" asked Robin.

"For one thing, he wanted to know when we were married," said Conrad. "I don't see how that could help him."

"Routine, old boy."

"No, he asked us funny questions too," said Marjorie. "He asked how long we were staying at the Towers, as if that mattered."

Charlie got up, and prepared to cut into a handsome walnut cake.

"The answer is, really, we none of us know what the devil it's all about. No use discussing it, I suppose."

But they were still skirting uneasily around the topic two hours later, when Marjorie decided matters had gone far enough, and took her husband firmly away.

*

A little later that same Sunday—early evening, when the rain had stopped at last—Colonel Hugh Torrington went down to Waterloo Station to meet his friend, Harry Wilmot, off the Portsmouth express. It was typical of him that he arrived in time, but only just in time; so that he came up to the barrier as Wilmot was fumbling for his ticket.

Harry was looking tired, he thought, the slightly worried look which was normal with him somehow intensified. Comes of trying to cope with all those brats at the school, he reflected; or was the other man rattled, perhaps, by this question of giving evidence?

"Quite a surprise, wasn't it?" he asked, as Harry found the ticket, handed it to the collector, and left the platform with an air of accomplishment.

"What? Oh, you mean, this Harland business? I thought it was all cut and dried except for the question of identity."

"Well, so did I. But I didn't expect him to admit who he was, you know."

Wilmot laughed shortly.

"Well, I wish he hadn't. It seems to have been that decided the Prosecution to call me, after all; and there's nothing I can tell them. Makes a nice change, of course, but that's a mixed blessing, with old Castleton throwing a fit." He was a junior master at Ulcombe Abbey, a prep school in Hampshire, and the vagaries of his headmaster were an endless source of grievance. Fortunately, Hugh was a patient soul; his own career in the Army gave him complete satisfaction, and he was inclined to think that any less fortunate mortal had some right to complain. He possessed himself now of Harry's small suitcase and asked cheerfully:

"What was it this time? Did he grudge you the time . . . after all, you've no choice in the matter. Or was it the publicity?"

"Both," said Wilmot briefly. "Well, I could have done without it myself."

"Oh, I don't know. Though I wish it were the Defence we were appearing for—" He towered above his companion, a burly, immaculate figure in his uniform. Beside him, Harry Wilmot had a bleached look; a much smaller man, fair, and well-dressed in a quiet way, a strong contrast to his friend's flamboyance. He said now, a little breathlessly, because Hugh had never learned to moderate his pace:

"But if it really is Harland—"

"You never liked him much, did you?" His tone was tolerant.

"I hardly knew him. But after what happened—"

"Well," said Hugh, positively, "I liked him. And now I'm damned sorry for him, whatever he did."

Wilmot had a sidelong look for that. "That Polish business—"he said.

"Enough to turn your stomach," agreed Hugh. "But I don't suppose he realised—"

"Don't you?" The query sounded, oddly, as though it were made in genuine interest. And as his friend looked at him enquiringly, Harry Wilmot added almost angrily: "The Dubenocz experiment is a matter of history. Do you think Harland was necessarily so much more squeamish than the men who made use of his work?"

Torrington grinned at his vehemence, and said pacifically, "Have it your own way." They had reached the station yard now, and he made a beeline for his car. Harry had barely time to notice that it was a new one, the latest MG, before he and his luggage were stowed away neatly and they were moving out into the traffic of the Waterloo Road.

"I booked you a room," said Hugh. "Strand Palace . . . okay? . . thought it would be convenient." He went on, without pausing for his friend's agreement, which he cheerfully took for granted. "Good thing the Motor Show's over. It is a bit thick, I suppose, calling on you at a moment's notice, like this. But I expect they felt a bit flummoxed, with the whole thing sprung on them like that."

"I don't see what they think I can do for them," Wilmot complained.

"It isn't only you, you know. The Defence are calling Charlie Conrad, and both the Thurlows. Clutching at straws, I expect," he added; and chuckled, as if the thought amused him.

"A chap called Horton phoned me," said Harry. His tone was still a trifle querulous, but he was relaxing now, with the comfortable feeling that Hugh's companionship always gave him. "Solicitor, or something. That was before he knew I'd been called by the other side."

"Well, I can see their point," said Hugh. "Deuce of a position, you know. Think you've got the whole thing tied up nicely, and—bang!—it's all to do again."

"I'll reserve my sympathy for myself," said Harry, drily. They were crossing the river now, and he looked out idly in the gathering dusk and saw—and did not see —the pattern of lights springing up along the Embankment.

"Did he give you any idea?" asked Hugh.

"No, just a lot of talk. There was one thing, though."(As he recalled the conversation, Wilmot sounded uneasy again.) "He wanted to know how long leave we had. I don't see the point of that, do you?"

*

Sir Nicholas, making his way up to his nephew's quarters late that same evening, found Antony still at the writing-table with an empty plate and tumbler beside him, and Jenny curled up in her favourite corner of the sofa. She had a book on her knee, which she put down thankfully as he went in. He marked, and sympathised with, her faintly rebellious expression, and spoke a trifle testily to his nephew.

"You've been over everything—surely—by this time. You'll be stale if you don't leave it."

Antony got up, and moved a little stiffly across the room. As always when he was weary, the dull ache in his shoulder added its own burden. He was so used to it by this time that he no longer troubled to tell himself that he was lucky to have come so easily out of the war; in fact, he barely noticed the pain at all until he saw the quick flare of anxiety in Jenny's eyes, and read there the question she would never put into words. He seated himself beside her, and stretched his legs across the hearthrug, and reached out, as though absent-mindedly, for her hand.

"And a pleasant time was had by all," he remarked; and let out his breath in a long sigh.

"Where," asked his uncle, "is Stringer?" He was looking about him as he spoke, rather as if he expected to see the subject of his enquiry lurking in a corner, or hiding behind the door.

"At the Hardakers'," said Antony. And Jenny laughed, and added, even more succinctly:

"Courting."

Sir Nicholas leaned back in the chair he regarded as his own. "I hope you haven't been match-making again," he said. Jenny assumed an expression of quite impossible virtue.

"It was all his own idea, Uncle Nick. I'd given up hope about Derek ages ago. But I admit, he met Ann here."

"I thought as much." He turned back to his nephew again. "Has Geoffrey finished his arrangements?"

"I believe so."

"Poor Geoffrey," said Jenny, without a jot of sympathy in her voice. "He is hating it so."

"That does not altogether surprise me." Antony looked up quickly, disliking the gentleness of his uncle's comment. "You may have to open your case tomorrow," Sir Nicholas pointed out.

"That doesn't really worry me. Having nothing to tell the court, I am at least saved the dilemma of deciding how best to present matters." His tone was light, but there was a tightness about his mouth and he looked desperately tired.

"And so far, Harland's story is all you have to oppose to the Prosecution's evidence?"

"Yes, I'm afraid so. And, of course," he added, apologetically, "I'm not even sure it's true." He felt Jenny's hand tighten on his own, but his eyes were fixed on his uncle.

"Then it seems you will find some difficulty," suggested Sir Nicholas, "in demonstrating his innocence to the jury."

"Don't worry, I can't!" He saw the older man's look of annoyance, and added to forestall comment, "There are still a few Prosecution witnesses . . . something may emerge."

"You must have some idea," said his uncle testily, "how you are going to proceed."

"Well, of course, there are things I'm looking for. Which of the party did Fraser dislike, for instance? If Harland is telling the truth, who completed the work and made the Dubenocz experiment possible? More important—and making the same assumption—which of the people at Burnham Green is really the traitor? Opportunity . . . it could have been any one of them, so far as I can tell. But motive . . . how the hell am I to know, from talking to them, just what makes them tick?"

"You're being extremely vague," Sir Nicholas protested. "There are two definite lines, you know . . . the cigarette case and the gun."

"Yes, of course. Well, I've got my own ideas, but even if I'm right I don't see yet how best to set about proving it. Look here, Uncle Nick . . . how would you open?"

Sir Nicholas was still expounding his views (and defending them as necessary) when Jenny went to bed at midnight. It was almost an hour later before her husband joined her, but he was asleep within five minutes, so she assumed the discussion must have done something to compose his mind. It was only then, with her personal anxiety momentarily stilled, that she began to wonder whether he was right to trust Guy Harland, and what the outcome of the trial would be.

CHAPTER 12

MONDAY, the fifth day

The weekend recess, and the perusal of the Sunday papers, seemed to have done nothing to lessen interest in the outcome of the trial. It was true that "the man in the case" was now identified, but this seemed only to have added to the fascination of the affair.

Mr. Justice Conroy, settling himself in his place on Monday morning, thought the amount of scrambling going on in the public gallery unseemly, and the usher bellowed officiously for silence. By the time the order was complied with, the first witness was already in his place, and was sworn without delay.

Patrick Hickman was retired from his position as butler to Sir Gervase Torrington, but resided still in the village of Burnham Green. A small man, with a lined monkey face and a lively air, he was not precisely what Antony had expected from reading the measured periods of his proof. Not an advocate of a quiet life, by any means; and the present business a pleasant change, most likely, from the unwelcome serenity of retirement.

Garfield was proceeding with his customary smoothness, past the preliminary matter to the first point of interest.

"And on the evening of the 16th October, Mr. Hickman—?"

"The family dined early, as was customary at that time because of Sir Gervase going out. I made a point of serving coffee promptly when they returned to the drawing-room, as he liked to leave the house by eight-thirty."

"So the time you served coffee would be—?"

"Just about twenty past eight, sir."

"The members of the household were all present in the drawing-room?"

"So I understood . . . well, sir, I didn't count them."

"No," said Garfield. Maitland stifled a grin that was not without a hint of malice. For himself, he had a weakness for a personality; but his opponent, he knew, would have been happier with the orthodox figure of the perfect butler.

"Not Doctor Fraser, though," the witness went on, happily regardless of having stepped in any way out of line. "And why I remember that, sir: Lady Torrington poured a cup of coffee for him first of all, and asked me to take it to him."

"And Doctor Fraser was in the study?"

"He was, sir. I put the cup on the desk beside him, and went about my duties."

"They did not take you back to the drawing-room?"

"Not then. I was between the dining-room and my pantry."

"Passing through the hall from time to time?"

"Yes."

"And on one such occasion, was it brought to your notice that Doctor Fraser had a companion in the study?"

"Yes, sir. I heard voices."

"Did you notice the time?"

"It was probably about twenty to nine. Certainly before a quarter to."

"Did you recognise who was speaking?"

"Oh, yes, sir. Well, not at first; but when he raised his voice I knew it was Mr. Guy Harland. A carrying sort of voice, he had." (And that, thought Maitland, was true enough.)

"And are you quite sure it was Doctor Fraser he was addressing?"

"Quite sure. I heard his voice too, plain as plain. Very heated, they were getting, raising their voices, like I said."

"Quarrelling, Mr. Hickman?"

"That's what it sounded like."

"So that you paused, perhaps, on your way across the hall? If you were startled by what you heard?"

"Well, sir," said the witness, ignoring the proffered byway. "I was curious, you know . . . wouldn't you have been?" (Maitland, who had drawn a very poor likeness of the witness on his pad, looked up now, not attempting to hide his amusement, and then added an outsize ear in his sketch.)

"And you heard, perhaps, something of what was said?"

"Not so much as I'd have liked," said Hickman frankly. "First it was just the voices, but sounding angry. Then I heard Mr. Harland say 'Not now . . . not when it's so near.' And then something like 'any fool would know that.'"

"Did Doctor Fraser reply?"

"I could hear his voice rumbling, sir. It was lower pitched than Mr. Harland's. He said: 'Any fool would know better than to ask—' but then the words became indistinguishable."

"Was that all you heard?"

"Not a thing more, sir."

"And did you see either of these men again that evening?"

"Both of them, sir. A few moments later, coming into the hall from the servants' quarters at the back of the house, I observed Mr. Harland talking to Miss Marne. That's the lady who was Doctor Fraser's secretary, sir."

"And is now Mrs. Conrad. You got the impression that he had just left the study?"

"Well, I knew he had. It wasn't above a minute or two—"

"No . . . exactly. Did you notice anything about Mr. Harland at that time?"

"He looked flushed, sir. Excited, sort of."

"And he was talking to Miss Marne?"

"He was lighting a cigarette for her. I suppose they were talking, but I don't remember about that."

"And then, Mr. Hickman?"

"I went into the study to collect Doctor Fraser's cup."

"Did you have any conversation with him?"

"No, sir. Not to say, conversation. I said 'excuse me,' I suppose. And I know he only grunted in reply. But then, sir, a clever gentleman like that, he'd be thinking, I wouldn't wonder. So I took the cup and went away."

"Did Doctor Fraser seem at all upset?"

"Well, sir . . . a bit put out, I'd say."

"No more than that?"

"No, sir."

"Now, I should like you to look at the silver cigarette case, which has been put into evidence by the Crown. Do you identify it?"

"Indeed I do, sir. It belonged to Mr. Harland."

"You are in no doubt about that, Mr. Hickman?"

"Oh, no, sir. I often saw him with it. And then, he was careless like, always leaving it about. Many's the time I've given it back to Mrs. Harland, when I found it down the side of a chair, perhaps, or lying on a table."

"You returned it to Mrs. Harland?"

"Well, usually I did. During the day, that'd be— she'd be home, you see, and he'd be at the works."

"Yes, I see. Did you see this cigarette case on the evening we have been speaking of . . . the evening Doctor Fraser was attacked?"

"Yes, sir, I told you. Mr. Harland had it in his hand when he was talking to Miss Marne. I took it he had just given her a cigarette, and was lighting it as I crossed the hall."

"Thank you. There is just one other thing. At ten- fifteen that evening, were you again in the front of the house?"

"Yes, sir, I was. Mr. Hugh rang from the billiard-room. Well, I knew that meant he wanted a nightcap, so I brought the tray."

"Will you describe to the jury—in detail, please, Mr. Hickman—what you did, and what you saw."

"I came through from the service door with the tray, and went into the billiard-room. Mr. Hugh was there, and Mr. Wilmot with him. They were both in their shirt sleeves, and had been playing, I supposed. Mr. Thurlow was sitting in one of the big arm-chairs by the fire." He paused, visualising the scene. "So I put down the tray, and Mr. Hugh said something, thanking me, you know. Then I went out into the hall again."

"Yes, Mr. Hickman?"

"As I closed the billiard-room door, Miss Marne came out of the morning-room, and Mr. Conrad just behind her. She said something like 'I'd better make sure,' and went across quickly to the study, and knocked. Then she opened the door and stood just a moment, and then she gave a . . . a sort of scream." This time his pause was deliberate, for effect. Maitland gave him credit for a sense of drama, but just here the evidence was more detailed than he liked.

"Miss Marne—the present Mrs. Conrad," added Garfield, in an aside to the jury. "Miss Marne was standing in the doorway of the study, and Mr. Conrad was behind her?"

"Well, not exactly, sir. He had no more than come out of the morning-room. Seemed as if he was waiting for her. Then, almost as soon as she yelled, Mr. Hugh came out and pushed past her into the study. He was there no more than a moment, then he came out, shutting the door behind him, and looked at me and said: 'Doctor Fraser has been hurt. Call Doctor Greenhalgh, there's a good chap. And you'd better get on to the police.' So I went away to phone."

A quarter of an hour later, when the witness had reiterated to Garfield's satisfaction the more important parts of his testimony, Derek Stringer rose to cross-examine. Maitland, watching him as he picked his way delicately through his opening questions, reflected that—well as he knew the other man—he had not the faintest idea of his feelings about the case. Derek had accepted the change of policy with his usual calm, a fact for which his leader was duly grateful. If his sympathies were engaged, he gave no sign of it; at the same time, he would put forward his best endeavours, no matter how sticky the going became; and that was certainly something to be thankful for.

"When you took Doctor Fraser's cup to the study, Mr. Hickman, what was he doing?"

"He was sitting at the desk, sir."

"Working . . . writing?"

"No, sir. There hadn't been time for him to settle down. He was getting some papers from his brief-case."

"And later, when you heard him talking with Mr. Harland . . . you are quite sure, I suppose, that they were quarrelling?"

"Well, sir, Mr. Harland was protesting about something. And his voice was raised, like he was angry, too. Doctor Fraser . . . well, he was just telling him off, I'd say."

"You were in no way worried when you heard this altercation?"

"Oh, no, sir. I just thought the doctor was at it again."

"An irascible man, was he?"

("My lord!" protested Garfield. "But, with respect," said Stringer, smoothly, "your lordship will no doubt feel that my question was merely designed to clarify for the jury a statement which the witness had already made . . . at least by implication." Conroy smiled his tight, impartial smile, and motioned him to proceed.)

"Well, sir," said Hickman carefully, "he had a temper, that I won't deny."

"And when you went the second time to the study, was Doctor Fraser writing then?"

"Yes, sir. A letter, I thought; not because I noticed specially, but because he spoke to me. Well, it was no more than a grunt, really, but when he was working things out he wouldn't even know you were there."

"When Miss Marne found that Doctor Fraser had been injured, you say she did not go into the room at all?"

"No, sir. Just stood in the doorway and yelled."

"And Colonel Torrington was the first person to reach her?"

"Yes, that's right."

"Yet he had to come from the study; and Mr. Conrad, if I understand you, was already in the hall?"

"Well, so was I," the witness pointed out. "Startled, I was, and I expect he felt the same."

"No doubt. How long was Colonel Torrington in the study?"

"No more'n a minute, sir. Then he came out, and—"

"Yes, thank you. Where did you go to telephone?"

"I used the instrument in the alcove, sir."

"You mean, in the hall?"

"Yes, sir."

"Then you can tell us, no doubt, what happened next?"

"Well, it was a bit of a muddle." (And not very important or interesting, his tone said clearly.) "Mr. Hugh, he stayed by the door. The other men . . . Mr. Thurlow and Mr. Wilmot came out of the billiard-room. They went across to him, and seemed to be arguing, but of course I was occupied, sir, with the telephone. Mr. Conrad got hold of Miss Marne and made her sit down."

"Did nobody else appear on the scene?"

"Oh, yes, of course. What with Miss Marne calling out, and then all of them talking."

"Did you notice who arrived first?"

This was a new thought to Hickman. He gave it his attention.

"Mrs. Thurlow, I think, sir," he said at last. "She came downstairs, and Mrs. Harland not far behind her. They were both in their dressing-gowns. Then Mr. Harland. He was still dressed, but he had his tie off. And after I left the telephone Lady Torrington came downstairs. Well, just about half-way, because Mrs. Harland ran up to tell her what had happened. And they both went back upstairs again, together."

"And after that, Mr. Hickman?"

"Nothing else, sir, not until the police came."

"Mr. Harland, for instance, did not enter the study?"

"No, sir." The witness was emphatic. "Nor anyone else."

Maitland permitted himself a glance round the court. The Judge was looking puzzled, as well he might. They had to get the facts somehow, but if it involved putting many more of the Prosecution's points for them . . . it had got even Derek worried. His manner was imperturbable as ever, but his colleague was close enough to see that he was sweating a little. Garfield was smiling . . . cold, cruel, secret, thought Maitland with sudden extravagance, and stabbed with his pencil at the papers in front of him, and swore under his breath as the point snapped off. Harland was in his shell, as usual. The jury . . . impressed, of course, by the police inspector's evidence; and by the backing it was getting, and would get—no doubt— from the other Prosecution witnesses. He brought his mind back to what was happening, and to Stringer, reaching the end now.

"There is one thing I have wondered, Mr. Hickman. You say Mr. Harland was in the habit of leaving his cigarette case lying about?"

"He was, sir."

"Nothing else, Mr. Hickman?"

Again there was a pause for reflection. "No, sir . . . no."

"A fountain-pen, perhaps? A pencil?"

"Well, sir, you see, if he had any writing to do he'd do it in his own room. I wouldn't be picking up after him there."

"A note-book? No. A lighter?"

"He didn't have one, sir . . . I don't think." He stopped, and then went on, as though relieved to have remembered. "No, I'm sure about that, sir, because there was a shortage of matches then, and he used to lose his box and then be asking for more."

"Was Mr. Harland unusually dexterous, do you remember?"

"I . . . I don't rightly know, sir."

"Counsel means, Mr. Hickman," explained the Judge, "was Mr. Harland particularly clever with his hands?"

"Thank you, me lord. But I don't remember, really, one way or the other."

"You say he was holding his cigarette case, and at the same time lighting Miss Marne's cigarette. Was not that rather a clumsy proceeding?"

The witness looked puzzled. "I don't think—"

"In which hand did he hold the case?"

"Would it have been his left hand? I don't really remember, sir, but it seems to me that must have been how it was. He'd be holding the match in his right hand, I should think."

"Yes, I should think so, too. And that means both cigarette case and match box were in his left hand,

Mr. Hickman. Not impossible, of course, but unnecessarily clumsy, don't you agree? When it would have been so easy to slip the case into his pocket."

"Perhaps that's what he did."

"Then let us be clear about it. You saw him with the case in his hand; then he put it in his pocket, took out the box of matches, struck one, and held it to his companion's cigarette."

"That sounds likely, sir. But—"

"But the door from the study is not very far from the service door. Am I right about that? You would not have taken very long to cross from one to the other. You didn't stand staring, I suppose?"

"Oh, no, sir!"

"But perhaps, after so long, your memory is not very clear."

"It's a long time ago," the witness agreed, in a tone of relief.

"And if you saw Mr. Harland lighting Miss Marne's cigarette—?"

"I'm sure I remember that, sir." He spoke positively, but added in a worried tone: "But I'm sure I saw the cigarette case, too."

"In Mr. Harland's hand? At that particular time? The evening of the 16th October, at a quarter to nine or thereabouts? While he spoke to Miss Esther Marne in the hall at Burnham Towers, and you were busy about your everyday duties?"

But there was no shaking Hickman. He was vague, he was worried, but at the last he was obstinate in his recollection. Maitland noticed that the prisoner, for the first time, was displaying an interest in what went on. Garfield was unconcerned, and disposed of the point summarily in three careful questions when he got the chance to re-examine. Not that he need have worried, Antony thought resentfully. It was so much more simple to assume, as both Sir Nicholas and Geoffrey Horton had pointed out with varying degrees of forcefulness, that the presence of the case in the study was merely another instance of Harland's carelessness, and that he had dropped it on a second, unadmitted visit, than to trouble to look for an explanation as to how else it might have got there.

The next witness caused something of a stir, and a craning of necks among the spectators to get a better view. Mrs. Charles Conrad was a strikingly handsome woman still. Maitland—remembering his client's description of Esther Marne and wondering if it prejudiced him— thought she had a hard look; and would have been surprised if he had realised how nearly, on this point, Mr. Justice Conroy's opinion paralleled his own; but Garfield was obviously pleased with his witness.

Certainly she gave her evidence well. A little vague, perhaps, about the finding of Doctor Fraser ... "I know it must sound stupid, but I was so upset I really don't seem to remember" ... but definite enough about her brief conversation with Guy Harland when he came from the study, and equally definite that when he offered her a cigarette it was from his own case, which she knew well and was quite willing to identify.

"He often left it lying about, on his desk at work, or on one of the benches in the laboratory." And it was at this point that Antony began seriously to wonder ... She wasn't a talkative woman, she wasn't nervous; whatever she said, he felt there was a reason for. But he rose to cross- examine, when the time came to do so, with no great feeling of confidence.

As she turned to face him, her eyes were alert and questioning, only too obviously assessing him. She was ready, he realised, to treat him as an ally ... for just so long as it suited her to do so ... for just so long as he, in his turn, would subscribe to the fiction that she was a disinterested bystander. That it was a fiction he was suddenly, illogically, convinced. The problem was, how far should he press his questions?

"You have told us, Mrs. Conrad, of your meeting with Guy Harland in the hall at Burnham Towers, 'after he left the study.' Did you actually see him coming out of that room?"

"Yes ... yes, I'm sure I did. I came out of the drawing-room, and closed the door; and then the study door opened, and he came into the hall."

"And you stopped to speak to him?"

"For a moment."

"He offered you a cigarette?"

"Yes. You see, Lady Torrington didn't really like us smoking in the drawing-room, so I suppose he guessed why I had come away. He said something like, 'looking for a fag, Esther?' and pulled out his case."

"And you took a cigarette, and he gave you a light for it?"

"Yes."

"You have told my friend that Guy Harland did not possess a petrol lighter, that he used matches. Do you remember what he did with his cigarette case?"

"Why ... he slipped it into his pocket, I suppose."

"You don't seem very sure of that, Mrs. Conrad."

"No ... well, only because he must have done, I think."

"He did not, for instance, pass it to you, to help yourself?"

"Oh, no. I should have remembered that, with all the talk there was later."

"But Hickman, the butler, has testified that he crossed the hall at the moment Guy Harland lighted your cigarette. At the same time, he saw the case, which he has identified—"

"My lord!" said Garfield, righteously indignant. "My learned friend is distorting the facts—"

"With respect, my lord, I was endeavouring to reconcile—"

"I think you must be more precise, Mr. Maitland."

"As your lordship pleases." He was angry suddenly, though the emotion was well hidden. Conroy heard the suspicious mildness of his tone, and remarked again the fleeting resemblance to his own contemporary, Sir Nicholas Harding. He was conscious of a half-resentful amusement; if these young fellers thought they could fool him with bread-and-butter airs and respectful words . . .

Maitland, meanwhile, had returned to the witness. "You have said, Mrs. Conrad, that Guy Harland was careless with his possessions."

"That is correct."

"You are quite sure what happened that evening? Think carefully, please, it is an important point."

"He gave me a cigarette. He lighted it. Is that so strange?"

Perhaps it was the sharpness in her tone which prompted Antony to his next question. "I suggest, Mrs. Conrad, that he passed the case to you—"

"No!"

"—and that, by accident perhaps, you failed to return it."

"That isn't true." Her voice was firm enough, but for the first time he noticed a sign of strain; the white gloves she carried were twisted together, until they looked no more than a cord between her fingers. "It simply isn't true," she repeated.

"Is it not, Mrs. Conrad? Perhaps I should be nearer the mark if I suggested that he passed you the case and you retained it by design."

Her lips were a thin line. She looked across unlovingly at the prisoner. "Is that what he told you . . . what he said happened?"

"My client, madam, is—as you have told us—of a careless disposition. But I think you could enlighten us, if you would."

"You are saying that I—"

"That you handed the case to some third party, Mrs. Conrad. That's the truth, isn't it?"

Strangely, he had forgotten the possibility of interruption, but whatever he might have goaded her into remained unsaid. Garfield was on his feet again, at his most icily formal. "My lord, I have every sympathy with my friend's predicament, but this attempt—"

"You m-may reserve your s-sympathy," said Antony, suddenly, giving his temper rein. The Judge directed a quelling glance at him.

"This attack on the witness, my lord—"said Garfield, ignoring the interruption.

"As your lordship knows, I am entitled to cross-examine."

"Can you justify this line of questioning, Mr. Maitland?"

"My lord, I am trying to find the truth!"

"A very laudable ambition," said Conroy, approvingly. He shook his head at Garfield, and spoke again to the Defence Counsel. "You may proceed," he said. And added, as Garfield sat down and Maitland turned again to the witness: "When you have found the truth, no doubt you will inform us?"

"Assuredly, my lord." But the interruption had served its purpose. There was no hope now that the witness would speak, unthinkingly, to her own disadvantage.

"You have said, Mrs. Conrad, that you left the drawing-room at approximately a quarter to nine. After you parted from Mr. Harland in the hall, how did you spend the remainder of the evening?"

Up to this point she had been answering readily enough, but now she paused to consider her reply. Antony could detect no sign of discomfort in her manner; rather, he had an uncomfortable impression that her dark eyes were mocking. She said at last, carefully:

"I went into the morning-room, to smoke my cigarette. I was there for the rest of the evening; until ten-fifteen, that is, when I went into the study."

"You were not, however, alone all that time?"

"Oh, no!"

"Please tell us who you saw during the course of the evening."

"Until the time I have mentioned, only my husband. He joined me at nine o'clock."

"At nine o'clock exactly?"

"Probably just before. The wireless was in the morning-room, and he liked to hear the news."

"I see. And you were together—"

"Until a quarter past ten."

"All the time, Mrs. Conrad? You are sure of that?"

"Quite sure."

"Neither of you left the morning-room, even for a moment?"

"I've told you . . . no."

"To fetch a newspaper, perhaps? . . some more cigarettes? . . your knitting?"

"We were just sitting and talking; my husband had plenty of cigarettes."

"And you are quite positive he did not leave you, during that hour? After so long a lapse of time you have no doubt—"

"No doubt at all."

"And at ten-fifteen—?"

"We were going for a stroll, and I thought I should see if Doctor Fraser had any letters for the post. That was why I went to the study."

"And during the quarter of an hour before Mr. Conrad joined you, you saw no other person?"

"No."

"And did not leave the morning-room?"

"I was smoking my cigarette there."

"Did you leave the morning-room, Mrs. Conrad?"

"No, I did not!"

"You have spoken of 'your husband.' You were not married at that time, I believe?"

"No."

"Engaged to be married, perhaps."

"Not then."

"But Mr. Charles Conrad was your colleague. You knew him well, I suppose."

"Very well."

"For how long had you been acquainted?"

"Since I went to work for Doctor Fraser . . . nearly two years."

"When were you married?"

She frowned at him. "In 1946," she said. "After the war was over."

"Four years after the events of which we are speaking?" He seemed to be meditating on her reply, then looked up at her and added suddenly: "A long courtship, Mrs. Conrad."

"I don't understand you."

"I mean what I say, madam, neither more nor less."

He looked at Garfield, saw the indecision on the other man's face, and added quickly: "Thank you, Mrs. Conrad, you have been very helpful."

Counsel for the Prosecution returned his opponent's look sourly, but declined to re-examine. As for the prisoner, he was not the only one who followed the witness with his eyes as she left the stand; but in his look, at least, there was no admiration.

CHAPTER 13

MONDAY, the fifth day (continued)

I t was afternoon before Colonel Torrington's evidence was reached, and Antony was feeling weary and harassed. He had spent the luncheon recess arguing with Stringer over the wisdom of the tactics he had adopted in dealing with Esther Conrad.

"All or nothing," Derek had maintained stubbornly "If you had to take that line—"

In spite of the uselessness of the proceeding, his leader had maintained his position with some heat; but the trouble was, he realised, that Derek was no more convinced than was Geoffrey Horton of their client's innocence . . . and was probably equally exasperated by his own, admittedly unreasonable, belief.

"I haven't got the picture clear yet," he admitted. "We shan't know who to rely on until we've seen the rest of the witnesses."

"We shan't *know* even then."

"Oh, for heaven's sake!" Antony's anger flared momentarily, and was as quickly suppressed. "That brings me back to what I was saying," he remarked; and though his sidelong look was apologetic, his tone was stubborn. "I've seen Mrs. Conrad, and I don't believe her."

His thoughts were running on much the same lines as he watched Hugh Torrington take the oath, and heard his answers to Garfield's opening questions. The witness was a big man, good-looking in his way, or was that just the effect of an abundance of energy, obvious even in these sober surroundings? For some reason he had not emerged from the pile of proofs as a personality, and now Maitland wondered how this had come about. One thing was obvious, Harland's opinion notwithstanding, the man was no fool.

His account of the evening of 16th October differed in no way from what they had already heard, up to the point where Guy Harland put down his half-full cup of coffee and left the party.

"It was just about ten minutes later," the witness went on, "when Esther Conrad went out of the room. And almost immediately Harland came back."

"Now I must ask you, Colonel, to look at this cigarette case. Thank you. Do you identify it?"

"Yes, I know it. It belonged to Guy Harland."

"Did you see it at any time on the evening of the 16th October, 1942?"

"Yes, I did."

"In the prisoner's possession?"

"No. It was when I went into the study, after Mrs. Conrad called out. Doctor Fraser was my main concern, of course; well, I don't pretend to be an expert, but I made sure there was nothing to be done for him until the doctor came. Then I took a quick look round, and came away."

"And, at that time, where was the cigarette case?"

"It was lying on the floor, not far from the window. The curtains were blowing, that's how I came to glance in that direction."

"The window was open, then?"

"So I supposed. I didn't go across to see."

"That is a french window, is it not?"

"It is."

"So you left the study. What did you do then?"

"I asked Hickman to phone the doctor. I stayed by the study door until he arrived. The police were with him."

"During this period, did anyone else enter the study?"

"No."

"We will go back to your account of the earlier part of the evening, Colonel, if you please. You say that Guy Harland left the drawing-room while the rest of the party were drinking their coffee, and returned after approximately ten minutes."

"That is correct."

"And on this occasion he spent about two minutes in the drawing-room?"

"Yes, he came in to speak to Mary, his wife. He said he was going for a walk. She didn't seem keen on the idea."

"And when did you again see the prisoner?"

"Now that," said Torrington, regretfully, "I can't tell you. Quite a bit later; Wilmot was with me in the billiard-room, and Thurlow joined us there, and I remember thinking Guy must have been feeling pretty energetic to be out so long."

"You have not explained, Colonel—"

"No, I'm sorry. I saw him as he came back to the house, coming round the side towards the front door. He passed the window."

"It was dark, was it not?"

"Yes, of course. But the room was lighted, and the curtains weren't drawn. Quite a lot of light fell across the path."

"And this path . . . you are naturally familiar with the grounds of Burnham Towers, Colonel Torrington—"

"It is my home," said Hugh, drily.

"Exactly. This path, then . . . a man walking on it, past the billiard-room window towards the front door, would also have passed the study window, would he not?"

"Unless he had forced his way through the shrubbery, he must have done so."

"And when you saw the prisoner that evening, there was nothing to indicate whether he had come straight round from the back of the house, or whether he had come from the study by the french window."

"There was nothing to suggest that one was more likely than the other."

Mr. Justice Conroy approved of the witness. An honest man . . . probably; a precise one . . . even more important for the smooth running of the course of justice; careful, not too garrulous, and with some knowledge of legal form. For all that, it was easy to see where his sympathies lay . . . not with the Prosecution. And that was perhaps odd . . .

Derek Stringer, his attention alert for any point that might help the Defence, was conscious of a growing dismay. This repeated account of a very ordinary evening held no suggestion of undercurrents. Nobody had behaved suspiciously . . . not even, at that time, Guy Harland. But for all that Torrington obviously did not relish having to give evidence, it was also obvious that he had never doubted the prisoner's guilt.

Guy Harland was watching the witness, with an interest he no longer endeavoured to hide. No use trying now for an objective approach. Strangely, he did not altogether wish to. There was Hugh, whom he had liked always in rather a condescending way: the man who worked with his brains, comparing himself a little smugly with the practical man. But Hugh Torrington, by any standards, had made a success of his life. While he, Guy Harland, had lived for fifteen years a shadow among real men; had lived a lie, because he feared the truth. That his fears had substance he dismissed as irrelevant; and perhaps, in this, did himself less than justice. But he found a strange comfort in Torrington's unexpressed sympathy, and when, later, its strangeness occurred to him (as it had already occurred to the Judge), he was unwilling to pursue the thought.

Garfield was proceeding with the expected repetition of his questions, underlining his points skilfully, and stressing as he did so the everyday nature of the events which had been interrupted so suddenly by violence and treachery. Maitland, listening, was caught by an unwilling admiration, the more so because he could hardly be said to have got anywhere with his attack on Esther Conrad. Not unnaturally, the failure rankled; and his recollection of Garfield's gibes, and his dislike of the man, gave him a personal interest in success. Nor did he know to what degree he was fighting for his own belief in his client, how much from an unselfish desire for justice. (Sir Nicholas would have told him roundly that all this introspection was a waste of time; adding that, if he had been governed by self-interest he would have taken the quite legitimate excuse to his hand, and dropped the case when Harland admitted his identity. But Sir Nicholas was in the living-room of his nephew's quarters in Kempenfeldt Square, growling over the teatime edition of his evening paper, while Jenny tried vainly to distract him with offers of tea and hot buttered toast; and his comments, had Antony been privileged to hear them, would have given the younger man no pleasure at all.)

"And before this occasion of which we are speaking, Colonel, how long had you known the prisoner?" That was Garfield, breaking new ground. Counsel for the Defence abandoned his abortive examination into his own motives and gave his opponent again his full attention.

"On and off, for about eighteen months."

"Ever since he joined Doctor Fraser as his assistant, in fact?"

"Yes."

"Will you explain to the jury, please, how that came about."

"He wasn't living at the Towers then, of course. But I was home pretty often at that time . . . we were stationed for a while within twenty miles of Burnham Green. He was a friend of Charlie's—of Charles Conrad. I met him several times when we walked down to the Wellington Arms for a pint."

"Did you have any conversation with him about shooting . . . about marksmanship?"

"My lord," said Maitland, getting to his feet in a hurry, "is this relevant?"

The Judge cocked an enquiring eye. "Is it relevant, Mr. Garfield?" he asked.

"I believe I can demonstrate, to your lordship's satisfaction—"

"Doctor Fraser was not shot," interrupted Maitland, flatly.

"But we have heard evidence that he was clubbed with a revolver." Conroy's voice was gentle, and Maitland compressed his lips. "I do not think I can allow your objection."

"As your lordship pleases."

"I was asking you, Colonel," said Garfield, smoothly, 'whether you remember any occasion—"

"Yes, I haven't forgotten the question. There was some talk of marksmanship, I recall; somebody said— perhaps it was Conrad—'You ought to be in the Army, Guy, you're wasting your talents in the lab.' I'm not suggesting, you know, that those were the actual words used."

"Was any mention made of a specific weapon?"

"Only in the most general terms."

"You were talking of rifle shooting?"

"Not particularly. Harland had been a member of a club at his previous firm, they'd gone in for target shooting, and I'm sure he said he was equally good with a revolver."

"He boasted about his ability, in fact?"

"Well, not precisely. He wasn't . . . he isn't . . . oh, well!" For the first time, the witness seemed confused, and he added, almost irritably: "I never found him a bombastic sort of fellow."

"Did he offer, perhaps, to demonstrate his skill with a revolver?"

"If it will make my learned friend happy," said Maitland, "we are willing to admit our skill in this connection."

"Does that content you, Mr. Garfield?"

"I am sorry, my lord, to refuse so kindly an offer from my friend. But he misses the point I am making."

"The point," said Maitland, casually, "would seem to concern my client's marksmanship."

"Do you wish to pursue this line of questioning, Mr. Garfield?" The Judge's glance between the two men was full of amusement; his words might be mild, but his intention was, at this stage, purely mischievous.

"With your permission, my lord. The point arises from the prisoner's skill—"

"The point, then, is not yet reached?" Counsel for the Defence was incredulous.

"You must be patient, Mr. Maitland."

"So I gather, my lord." He sat down again with a swirl of his gown and a look of resignation. Garfield said icily:

"If your lordship will permit me—"

"By all means, Mr. Garfield."

"I was asking you, Colonel, whether the prisoner had offered to demonstrate his skill with a revolver?"

The witness did not seem to have been attending to the exchange, or even to have heard the question. He did not answer directly, but said in a tone of pleased recollection: "The Peacehaven Hand-Gun Club . . . that was the name of the outfit he belonged to. I knew I ought to remember it."

"The . . . the outfit, Colonel?"

"The club . . . I told you. And as for a demonstration, well, nobody doubted his skill, you know. But I think there was some talk of target shooting, only nothing came of it. And if you're thinking," he added, shrewdly, "that you can infer from that he must have had a gun in his possession, I don't agree. He might reasonably expect Wilmot and myself to provide the artillery, you know."

"I think we can safely leave the question of inferences to the jury, Colonel Torrington," said Garfield, at his blandest. Maitland exchanged a look with his junior. He couldn't help feeling a reluctant admiration for his opponent, even while he found his tactics inconvenient. As he rose to cross-examine a few minutes later, it was with a strong feeling that the tide was running against him.

Torrington turned a little, and eyed the Defence Counsel appraisingly. A look of strain there, he thought, that wasn't entirely to be accounted for by long poring over his brief. He had thought before that the other man's continued denial of his client's guilt was disingenuous, but looking at him now he began to wonder. And for the first time it occurred to him that because Guy Harland's guilt had been taken for granted for twenty years, it wasn't necessarily an established fact. But he didn't entertain the thought for long.

Maitland, meanwhile, had completed his own stocktaking, and had started to skirmish. "With your good will, Colonel, we will return to the drawing-room at Burnham Towers, at the time my client came back from his brief conversation with Doctor Fraser in the study." He paused, and the witness nodded encouragingly. "You have identified a cigarette case, which my friend put into evidence, as belonging to Guy Harland."

"Yes."

"And when he returned to the drawing-room, at a quarter to nine, did you see this case in his possession?"

It was clear that Torrington understood the import of this question; clear, too, that he did not relish it. "He was only in the room a couple of minutes," he said, temporising. "And we never smoked in there, my mother didn't care for it."

"You didn't see the case?"

"No."

"He did not, for example, take it from his pocket and lay it on one of the tables in the drawing-room?"

"I wasn't watching him."

"But you did not see him do so?"

"I did not."

"And after that—you will forgive the repetition, Colonel, but I am anxious to have the events of that evening clear; after that you went into the billiard-room with Mr. Conrad, who stayed with you until nine o'clock."

"Until about nine."

"A little later Mr. Wilmot joined you; and later still, Mr. Thurlow?"

"Yes, that's right."

"When you went into the study, Colonel Torrington, after Mrs. Conrad screamed . . . why did you not check the window?"

"I don't quite understand?" He seemed genuinely bewildered.

"It was obvious, I suppose, that Doctor Fraser had been attacked. Surely your first thought would have been that his assailant came from outside the house?"

"Well, yes, I did think that. But it never occurred to me that it might only just have happened."

"The question does not seem material, my lord," protested Garfield.

"My learned friend is right, of course," said Maitland, in an injured tone. "But I am trying to get clear the events of that evening; surely your lordship will grant me so much latitude?"

"You may proceed, Mr. Maitland. For the moment."

"I am obliged to your lordship. Now, Colonel, when you saw Guy Harland . . . in spite of the blackout, you saw him clearly in the light that streamed from an uncurtained window."

The witness grinned. "There was hell to pay about that," he admitted. "But the room got so stuffy, I thought I'd chance it for ten minutes. That's how I happened to see Guy."

"And when you did . . . again I must put a suggestion to you. If Guy Harland had walked in the direction of the village, and had turned down Packer's Lane and returned to the house by way of Whitfield Cross, by what route would he have approached the front door?"

"The way I saw him come. By the path from the back of the house."

"Thank you, Colonel. Now, you have spoken of certain convivial evenings at the Wellington Arms in Burnham Green. Do you remember anything of the conversation on those occasions?"

"No." He smiled suddenly at the man who was questioning him, and added: "Not because we were drunk, you know; they weren't as convivial as all that!"

For a moment, Counsel's look of strain left him; there was something infectious in the witness's good humour. But even as he returned the smile, he was conscious of a feeling of envy: Hugh Torrington, he supposed, was at least five years his senior . . . but was I ever as young as that, relaxed, completely unselfconscious?

"I am sure the occasions we refer to were models of decorum," he said. "But perhaps you will remember if I put it another way. Did Guy Harland ever speak to you of his work?"

"I suppose he did. No man can avoid shop all the time. But nothing that mattered; certainly nothing that infringed security, if that's what you mean."

That was exactly what Counsel had meant.

"You can assure me of that, Colonel, even though you do not remember much about these conversations?"

"Of course I can." (So he had been right, after all, to press the question.) "I don't remember what we talked about, because it was twenty years ago, and only trivial matters. But something like that . . . in wartime . . . I'd certainly have noticed, you know."

"So I suppose. Now, at the time of which we are speaking you were on leave, I understand?"

"Yes."

"Embarkation leave?"

"Yes."

"And you came home on the Wednesday preceding these events? Wednesday, the 14th October, 1942?"

"We did."

"We—? Ah, yes, Mr. Wilmot was with you. Now, Colonel, how long did your leave extend?"

"We were due back at midday on Monday. That meant leaving home early on Sunday afternoon."

"And when were you next in England?"

"Not until 1946. September."

"Thank you, Colonel. That is all I wanted to know."

Maitland's gratitude appeared so heartfelt that Garfield eyed him suspiciously; and declined to re-examine when, after a few more casual questions, his opponent signified that he had finished with the witness.

Was Harry Wilmot's evidence an echo, merely, of that given by his friend, Hugh Torrington? It was clear that Garfield regarded it in this way, the only new piece of information was that the witness had seen Guy Harland leave the house on Saturday morning; hardly a matter of earth-shaking importance. But Maitland, as he listened to the repetition . . . the same story of the events of the evening, the viewpoint only a little varied . . . found himself more and more interested in the witness. A pale, quiet man he seemed; it would be easy enough to write him off as a nonentity, a foil for his friend's exuberance. But that, he was sure—and became more sure as he listened—was to over-simplify the relationship between the two men. Paradoxically enough, it was Hugh Torrington whose character he began to find more interesting. What was the bond that held these two together, in close friendship, for so many years?

So the same points were made . . . the events of the evening . . . the cigarette case . . . the talk of target shooting. And at the risk of wearying the jury, he must make the same attempt to minimise their effect.

"Your embarkation leave in October 1942 was not the first time you had met Guy Harland, I understand."

"I had met him on previous occasions, both before and after he went to live at the Towers." Wilmot seemed resigned to the repetition of statements he had already made, and his tone gave no sign of impatience.

"And of what duration was your acquaintance with Colonel Torrington at that time?"

"From the time I joined the Army . . . a little over two years."

"You knew when you went on leave that you would be going abroad?"

"Yes, we knew that."

"And that you were due back in camp by Monday, the 19th October?"

"Yes."

"Had you ever heard Guy Harland speak of his work?"

"I . . . suppose so." Wilmot's quick look towards the prisoner was oddly uncertain. "He must have done sometimes. We all do."

"I will be more explicit. Had you ever heard him speak incautiously of matters you knew must affect security?"

"No."

"You are sure of that, Mr. Wilmot?"

"Quite sure." He paused and, as his friend had done, added positively: "I'd have remembered that."

"Yes, I suppose you would. Now, when you saw Guy Harland leave the house—I am speaking of Saturday afternoon, the 17th October—did anything particular strike you about his appearance?"

"I don't think so."

"He was running down the stairs, you say, but slowed his pace when he saw you in the hall. That is guesswork, is it not? You cannot know his reason."

"That's how it seemed to me."

"So he crossed the hall, and went out of the front door. Did he not speak to you?"

"I think he said something about going over to the lab."

"Did you tell this to the police when you knew they were looking for him?"

"Of course. But it was quite a bit later. I'd gone out for a stroll myself."

"So there was nothing to put the police on his track for—how long, Mr. Wilmot?"

"Well, an hour anyway, I'd say."

"Thank you. Now, when you left the drawing-room that Friday evening, it was in Guy Harland's company?"

"I think, to be accurate, I was just ahead of him. He caught me up in the hall, and we went upstairs together."

"Did you see where he went?"

"To his bedroom. He said he wanted a pullover."

"And you, Mr. Wilmot?"

"I went to my room, too. I wanted to fetch a book."

"And then you went downstairs again, and joined Colonel Torrington in the billiard-room?"

"Yes."

"Immediately, Mr. Wilmot?"

"I think . . . no, it can't have been. He was alone, and I'm sure someone said Charlie didn't go into the morning-room until it was time for the nine o'clock news."

"Did you see Guy Harland coming back from his walk?"

"No."

"But you remember the curtains being drawn back for a time?"

"Oh, yes." He smiled a little as he recalled the incident. "Hugh said he wasn't afraid of an air raid, but he was terrified of the wardens."

"But still, he opened the curtains?"

"Yes." For the first time Wilmot sounded startled, and shot a quick look at the man who was questioning him. "The room was unbearably hot," he added.

It was growing late. Antony, observing from his eye corner that the Judge was consulting the pocket-watch which he placed every day on the bench in front of him, was aware suddenly of weariness. He said, abruptly,

"I have no more questions." And remembered only belatedly to thank the witness for his help.

It was not long after this that the Judge adjourned the court. Of the Prosecution's witnesses there remained only the laboratory technician, Hans Gunther, who had been Harland's assistant at Litzen. And after that, the Defence must put its case.

CHAPTER 14

MONDAY, the fifth day (continued)

"I t does not seem," said Sir Nicholas drily, "that you have done much to-day towards proving your client innocent." He eyed his nephew challengingly over the rim of his coffee cup, and Antony looked back at him, frowning.

"No, I didn't," he said shortly. And added, on a note of protest: "Dammit, Uncle Nick, we've nothing to go on . . . nothing to use as a lever."

"So much is obvious." Sir Nicholas spoke with clear intent to annoy, and Jenny and Derek Stringer—sitting, as it were, on the sidelines—exchanged glances of mingled annoyance and resignation.

"Were you in court to-day, sir?"

"I was not." At the recollection of a grievance, he allowed himself a momentary diversion. "I spent the morning wrangling with Mallory—he wants me to take that brief from Hetheringtons, Antony, but I'm almost sure the case will be called at the same time as Brierly comes up for trial; as for the early afternoon, *that* was devoted to one of Bellerby's clients, who has been swindling his partner for years, apparently."

"Hence," said Antony, looking at the ceiling, "these tears."

"Not at all. His efforts to put a good face on the business were not without their amusing side. But as for your affairs—"

"If I could have made more impression," said Antony sadly, "on that wretched woman—"

"Are you so sure there was anything to be got from her?" Glancing with apparent casualness from his nephew to Derek Stringer, Sir Nicholas noted the latter's expression and formed his own estimate of the situation.

"Sure? Sure enough," said Antony. He looked at Stringer and added deliberately: "I didn't like the lady."

"If we'd a scrap of proof—"

Antony did not answer directly. He turned to his uncle and said, as though it were he who had raised the objection: "There isn't anything, sir. Even Sykes—"

"Had he nothing to tell you?"

"Nothing to the point." He thrust a hand into the breast-pocket of his jacket, and presently brought out some folded sheets of paper. "A collection of innocents," he mourned. "Every one of 'em."

"I don't know what you were expecting," said Derek. Antony got up and attacked the fire, a little too viciously.

"A few skeletons at least," he answered. "One might expect something, don't you think, sir?"—again he appealed to his uncle.

"In most groups of people, certainly," said Sir Nicholas. He put down his coffee cup, and directed a searching glance at the table beside him to make sure that every requirement was at hand for the peaceful enjoyment of a cigar. Jenny, who had been taking no part in the conversation, twisted a little in her chair so that the light fell more directly on her sewing. Antony wondered for a moment what she was thinking: most likely that it was tiresome of him to be so preoccupied with the affairs of strangers.

"I was wondering," said Jenny, "about that Mrs. Conrad—"

"What about her, love?"

"Someone said she was in love with Mr. Wilmot."

"But she spent the evening with Conrad, and married him in the end. Anyway, that was Harland's idea; and even if you grant he's a disinterested witness on that point, I should hardly call him an authority on matters of sentiment," said Derek. "If Antony's right about *her*, we ought to know more about her husband."

"Well, there's nothing to his detriment," said Antony. "Which is what you really mean."

"I am beginning to see," said Sir Nicholas, "why you found little to encourage you in what Sykes had to say."

"There's worse to come, sir. He gave me an explanation of why Fraser wasn't completely at ease with Garfield's question concerning possible enemies."

"Come now," said his uncle, "surely that's all to the good."

Jenny looked up. "Who was it that Doctor Fraser disliked?"

"Robin Thurlow. He wrote a book—" He broke off, and Jenny said, a little impatiently:

"Of course he did. He's a writer, isn't he?"

"I'm talking about his first novel. It was called *The Great Must Live*, and was published just about the time the war broke out."

"I got it out of the library the other day," said Jenny, "after you'd been talking about him. I didn't like it much."

"Then you'll remember the main character, a scientist—"

"Well, he wasn't exactly the main character," said Jenny. "At least, not the hero. He was very famous, and he'd made some sort of mistake in the past—I'm not sure what, because I skipped that bit. His assistant found out about it, and didn't tell anybody; only then they had a quarrel, and the assistant began to think it might be his duty to tell people, after all. It was all very high-minded, and rather silly."

"A fascinating synopsis, my dear," remarked Sir Nicholas. He looked at his nephew. "Is it relevant?" he demanded.

"People thought the scientist was Fraser. He wasn't shown in a favourable light."

"I seem to remember," said Sir Nicholas, slowly. "They took Hovingdons' opinion—Fraser's solicitors, I mean. But in the end no action was taken."

"Thurlow had been Fraser's secretary," said Derek, "which lent some colour to the story. I don't see why we can't use it."

"I don't want to confuse the issue." Antony's tone was positive. "There's plenty of evidence of envy, hatred and all uncharitableness . . . but none at all of treason."

"All the same," said Stringer, stubbornly, "it seems to me—" As his colleague was in no mood for argument, it was perhaps fortunate that at this moment the telephone rang. Jenny crossed the room to answer it, and said a moment later:

"It's Inspector Sykes. He said he'd like to see you, Antony, so I told him to come round right away." She picked up the coffee-pot and shook it enquiringly. "I'd better make some more," she said.

Sykes, who arrived some fifteen minuter later, brought a note of calm to an atmosphere which by then had grown rather heated. He had a decided partiality for Jenny, and enjoyed the fuss she made over his comfort. Antony, who had given the newcomer his chair and taken up his favourite position with a shoulder against the mantel, looked down at them with amusement, more relaxed than he had been all day.

"I hope you have some more news for us," he said, after a while.

Sykes shrugged. "Summat . . . and nowt," he said. "Don't be expecting too much, Mr. Maitland."

"Oh, lord," said Antony, still amused. "Another Jeremiah! I'll take what you can give me, Inspector . . . and no doubt I shall be thankful."

Sykes stirred his coffee, and Jenny pushed the sugar bowl towards him. He helped himself absent-mindedly to three extra lumps, tested the mixture and found it to his satisfaction, and turned again to his host. "You asked me," he said, "if I could make an opportunity to see Inspector Cummings; so I asked him round for Sunday supper, and afterwards we had a bit of a talk."

Jenny leaned back, and picked up her sewing. Derek looked up quickly at Antony, remembering some questions he had meant to put to him. Sir Nicholas deposited an inch of ash carefully.

"I knew," he remarked, "that we could rely on you."

"Well, now, wait a bit. I've nothing very sensational to offer you, I'm afraid."

"Not even," said Maitland, "the answer to the questions we didn't ask in court?"

"I can tell you that, I think. I don't think it will be helpful. The details of what they found in the study, for instance. The window was open, and the curtains blowing. The gun was on the floor, about two feet from the window, and a little over a foot behind the chair Doctor Fraser was sitting in."

"Garfield asked him that," said Maitland. He spoke a little irritably, but Sykes showed no sign of having noticed.

"Yes, it was made abundantly clear that the man who attacked Doctor Fraser came by the french window and took him unawares," he agreed. "Just as I understand the Prosecution maintain Guy Harland did."

"Anyone could have come that way. With the blackout—"

"Guy Harland . . . or anyone," said Sykes, nodding.

"It has occurred to me to wonder," interrupted Sir Nicholas, "why Harland permitted himself to be seen on the path outside the billiard-room."

"If he'd hidden the doings," Derek suggested, "he might have wanted to be seen empty-handed. The most likely thing would have been to put what he had taken into a brief-case of his own, and hide that in the shrubbery—probably in a pre-arranged spot for someone else to pick up. That would apply to whoever the thief was, of course."

"What Colonel Torrington told Inspector Cummings," said Sykes, ignoring the digression, "was that Harland seemed completely preoccupied—'in a dream,' I think he said—and didn't seem to notice the light, or look towards the window, or anything."

"Something *told* me not to ask that question," said Antony. His uncle gave him a withering look and said coldly:

"Your guardian angel, no doubt." Antony grinned at him.

"However," said Sykes, "that wasn't my point. Harland said Doctor Fraser was writing a letter, and the butler had the same impression. Actually, when he was attacked he was working on his notes, but it was months later, when he recovered, before the police knew that. Everything had gone that might possibly relate to the experiments he had been doing."

"As a matter of interest," said Sir Nicholas, "at what stage did the police know that there was more to the affair than just an assault, or even attempted murder?"

"They were fairly sure of it the evening after Harland disappeared. The other assistant, Montague, telephoned from the laboratory; he was wondering where Harland had got to. So then Cummings asked him some questions."

"There were two matters which puzzle me: why should Harland have gone to all that trouble to steal reports which must have been readily available to him at work? And why should he, if guilty, have drawn his colleague's attention to the fact that they were missing?"

"Harland answered the first question for me, sir. Security at the lab was pretty strictly observed—but not so far as Fraser was concerned. He was the only one who could have got away with the stuff."

"Yes, that's reasonable. And the other point?" Sir Nicholas looked round for enlightenment.

"Cummings thought he wanted to make sure nothing important had been left behind," said Sykes. "If you're thinking of recalling Mr. Montague on that point, I don't think I should," he added, apologetically. "His last conversation with Harland on the telephone, as he reported it to the police, would certainly bear that construction." He paused to sip his coffee, and to take stock of his companions. Jenny's head was bent again over her work; Sir Nicholas was gazing at the ceiling, apparently dissociated from the whole affair now that his questions were answered; Derek was making notes in his pocket book; and Antony was frowning, as though what he heard displeased him.

"It was some months before Fraser recovered sufficiently to give his evidence." Sykes was in no degree put out by the reception his listeners were giving him. "The fact that the laboratory reports were missing was all that seemed to matter, but as you're looking for out-of-the-way points there is just one thing, Mr. Maitland. A few days before he was injured Doctor Fraser, being short of personal stationery, had bought a package of note-paper in the village shop at Burnham Green. When he got home he was disgusted to find that the paper was coloured pink and impregnated with a strong, disagreeable scent. He wouldn't use it for his correspondence, but because it was wartime he didn't want to waste what he had bought, so he had written some comments on the day's experiments on the scented paper. These notes were gone, as well as the file of laboratory reports."

"The notes were technical, I suppose?"

"They were. I gather," said Sykes, "that the discovery—whatever it was—is still on the secret list."

"Unfortunately," said Antony. He glanced across at his uncle. "We had all that out in court to-day. There's nothing to be done about it."

"You felt, I suppose, that some detail might help your cross-examination of the witness, Hans Gunther?"

"Well, it might," said Antony. "Besides, as it is, my researches into the subject are completely wasted." His uncle smiled at him.

"Annoying," he agreed. But Maitland had turned his attention again to the visitor. "Is that the lot?" he asked.

"I'm sorry, Mr. Maitland. That's all there was, and I don't see how it can help you, any more than the rest of my report."

"Well, neither do I," said Antony. "But I'm no less grateful, and of course I may be wrong." He glanced at his uncle, and then at his colleague who was stowing away note-book and pencil.

"Who lives may learn," he said; but he did not sound particularly hopeful.

CHAPTER 15

TUESDAY, the sixth day

There was certainly nothing in Hans Gunther's appearance when he was called to give evidence next morning to encourage the Defence in any extravagant hopes. He was stocky, fair-haired; and might have been drawn, reflected Antony, breaking his pencil point on a savage and ill-contrived sketch, by any cartoonist in search of the German equivalent of the man-in-the-street. Nor was there any encouragement to be found in his answers to Garfield's questions; his English was unexpectedly excellent, but he seemed a creature of no imagination, a little stupid even . . . everything, in fact, that the proof of his evidence had foreshadowed, and that Maitland had least wanted to find.

There was nothing unexpected in his story, of course. He had been working at Litzen already for some time when Guy Harland came there, as assistant to *Herr Doktor* Braun. When he was assigned his new duties by the *Direktor* he had been told, certainly, to be alert, but there was nothing strange in that. The work was difficult . . . no, *Herr* Harland had not confided in him to any great extent . . . he was a clever man, the witness thought, but not communicative.

Mr. Justice Conroy, watching the Defence Counsel's expression without getting very much enlightenment, wondered idly what sort of an answer he was going to provide to all this weight of evidence. Paul Garfield's reflections followed much the same track . . . things were turning out well, and his case bade fair to be overwhelming. He was sure of his victory now, but equally sure that it would be a righteous one. Maitland, who realised this well enough, could only wish he had one quarter the certainty in the cause for which he was fighting so stubbornly.

Harland's thoughts were a jumble . . . a little hope, and a great deal of fear. After this witness—and what could be got out of a chap like Gunther to favour his own case?—after this it would be the Defence's

turn. Maitland had warned him that his opening remarks would be brief
. . . and his own evidence would follow. Nothing to worry about . . . just
take it quietly and tell them . . . and tell them . . . His mind was blank
suddenly, there was nothing, *nothing* he could say. For a moment the
courtroom receded, and Gunther's voice, and the half-smile that was on
Garfield's face as he put his questions; there was only the suffocating
feeling of panic. But after a time he had mastered it; the present was
vivid and frightening, but he was calm again. "One more river," said Guy
Harland to himself, watching the witness and wondering what sort of
show he in his turn would make. "One more river ". . . but he couldn't
even see the other bank, and who knew how far it was across?

The Foreman of the Jury felt the Prosecution's case was a strong one.
He must keep an open mind, of course; that was his duty, and there was
bound to be something to be said for the Defence. Though once Harland
had admitted his identity, it was difficult to see what could be put forward
in his favour. The Defence Counsel looked confident enough, but what
could you make of that? "Window dressing," thought the Foreman,
shrewdly enough, and would have been startled to know how nearly his
own thought ran with the reflections of the prisoner's solicitor.

Geoffrey Horton, equally with Counsel, had lost his equanimity over
this affair. He was conscious of conflicting emotions; and uncomfortably
aware that Garfield's case was almost complete now and the end couldn't
be far off. Even as he thought that, Counsel for the Prosecution finished
his examination and seated himself again; and Maitland got up in his
turn and stood looking at the witness.

He allowed the pause to lengthen, borrowing unconsciously the trick
his opponent used with such effect; although he had already observed
Gunther with some care during the examination-in-chief. At last he said,
apparently casual: "You knew, of course, the nature of the work Guy
Harland was doing?"

"I had no detailed knowledge—" His tone was sharply defensive.

"You knew his experiments concerned a development of the bacillus
cholera sicca?'

"Yes, that, of course."

"And that it was hoped to find the means of infecting large numbers
of people with a disease for which there was no known remedy?"

"I knew that." Gunther spoke slowly, and seemed to be weighing each
admission. Maitland's tone remained disarmingly friendly.

"When you were told you would work as Harland's assistant, what were your instructions?"

"I was told to help him in his work."

"To watch him, perhaps?" His manner changed as the witness hesitated, and he repeated sharply: "You were told to watch him, were you not, *Herr* Gunther?"

"To help him with his work, and—yes—to keep my eyes open."

"And which of these assignments would you say was the more important?"

"To assist with the experiments." The answer was given quickly . . . a little too quickly, it might be felt.

"Why did you think that?" Maitland had reverted to his quiet tone.

"Because . . . because *Herr* Harland was working with us."

"You did not regard it as important that you were asked to watch his movements. To report—I suppose—to the *Direktor* on his behaviour." The insinuation was smoothly made, and passed unchallenged.

"It was important, of course. But there was no reason to believe him untrustworthy."

"He is an Englishman, *Herr* Gunther. We were at war. Would that not have made him worthy of suspicion?"

"One who had come to us in such circumstances? I did not think there could be anything to fear from such a one."

"It was all just part of the game you were playing." There was an edge to Maitland's voice, that Stringer heard with a feeling of unease. "You watched Guy Harland; the cleaners, no doubt, watched you; and the *Direktor* himself, you will perhaps tell me, watched the cleaners?"

"It is true," said Gunther seriously, "that there was need of care."

"But no special precautions were observed in Harland's case?"

"None that I knew."

"He was free to leave the house when he wished? To leave the grounds?"

"Well, as to that, the grounds were guarded. It was secret work we were doing, that was why we had been moved into the country in the first place. To get out, one must have a pass."

"Do you recall Guy Harland having such a pass? To go into Litzen, perhaps?"

"I do not remember."

"He would have gone out sometimes, surely, if he had been free to do so."

"He might have felt it wiser—"

"You admit then that he had need of caution?" The question came swiftly, but Gunther was not to be shaken. He said woodenly:

"I do not understand," and Maitland laughed.

"Shall we call for an interpreter?" he offered.

"I do not think—"

"No, you speak English very well, as we have heard. Was it for this reason that you were given the job of watching Guy Harland while he worked at Litzen."

"I think that was perhaps the reason."

"Had you no other qualifications to recommend you? You knew something, did you not, of the work he was doing, of the sort of problems he would meet?"

"I have explained to you, I knew very little—"

"This *Direktor* then. Was he a fool?"

Gunther did not answer immediately, but looked frowningly at the man who had questioned him. Then he said carefully:

"I hear what you say, mein Herr; I understand the words you use; but I do not know their meaning." Maitland, sensitive and alert, was sure now that the witness was afraid. And—for all his stolidity—definitely not a fool. Perhaps, after all, there might be something to be salvaged. He said quietly:

"Why did he give you this work, if it was beyond your capacity?"

"You have given the answer. Because I knew English well."

"Did Harland speak German?"

"Not when I first knew him. He learned quickly."

"Then would not that have been the time to give him a more capable assistant?"

"He found me useful enough, I think."

"And by then you were familiar with the work."

"A little familiar."

"With his aims, and how he hoped to bring them about?"

"I had learned something of what he was doing."

"Something?" said Maitland, drawing out the word sceptically. "No more than that?"

"He was, as I have said, a secretive man."

"You do not think, then, that he had no confidence in you?"

"That may well have been the case."

"It would certainly have been the case, would it not, if he was trying to trick you?" The witness stared at him even more woodenly than before, and he added impatiently: "Do not say again, you do not understand. I think you know very well what I mean."

"There was never any question of his sincerity. He came of his own free will to Germany," said Gunther, spitefully, "and brought with him the laboratory reports—"

"Who told you that?"

"The *Direktor*, I suppose. Perhaps *Herr* Harland himself."

"Did he tell you how he had escaped from England?"

"No. I do not remember." (But, not a doubt of it, the man was afraid.)

"He did not speak to you of the matter. That is the truth, is it not?"

"I do not remember. But what had happened was common knowledge."

"We have your word for that." He sounded scornful. "At what stage was the work when Harland was ordered to remove from Litzen?"

"I cannot say. The reports he brought from England, the reports of his own experiments, he took everything with him."

"You are sure of that, *Herr* Gunther?"

"They were certainly gone from our laboratory."

"Had he completed his work?"

"No. I . . . I do not know."

"That is two answers you have given me. Which was the true one?" The witness did not answer, and he added gently: "I think your first thought was best, my friend, but perhaps you feel your second thoughts were . . . safest."

Garfield came to his feet in a leisurely way. "My lord, I must echo the witness. I do not understand this line of questioning," he said plaintively.

Maitland smiled at him. Just for the moment he felt in command of the situation, and he did not even resent the interruption. "Is it necessary that you should understand?" he asked softly.

"It would be a convenience, perhaps." The Judge leaned forward. "I do not understand myself, Mr. Garfield; but I shall rely on Mr. Maitland to spell it out for us when he comes to address the jury."

"I shall be happy to do so, my lord." The deference in his tone was just a shade overdone. Garfield sat down again, not ill-satisfied; Maitland, with no thoughts to spare for side issues, turned back to the witness.

"So we are agreed, are we not, that Harland had not completed his experiments at the time he left Litzen?" He made the assumption blandly, and half expected to see Garfield on his feet again.

"I do not know." Gunther sounded sullen, but his denial lacked assurance.

"And as he is known to have been in Switzerland some six weeks later, you will agree, I think, that there would hardly have been time—" He broke off at the precise moment that Garfield started to get up, and did not give him a chance to voice his protest. "I apologise, my lord. I spoke my thought aloud." Unexpectedly, Conroy smiled at him almost benignly.

"You will have opportunity later to address the jury, Mr. Maitland. If they are not too weary to attend by that time, no doubt you will be able to convey your meaning to them."

Again Maitland smiled, and again with genuine amusement. "I will endeavour to be brief, my lord," he said.

"I believe you would be wise to do so." Conroy nodded his head at him portentously. Counsel bowed, and turned back to the witness.

"I was asking about your qualifications, *Herr* Gunther. You did not tell us—"

"My work had not been of that kind—" But the evasion was clumsy. Maitland judged it time to press the question further.

"You are a graduate, I believe, of the University of Tubingen?"

"Yes." The admission came reluctantly, and Antony had time to note Garfield's frown. He hadn't known, then? Well, it was likely Gunther would have kept quiet about it; he'd been playing the part of the rather simple-minded assistant who followed instructions blindly ever since the end of the war, no doubt. And no doubt would go on playing it, if given the opportunity.

"And your studies for your degree were in the field of bio-chemistry?"

"They were."

"You have then, I expect, some elementary knowledge at least of cholera . . . of its causes and its treatment?"

"My work was not concerned—"

"But even the most general studies would give you a suitable background, so that you could quickly master the details of work in any related field?" He paused, expectantly; but as no answer was forthcoming added insistently: "Is that not so, *Herr* Gunther?"

"I suppose it is." He spoke grudgingly.

"When you were approached to give evidence, you did not mention this very significant fact?" The court was still now. The witness looked round quickly before he spoke, as though he hoped to find inspiration.

"I was not asked. It did not seem important."

"It would have been an odd thing, would it not, for a man of your qualifications to act as assistant."

Gunther did not let him finish, but broke in with an eager explanation.

"It was his own subject . . . he had followed the experiments from the first . . . he had the notes *Herr Doktor* Fraser had made that last day—"

"And still you tell us you were employed only to help Guy Harland?"

"That is the truth."

"Without speaking to him of your qualifications?"

"There was no need." He paused, and swallowed; and added more confidently, "Obviously he knew."

"But not because *you* told him. The game you were playing was too deep for that."

"I was only there to help him—"

"I will tell you why you were there, though Harland never suspected. *He* thought you stupid, and did not believe what he had been told. But one thing he did notice—this rather unobservant enemy of yours. What were you doing in the laboratory at night, *Herr* Gunther? Not once, but many times?"

"I was working." The question had been shot at him without warning, and in his anxiety to present an explanation the witness did not stop to reflect that a simple denial would have been more to his purpose.

"Working?" said Maitland. "At a problem about which you know so little? Do you expect us to believe that, *mein Herr*?"

"There were things I had to do—"

"Yes, that is the truth for once, I think. There were things you had to do. Such as photographing the reports that had been brought from England . . . that was one of your duties, was it not?"

"No . . . no!"

"You are telling me that never—never, *Herr* Gunther!—did you use a camera in the laboratory?" He leaned forward, and struck the flat of his hand on the table in front of him. "Answer the question!" he said.

"It was . . . a precaution," said Gunther.

"A sensible precaution," Maitland approved. He straightened himself again, but his whole attention remained fixed on the witness. "Because Guy Harland was not trusted; because it was known he was playing for time."

Gunther looked at him blankly. "It was a precaution," he said again. "We had need of care."

"Yes, indeed. Now, you have spoken of Doctor Fraser's notes. How did you know, with your so limited knowledge, what progress he had made?"

"There was a note . . . it was dated—"

"A note on pink paper?" Maitland's tone was quietly reflective. Gunther, feeling perhaps that he had here some chance of being believed, rushed into eager agreement.

"On pink paper, *mein Herr* . . . incredibly. But it recorded a great step of progress—" His voice faltered, as he realised that his words came perilously near to an admission of knowledge. Maitland smiled at him amiably.

"I am sure you found it of the greatest assistance. And by the time you were finished, no doubt, you were certain that Harland had no intention of completing the work—"

"I did not know that."

"But you had told your superiors that you had now all the background knowledge you needed . . . that Harland had made no progress . . . that he might well be disposed of."

"No . . . no . . . I had not the ability—"

"You are too modest, *Herr* Gunther."

"It was *Herr* Harland's own field of work . . . not mine."

"Yet you have admitted to us that you spied on him . . . that you photographed his papers at night . . . that you understood his work very well."

"I . . . no, I did not say that. If you wish I will admit . . . that I was told to watch him. But I thought only that he was, perhaps, not so clever as had been believed."

"Not clever enough, for instance, to complete the experiments himself."

"But he . . . no, that is not fair, *mein Herr*. The work was his."

"Work which you understood, no doubt, as well as he did."

"Well . . . perhaps . . . after a time." He was growing confused now, and his fear was evident, but he returned stubbornly to his denials. "The direction of the experiments was his affair."

"Yes . . . no doubt. But you completed them, did you not, after he left the laboratory at Litzen? And in spite of the fact that he destroyed his own notes and the only reports he knew existed, before he was taken away." He paused, deliberately, for a moment, as though giving the witness time to answer. But though Gunther's lips framed a denial, he did not utter it. He shook his head in a dazed way, at last, but doubtfully, with no sense of conviction. Maitland let the question lie unanswered between them for a moment, and then asked softly:

"What plans had been made for Guy Harland's future, I wonder, if he had not escaped?"

As he seated himself, Derek Stringer let out his breath in a long sigh.

"I didn't think you could do it," he said.

"G-garfield's not f-finished yet." Antony put his hands on the table in front of him, and clasped them together to hide the fact that they were shaking. When he spoke again the slight stammer was mastered, but the look he gave his friend held a hint of apology and a good deal of self-derision. "It doesn't really mean much," he said. "But I think we've got a chance now. Don't you?"

The Case for the Defence

CHAPTER 16

TUESDAY, the sixth day (continued)

Maitland was right in his surmise, the effect of his attack on this last of the Prosecution's witnesses was out of all proportion to the value of Gunther's admissions. Perhaps because it was the first hint that the prisoner's guilt was not to be taken for granted on every point, there was— for the moment at least—a reaction in his favour. Derek Stringer, summing up his impressions in the pause which followed Garfield's short re-examination of the witness, said bluntly:

"It all depends on Harland now." And if he added to himself, a little grimly, as his colleague got up to open his case: "But he'd better be good," there was nothing in his expression to convey the smallest doubt.

Mr. Justice Conroy, a cynical auditor, thought that Maitland should feel some satisfaction over the way he had handled the last witness. Obviously, he intended to fight every inch of the way; but Garfield's case was well-constructed and convincing, and so far the Judge had heard nothing to shake his belief in the prisoner's guilt. But it was the effect on the jury that mattered, after all.

The witnesses who had already given evidence were now seated in the court. Esther Conrad was giving Counsel only half her attention while she grappled with a problem that had presented itself for the first time while Gunther was giving evidence. Just how fully would to-day's hearing be reported in the Press? And how far should she go in telling Charlie what had happened? She wasn't quite easy about his attitude the previous evening; he had seemed preoccupied, and far less indignant than she had expected over her treatment by the Defence Counsel. Almost as if . . . as if he didn't trust her. The thought was unpleasant, and she pushed it away from her, only to have it return a moment later with a new twist added.

If it came to the point, how far could she trust Charlie? She had seen something in the past of his ruthlessness, but it hadn't mattered because never before had she had occasion to question his devotion to herself.

Beside her, Hugh Torrington whispered to his other neighbour, "Chap's got the bit between his teeth now." His eyes were on Maitland's face; he thought his confident air impressive, and his words convincing.

Harry Wilmot, also watching Counsel, acknowledged the comment with a slight smile, but did not reply to his friend's observation. He was occupied with the implications of Gunther's evidence, and wondering how long it would delay matters, and what the end would be. Seeing Esther had unsettled him, he supposed; she was even handsomer now than when she was a girl, the slight hardness which had then been apparent having somehow transmuted itself into poise. It was a good thing that Hugh, for all his clumsy tact, did not realise just how upsetting he found it, meeting her again.

Maitland, weighing each point as he brought it forward, found each in turn inadequate. Garfield knew that—damn him!—and Conroy too, from his sardonic look. Better finish quickly, before the Judge's amusement became more apparent; he'd something to build on now, no need for the jury to realise how shaky a foundation it was. And heaven help the lot of us, he thought as he seated himself, if Harland doesn't come up to proof.

The prisoner's demeanour was quiet enough as he moved from dock to witness stand, but his Counsel, noting his tense air and general look of strain, found himself shaken by something sympathetically near to panic. As he got to his feet again he was smiling faintly, but Stringer (who knew the signs) scribbled "Take it easy!" on the pad in front of him, and pushed the note along until it was under his colleague's hand, Maitland glanced down, and acknowledged the message with the briefest of smiles before he began, in his easy, casual way, to take the witness through the preliminary part of his evidence.

Under his handling, Harland relaxed a little, his answers came easily. Stringer noted with satisfaction that the story sounded convincing, but when the court reassembled after a late luncheon recess the prisoner looked apprehensive as Garfield rose to cross-examine.

It was at such moments as this that Paul Garfield was most impressive. Conscious of his own virtues, he could press his attack without any of the misgivings which might assail a lesser man. He eyed the witness for a moment and then asked quietly:

"You went to work for Doctor Fraser, you say, because you thought it was your duty."

"I don't think I said that . . . exactly." Guy Harland paused, and cleared his throat nervously before he went on. "But it was near enough what I meant."

"You knew before you went to him that the work he was engaged on was secret?"

"I might have guessed that, I suppose. I didn't know until after I joined him, of course, but actually it was 'most secret,'" said the prisoner. And glanced at his Counsel, a look half apology, half appeal.

"So that an opportunity would occur, no doubt, for a man with connections abroad—"

"My lord!" Maitland's tone was scandalised. "My friend has laid no grounds for this suggestion." The Judge gave him an admonitory look.

"It is open to the prisoner to deny the charge, Mr. Maitland."

"An open accusation, my lord, would be easier to counter. But these insinuations—"

Conroy shook his head at him. "Perhaps you have not read your brief, Mr. Maitland, but at least you have had the opportunity of listening to the indictment."

"We are prepared to counter the charge of treason, my lord." He met Conroy's eye as he spoke, and uttered the lie blandly. "But to allege—"

"No, Mr. Maitland." His tone was final, and Maitland subsided with a mutinous look. "You may answer Counsel," the Judge added, speaking for the first time directly to the prisoner.

"I suppose I must, my lord." His glance flickered for a moment to his own Counsel, seated again but no more relaxed than a coiled spring, and then returned to Garfield's face. "'The words of Mercury are harsh,'" he said regretfully, "'after the songs of Apollo,'"—and apparently did not see anything odd or outrageous about the remark. Conroy gave one startled look from the Defence to the Prosecuting Counsel, and disappeared behind his handkerchief. Antony, half-way between annoyance and amusement, succumbed to the latter emotion on catching sight of his opponent's expression. Well, it would take them both some time to live that down; but Garfield, poor chap, would find the inevitable ridicule harder to bear.

Harland, meanwhile, had turned back to the man who was questioning him. He waited for the laughter to subside, and then said as though nothing had happened: "I didn't think about . . . what you suggested. And I hadn't any 'connections abroad,' that I remember."

"Your memory is an accommodating one, Mr. Harland. Let me help you a little." Garfield paused there, for effect, and the prisoner looked back at him, as fascinated as a rabbit by a snake. "There were two young men at your college, were there not? A Dutchman, Pieter Vandervoort, and a German, Erik Mueller?"

"Well, yes, there were, but—"

Maitland, half-way to his feet, sat down again. Too late to stop the admission . . . better air the matter a little, perhaps. He was conscious of irresolution, but Garfield was pressing his point.

"You knew them well?"

"As one knows fellow students. Not intimately."

"You had no communication with them after you came down? You did not know, for instance, that Vandervoort was shot by his own countrymen during the occupation, as a collaborator? Or that Mueller's father was well known as a Nazi, and that Erik Mueller himself was a member of their military intelligence?"

"No."

"I will repeat the question. Did you have any communication with either of these two men after you left your university?"

"No."

"Did you know what became of them? What happened to Vandervoort?"

"No."

"Or of Mueller's party affiliations?"

"No. At least . . . not until later."

"Later?" Garfield pounced on the admission. "Later? What do you mean?"

"That I saw him, when I was in Germany." He sounded defensive now, and again there was that sidelong look at his own Counsel. Maitland's lips were set in a thin line: just one more thing he hadn't been told, and perhaps Harland really hadn't thought it important. He doubted if he could stop the questions now . . . he thought it might do more harm than good to try. Beside him, Derek muttered "Leave it," and he found himself grateful for advice which in a more confident mood would have irked him.

"You saw Erik Mueller when you were in Germany. During the war. Perhaps you will tell us how this came about."

"I saw him several times when I was in Litzen. I think he was trying to find out if I was really doing my best to complete Doctor Fraser's experiments."

"And you ask us to believe that this was a coincidence?"

"I'm telling you what happened."

"I suggest, Mr. Harland, that you knew very well you would see Erik Mueller at Litzen."

"No! But once I knew he was there, it was partly that which made me decide—"

"We will come to your motives later. Just answer the questions, if you please. You have admitted that after your interview with Doctor Fraser on the evening of October 16th your silver cigarette case was still in your possession?"

"Yes, I—" Harland seemed bewildered by the change of direction. Garfield spoke quickly, underlining the hesitation.

"That is not a very difficult matter, surely. You have already told the court—"

"I remember talking with Miss Marne . . . with Mrs. Conrad. And as I gave her a cigarette, I must have had my case then."

"But you deny that you went back to the study?"

"I didn't go back."

"How then do you account for your case being found there?"

"I don't account for it."

"Come now, Mr. Harland, you must surely have given this matter some thought. Do you suggest that Mrs. Conrad took it from you?"

"No."

"Or that you left it in the drawing-room?"

"No." His tone was dogged now. "I don't suggest anything, either of those things might be true. I only know I didn't go back to the study."

"Where did you go when you left the house?"

"For a walk."

"Please tell us where you went."

"But I've already . . . oh, all right! I went out by the front door, and down the drive. When I reached the gates I turned left, towards the village, and turned left again before I reached it, down Packer's Lane. About half a mile from the main road I took to the fields, as far as Whitfield Cross, and so back to the Towers again."

"Where you lived for a little over six months?"

"Yes."

"And you had been at Burnham Green for about a year before that, had you not?"

"Yes."

"Are you fond of walking, Mr. Harland?"

"Yes." With each repetition, the word was spoken more doubtfully.

"You were presumably well acquainted with the countryside . . . with that particular walk you have described to us?"

"Yes. Yes, I was."

"So if you had to explain how you came to be seen walking back to the front door from the direction of the study window, a suitable story would not be far to seek?"

"My lord!" protested Counsel for the Defence, and this time the Judge's admonitory shake of the head was for his opponent. "You must be more precise, Mr. Garfield," he said firmly.

"It will be a pleasure, your lordship." (Maitland sat down again, scowling.) "I suggest to you, Mr. Harland, that when Colonel Torrington saw you that evening on the path outside the billiard-room window, you had just left the study."

"No."

"And that Doctor Fraser was at that time unconscious, and his papers in your possession."

"No . . . no! It wasn't like that."

"How then, Mr. Harland?"

"I just went for a walk."

"You have described this excursion to my friend in some detail, and have gone over the main points for me again. But you have not mentioned the possibility of corroboration."

"No."

"Why not, Mr. Harland?"

"I didn't meet anyone. Not that I remember."

"Is it possible that during all that time—well over an hour, was it not?—you saw no one?"

"It must be possible, because I didn't."

"Nobody walking down to the Wellington Arms?"

"I saw no one."

"No member of the Home Guard? No air raid warden about his duties?"

"No."

"What time was it when you left the house?"

"I . . . I don't know exactly. I think . . . about ten to nine."

"And no member of the household was about: none of your fellow guests?"

"Mrs. Thurlow was on the terrace. I saw her standing there, but I don't think she noticed me."

"Was that not rather unobservant of her . . . if, in fact, you walked down the drive, as you say?"

"Not especially. She didn't look round. She was listening."

"Listening? Listening to what?"

"Someone was whistling."

"A serenade, no doubt." Garfield's tone was at its most sarcastic, but the witness answered seriously enough.

"No, I don't think so. Someone was walking down one of the paths in the shrubbery, and whistling as he went."

"Mr. Harland, why are you trying to confuse the court with these irrelevant details?"

"Details which my friend has insisted upon hearing," said Maitland, on his feet again. To his surprise, the Judge took up the point.

"I do not think your complaint is justified, Mr. Garfield." He turned to look at Guy Harland. "Do you remember the tune?" he enquired. (Maitland exchanged a look with Derek Stringer, who was grinning; they both knew his lordship's purpose was merely to annoy the Prosecution.)

"No, my lord." The prisoner answered promptly, but cleared his throat nervously again before he went on. "Well, I can tell you one thing. It wasn't a song hit."

"Not—er—'Roll out the barrel,' or some similar popular melody?"

"Oh, no, my lord. Nothing like that."

Conroy leaned back again. "You may continue, Mr. Garfield," he remarked affably.

"I am obliged to your lordship. You are not suggesting, I suppose," he added, turning back to the witness, "that this man who was whistling saw you, and can substantiate your statement?"

"I didn't see who it was. I don't suppose he knew I was there."

"So we are still without corroboration of your account of your movements that evening."

"Well, if I'd met a dozen people," said Harland, suddenly abandoning his passive attitude, "I don't see that it would help. I'd still have had 'world enough and time' to attack Fraser if I'd wanted to."

"You really must control your witness, Mr. Maitland," the Judge protested.

"With respect, my lord, the line of questioning which my learned friend is following—"

"Is no excuse for so improper a comment. However," he added, rolling a steely eye from the prisoner to Counsel for the Prosecution, "I am sure, Mr. Garfield, that there are other points you wish to cover."

Maitland's expression lightened, and he grinned almost cheerfully at Derek Stringer as he sat down again. When not personally directed, the Judge's tactics had their amusing side. Garfield, as might have been expected, had taken the implied rebuke smoothly, and was moving to his next position.

"Yes," he said, impressively. "Yes, Mr. Harland." And though he knew it was a deliberate trick, Maitland was aware of a chill as his opponent paused. He permitted himself a glance at the prisoner, and meeting his eye for a moment was conscious that the facade was crumbling, the veneer of calm wearing very thin indeed.

"We have heard evidence," Garfield went on, "that a gun found in your possession was the weapon used in the assault on Doctor Fraser. How long had you owned the gun?"

"It wasn't mine!" The denial was over-emphatic. Maitland looked up, and the frown was back between his eyes.

"It was found in your suitcase. How do you explain that?"

"I can't explain it."

"I suppose, like the cigarette case, it was 'planted?'" Garfield's tone was properly scornful of the suggestion.

"I suppose so."

"You think it likely?"

"I didn't say that. Just that it happened."

"Someone who bore a grudge against you, no doubt?"

Harland took time to consider that. "I shouldn't think so," he said at last. "I expect it was because I was Fraser's assistant, and living in the house. That would make me a likely suspect, wouldn't it?"

"You admit that?"

"It wasn't exactly an admission—"

"However, you were arrested?"

"Yes."

"And you have told us that, as soon as opportunity offered, you attacked the constable who had you in charge and made your escape." Harland did not reply, and he added, sharply: "You admit that?"

"Well, yes . . . it wasn't quite like that."

"You attacked him, did you not, with the intention of rendering him unconscious?"

"Yes, but—"

"We have heard your explanation, Mr. Harland, The jury, I am sure, are bearing it in mind. This story of how you were kidnapped and taken to Germany . . . do you really expect us to believe that?"

"I don't know."

"The fact was, of course, that you went willingly—"

"No."

"—that the journey was already carefully arranged—"

"No . . . no . . . no!"

Again Garfield paused. "You are vehement, Mr. Harland. But you haven't explained, you know, why your enemies should go to so much trouble."

"If I wasn't there . . . at Burnham Green . . . I couldn't deny I was responsible—"

"They could have killed you—surely?—more easily than carry you out of the country."

"Yes, but there were the experiments . . . the work not quite completed."

"Again, far simpler to have waited until the work was done."

"No, it was because . . . I heard them say their plans had changed. The theft had been carried out earlier than was intended. I don't know why."

"You heard—? This was during the time you were working for the Nazis in Germany, was it not?"

"I never did that."

"You *seemed* to be working for the Nazis?"

"That was my intention."

"And, as you have explained to us—from the very best of motives." Garfield was heavily sarcastic; the witness flushed, and his answer came haltingly.

"I was trying."

"We are interested only in facts, Mr. Harland. The facts are that you were seven months in Germany, from October 1942 to the spring of the following year; that during that time you were continuing Doctor Fraser's research; and that ten months after you left England the so-called Dubenocz experiment took place . . . quite obviously based on the work Doctor Fraser had done, which presumably you had by then completed."

"I didn't know about that until I heard Fraser's evidence."

"You were gratified, no doubt, at the excellent results—"

"It was none of my doing! I tell you—" He broke off, and made an obvious effort to calm himself; speaking after a moment on a lower key, and almost unemotionally. "You're going to ask me . . . how it came about? I don't know. I tell you, I don't know!"

"Then perhaps you will instead explain, if what you have told us is true, why you did not take the first opportunity of destroying the reports?"

Harland took this question quietly, with one of his abrupt changes of mood. "Have you ever thought about death?" he asked; and oddly, his tone was conversational. And in the pause which followed, unpremeditated for once on Garfield's part, he added: "That chap Claudio had the right of it . . . he wasn't keen on the idea either. '—to go one knows not where; to lie in cold obstruction, and to rot!'" His voice rose on the last words; in the sudden stillness of the courtroom the quotation sounded harsh, and vividly evocative. "That's my answer . . . I didn't want to die before I need."

"I . . . see." He added coldly: "We can dispense with the dramatics, I believe, Mr. Harland." (But again —though it might be briefly—the tide of sympathy in the room was running in the prisoner's favour.) "You say you did—at last—destroy the papers?"

"When I knew there was no more time . . . that the project would be taken away from me."

"But in all those months, when you were going about Litzen freely."

"I wasn't free."

"You have heard the evidence of a number of your compatriots."

"It may have seemed . . . I had the run of the grounds. But they were fenced and guarded. There wasn't a chance, there just wasn't any chance at all."

"You heard Squadron-Leader Myles's evidence. Do you deny that you had several conversations with him?"

"Three," said Harland, "to be exact."

"And in the course of these three conversations, you said nothing to disabuse his mind of the idea that you were collaborating?"

"I was concerned to keep up the pretence. Besides, for all I knew, it might have been a trick."

"You are telling us," said the Judge, leaning forward and peering at the witness in an interested way, "that you thought Squadron-Leader Myles might himself be assisting the Germans?" There was an incredulous note in his voice which Maitland felt was natural enough, considering Myles's apparent determination to conform exactly to type; as well, one felt, might the integrity of the Tower of London be called to question.

"Not exactly, my lord." Harland had his answer ready enough, but the Judge's interruption seemed to add to his uneasiness. "But I couldn't know, you see, so I had to be careful." Mr. Justice Conroy coughed, and sat back with an inviting wave of the hand in Garfield's direction. Counsel again took his time, eyeing the witness reflectively before he said:

"So, you escaped again? A lucky chance, was it not?"

"Very lucky." But as the pause lengthened he added, unhappily: "At least, that's what I thought."

"No previous opportunity had offered?"

"I told you . . . no."

"But now, in the nick of time—" Garfield's voice sharpened, he leaned forward a little, forcing the prisoner to meet his eyes. "You're lying about that, aren't you, Harland? You didn't want to get away before."

"Why should I ever have left . . . my friends?" His tone was bitter. Counsel for the Prosecution shrugged, and spread his hands—one of the unexpected gestures which from time to time gave emphasis to the point he wished to make.

"You had bungled your work, perhaps," he suggested, "and so grown afraid of them. But I think it more likely that the whole thing was concerted with your employers." From the corner of his eye he saw Maitland on his feet again, and forestalled his objection with an apologetic bow in the Judge's direction. "Precisely, my lord," he said, as though his opponent had, in fact, spoken. "This is not the time for these explanations." He turned again to the witness. "Tell me, why did you give a false name when you arrived in Switzerland in 1943?"

"It seemed the safest thing to do."

"It had been arranged, had it not, before you left Germany?"

"No. How could it have been? It was the merest chance that I fell in with Godson."

"So strange a chance that you will forgive me for suggesting the matter had been organised for you. No doubt Michael Godson had been in a concentration camp, as you say, and died there. Or was he murdered for your convenience?"

Harland did not attempt to reply to this. He was staring at Counsel with a look at once vague and worried, which seemed to bear no relation to the seriousness of the charge. Stringer thought, 'he's losing his grip again,' and was aware that the feeling of the court had once more changed; he could sense now no trace of sympathy among the spectators.

"Well, Mr. Harland?" said Garfield.

"Do I have to answer . . . when you suggest things that aren't true?" There was no conviction in his voice.

He sounded tired, and again there was the appealing look at his own Counsel, and the nervous cough before he spoke.

"If they are not true," said Garfield, "at least, you can say so."

"I told you the truth before . . . when I gave evidence."

"You ask the court to believe that?" His tone was incredulous. "When you admit you lied about your identity in Switzerland; that you lived under a false name for years; that you lied again to the police, and even— until a few days ago—to your own lawyers."

"I was afraid," said Harland. The words were gently spoken, but they were followed by a moment of silence; and once again to Maitland the stuffy court seemed chilly. Or was it merely the stir of his own memories, the recollection of fear?

"But now, of course, you have nothing to be afraid of?" Antony tightened his lips . . . even at second hand the mockery in Garfield's voice was almost intolerable. Whatever grip Harland might have had upon the situation was gone now. He was defending himself at random, and seemingly without hope.

"I thought . . . I tried to explain . . . I thought, if it wasn't cleared up now—"

"My lord, this has all been gone into at length—"

He knew as he spoke it was useless; the Judge rolled a sardonic eye, but the movement of his head was sharply negative. Stringer muttered, "Seconds out of the ring," as his leader sat down again; for himself, he doubted whether the witness was any longer collected enough to profit from the respite an objection gave him. Garfield was in the right of it here, with every justification for pressing his questions.

And press them he did; as the afternoon wore on, and Stringer eyed his watch furtively and wondered if the ordeal might be ended, for a time, by the court's adjourning. Maitland, as he listened, ("Why, Mr. Harland? ... why? ... why? ...") thought he knew now, only too well, his client's reason for that sudden, disastrous burst of candour. If the prisoner were to say, "I spoke because I saw my wife, because as Godson I could never go back to her," the way would be wide open for Garfield's counter-attack. He had advised silence, but now he wondered (with the indecision that seemed to be becoming his natural reaction to every aspect of this case) whether he had been right about that. Surely nothing could be worse than these unconvincing denials, and if Harland broke at this point, as he seemed in danger of breaking, the preliminary evasion would only tell against him.

But Harland was holding his ground. "I can't explain any better than I have done . . . I knew I was innocent, I thought there must be some way of proving it . . . I can't explain . . . I don't remember . . . I just don't know!" Maitland clenched his hands as he listened; like Stringer, he felt that an interruption at this stage might do more harm than good. But the witness's protests carried no conviction, he was over-emphatic and stood little chance, his Counsel reflected gloomily, of being believed.

And suddenly it was over, this demand that the inexplicable be explained. Garfield relaxed, his question came casually: "You belonged once, did you not, to the Peacehaven Hand-Gun Club?"

"Yes," said Harland. He paused, and his eyes were wary. "Yes, I did."

"It was connected with your place of business?"

"Yes."

"I should like you to give us some account of the club's membership, and its activities."

"I . . . don't understand."

"The question is—surely?—a sufficiently simple one—"

"And completely irrelevant," snapped Maitland suddenly. But again, as he had expected, the decision was against him. Garfield returned firmly to his point.

"Membership was confined, I believe, to employees of the firm?"

"Yes. There were about twenty of us."

"And the club's purpose?"

"Target shooting."

"Did you own your own weapon?"

"No."

"And your fellow-members?"

"Nobody did . . . not that I remember."

"They were provided by the firm?"

"Yes. I know it sounds unusual," he added, defensively, "but it was a hobby with the Managing Director. That's how we came to have the facilities."

"A pleasant diversion," said Garfield. "And you were, I believe, an expert at this . . . sport?"

"I was."

"But all good things come to an end, and the club was disbanded at the end of 1940."

"Yes; some of the chaps had already gone into the services, and others were expecting their call-up. And Compton got the idea we ought to hand the guns over." Maitland raised his head, and looked at the witness; a long, questioning look. Stringer, disturbed by this sudden rush of words, without understanding why, scribbled "What the hell?" on his pad, and pushed it along in front of his colleague. But Antony ignored the query, his attention still concentrated on the man who was giving evidence.

"It was a silly sort of idea, of course," Harland was saying; "but I expect it didn't look like that to him at the time."

"You are telling us, if I understand you rightly, that when the club closed the guns you had used were handed over to the authorities?"

"Yes, that's right."

"All of them, Mr. Harland?"

"Well, so far as I know. You could ask Mr. Compton." (But that, Maitland reflected, was just what they couldn't do. The former Managing Director had died some years ago; and he remembered quite well that he had himself informed the prisoner of this.)

Garfield gave no sign that he had noticed the advice. "Among the collection," he asked, "had you a favourite weapon?"

"Not that I remember."

"A revolver, perhaps, similar to the one which the Crown has put in evidence." The suggestion was offered casually.

"There probably was one like it . . . we had a pretty good selection."

"Do you remember the occasion when you shot in a competition, not long before the club was closed?"

"There were several such occasions."

"When you beat all previous records, your own included."

"I . . . yes, I remember vaguely."

"You shot that night with a revolver."

"I may have done."

"Come now, Mr. Harland, surely you remember that. You said it was a favourite of yours . . . that it always brought you luck!"

There was a silence. Harland was paler than ever now; he was looking straight ahead of him, and answering each question as it came with dogged precision. That couldn't last, the break was sure to come. Maitland was on his feet again, speaking quietly to conceal the sudden, bitter taste of failure. "My lord, I have already protested . . . the matter is irrelevant . . . my learned friend has entered no evidence—"

"Except the gun, Mr. Maitland," Conroy reminded him. But his expression was undecided, and he turned a questioning look on Counsel for the Prosecution. "Perhaps, Mr. Garfield."he began. Garfield turned to him, his calm not even ruffled by the query.

"A matter has come to my attention, my lord—"

"Of which the Defence has not been advised," the other man complained.

"My friend would have been told, of course, of our desire to call fresh evidence. It came to my notice as recently as lunchtime to-day. In the meantime, I naturally supposed—"

"I cannot agree," said Maitland; and saw that the Judge was still irresolute. But before he had a chance to press his argument Harland interrupted. He put his hands on the ledge in front of him and said calmly, almost conversationally:

"It is the same gun, of course . . . the one you've got down there. Compton gave it to me as a souvenir. I didn't think anyone else knew that."

Garfield allowed himself one triumphant glance in his opponent's direction, before he said ironically: "Thank you, Mr. Harland, that is all I wish to know," and sat down again.

In the silence that followed, Geoffrey Horton leaned forward.

"*Now* will you let me—?" He spoke softly, but with an urgency that was almost vicious.

Maitland turned, and the look on his face silenced the impulsive words, though he spoke as quietly as his friend had done.

"No," he said. "No!" And then, almost under his breath, "I don't think there's anything to be done in the face of that. But I can't stop now . . . I've got to know—" He looked up, and caught the Judge's eye, and came to his feet again with no sign of the weariness he felt.

"My learned friend," said he, "has succeeded very successfully in confusing the issue. So I must trespass on the court's time, my lord, to show that the ownership of the gun is not, in fact, relevant." He looked across at his client, but without really seeing him; his whole attention was focused on the form of words he must use, on the exact framing of his questions. "Tell me, Mr. Harland—"

*

The arguments raged long that evening, and it was turned eleven o'clock when Maitland, closing the door of the Kempenfeldt Square house behind Horton and Stringer, crossed the hall and tapped on the door of his uncle's study.

Sir Nicholas had been out, and the fire was not lighted, although the evening had turned chilly. He moved from the desk as the younger man went in, and crossed to the table where Gibbs had left a tray. "You look," he remarked, with his back to the room, "as though a drink would not come amiss."

Antony stood with his back to the empty grate. He said, wearily: "You have seen the papers . . . of course."

"Of course." Sir Nicholas crossed the room with a glass in each hand, placed one on the mantelshelf at his nephew's shoulder, and settled himself comfortably before he went on. "I was dining with Trent. Halloran and Bird were there. The matter was—er—touched upon in conversation."

"No doubt it was." The younger man sounded grim. "And you concluded, I imagine—as my instructing solicitor has concluded—that it's high time I threw in my hand."

"You'll not deny," said Sir Nicholas, "that Harland has lied to you, again and again."

"I know that. All the same—"

"You're very stubborn about this, Antony."

Maitland turned, and picked up his glass, and raised it as though he were giving a toast. "'What a fool honesty is'" he quoted, bitterly; "'and trust, his sworn brother, a very simple gentleman!'" He took a drink, and grimaced a little, as though he found the whisky stronger than he had expected. "I'm staking a lot on his innocence," he added, soberly. "And I don't even know —God help me!—whether I believe him about that."

"But in spite of these doubts, you feel you cannot at this stage abandon your position." The older man sounded reflective. "Well, that's quite reasonable."

"It's not quite as simple as that."

"Why not? You've lost cases before," said Sir Nicholas, flatly.

"Yes . . . of course. But this . . . it's a wretched business, Uncle Nick. When I'd finished with Gunther, I'd just about settled my own doubts. The chap was deadly afraid, which makes me think he really had a hand in the Dubenocz experiment. And if that part of Harland's story is true—"

"They might still both be lying. If they worked together, Gunther could not implicate Harland more positively than he did without incriminating himself."

"Do you think I don't know that? And if he really is guilty—"

"It is not," agreed his uncle, "a pleasant thought." He looked at Antony curiously. "What would you do," he asked, "if you defended him successfully, and then found proof of his guilt?"

"Shoot him myself, I should think," said Maitland. And Sir Nicholas, replying in kind, was aware of an uncomfortable doubt as to how much of the truth might lie behind those lightly spoken words.

CHAPTER 17

WEDNESDAY, the seventh day

There was a feeling of anticlimax about the proceedings next morning, when the Defence continued. Maitland, trying to think constructively while he listened to Derek Stringer's examination of the first witness, was conscious above everything else that for the majority of the people present the case was over already and the prisoner condemned. And immediately there came the now familiar uncertainty: should we have called Mary Harland after all? He knew that the decision had been reached logically, and was agreed by his colleagues, but in his present state of mind that counted for very little.

He turned his thoughts to Harland, as he had seen him the evening before, sitting in an attitude of dejection in the interview room below the court.

"That's it finished, isn't it?" he had said. His tone had been flat, unemotional. "I'm sorry about Mary . . . tell her that, will you?" But though shaken by what had happened, the prisoner—unpredictable fellow—had been quite unrepentant. "What I told you was true," he had insisted. "Everything that mattered. The gun was just a detail . . . I didn't want to make things any more difficult for you than they were already." Antony, stifling a bitter comment, had again been shaken by doubt. Was this a piece of calculated subtlety, or simplicity carried to the logical end . . . admittedly beyond the point to which his own mind could travel?

The Foreman of the Jury was disappointed, and a trifle resentful, that the case had turned out to be so simple, an open and shut affair with no scope for his talents in guiding his fellow-jurors. After what had happened yesterday, surely not even the least attentive of them could be in any doubt . . .

The youngest of the women jurors found the prisoner more interesting now his identity was established . . . and his villainy too, so far as she was concerned. She watched him covertly as the further evidence unfolded; he had a look of strain about him this morning, and that was no wonder. She felt a chill of distaste as she thought of the cross-examination, and turned her eyes towards the prosecuting Counsel. A hard man, she thought him, and cold . . . undoubtedly. But why deny, in the privacy of her own thoughts, that she was fascinated as well as repelled. She had sufficient detachment to find amusement in the thought; it's only because Denis is so dull, she told herself impatiently.

Maitland was leaning back with a fair assumption of ease to listen to his junior's handling of the witnesses. Harland's London landlady . . . two colleagues from the firm he had left to join Doctor Fraser: they could testify with sincerity to the accused man's state of mind when the position was offered to him . . . to his indecision . . . by inference, to his patriotism. Damned unconvincing, he thought, suddenly impatient, why the hell are we bothering to drag in all this? And there came into his mind Harland's appraising look, the evening he admitted his identity, his comment "you're a fighter;" and he thought bitterly, "he might more aptly have put it, you're a fool." Meanwhile, there was Derek's handling of unpromising material to admire . . . and Garfield's successful demolition, each time his turn came to cross-examine, of any expectation that the evidence might carry weight.

He had to make a deliberate effort to shake off his lethargy when Marjorie Thurlow was called. Stringer seated himself again, with a grimace at his colleague that was expressive of the frustration he felt. Maitland had no time to respond; as usual, as soon as he took over the witness he became absorbed in her. He took her quickly through the preliminary questions.

"—and so we come to the evening of the 16th October. You had been at Burnham Towers for four days, I understand?"

"Yes, since the Monday."

"And how long was your visit to last?"

"Until the following weekend. Until the 24th or 25th, I mean."

"You remember the events of that Friday evening?"

"Yes, very well. You see, we had to go over and over everything with the police, and after that you just couldn't forget what had happened."

"During the course of the evening you went for a walk, you and your husband?"

"Yes, we did."

"When you left the drawing-room, did you set out immediately?"

"Robin went upstairs to get my coat, and I waited for him."

"In the hall?"

"No, I went out of the front door, and stood on the terrace. It was a little chilly, but the room had got stuffy—you know what it was like in the blackout, one could never get enough air."

"How long were you on the terrace?"

"Perhaps . . . five minutes." She sounded doubtful. "It isn't easy to judge when you're waiting—"

"But you were standing there for at least five minutes?"

"Yes."

"Did you see anything while you were standing there . . . anything, or anyone?"

"It was quite dark, you know. No, I didn't notice anything."

"Did you hear anything, Mrs. Thurlow?" Insensibly, his tone had sharpened. Not that corroboration on this minute point would serve to make Guy Harland's story as a whole more credible, but for some reason it seemed important suddenly . . . terribly important.

Marjorie Thurlow was looking doubtful. "Nothing that could interest you," she said.

"Anything?" he repeated.

"Only the whistling." She looked at him enquiringly, and apparently found his expression encouraging. "It was just . . . someone walking in the shrubbery, I think. At the other side of the drive."

"Did you recognise the tune?"

"Oh, yes, it was Schubert's 'Serenade'." (In a happier mood, Antony might have been amused by this echo of Garfield's suggestion.)

"Do you know who it was, in the shrubbery?"

"No, I don't know that."

"But someone was walking there, and whistling as he went?"

"Yes."

"Your attention was occupied so that, perhaps, you would not have noticed a man leaving the house and walking down the drive?"

"Well, I didn't notice anybody. I think it's quite likely I wouldn't have."

The remainder of his questions elicited nothing further of interest. Such a small point, he thought, a little wearily, as he sat down again; and here was Garfield, all set to demolish its effect. The Judge looked withdrawn to-day, the jury bored and restless, Garfield so complacent that it was painful to watch him. Of his own team, Geoffrey was a little sulky still, and Derek, doing a good job of concealing his feelings, was strangely as nervous as a cat now he had nothing to do but take the notes.

Counsel for the Prosecution was wasting no time on anything but the one point which had caught his attention.

"This song you heard, Mrs. Thurlow . . . your memory is quite clear on this point, even after so long?"

"Oh, yes, I know it so well. Besides, I'd heard someone whistling it not long before, and I was trying to remember who it could have been."

"Not long before the evening of October 16th, 1942?"

"That's what I mean." Maitland, frowning, looked up at her; and as though in response to his unspoken urging she added: "While I was at Burnham Towers. So I was listening carefully, because I couldn't remember who it had been . . . and you know how a thing like that can annoy you sometimes."

Garfield was not to be drawn from his aloof air. "Did it not occur to you, Mrs. Thurlow, that the man who was whistling might well have been Guy Harland?"

"It didn't occur to me. I'm sure it wasn't."

"And you have never thought to mention this before, Mrs. Thurlow? You did not, I believe, speak of it to the police at the time of the original enquiry?"

"Nobody asked me. Besides . . . it didn't matter. How could it?"

"Exactly!" Garfield sat down again with a self-satisfied thump. "How could it matter?" Which was exactly what Maitland, scowling frantically and drawing an unlikely-looking troubadour on the back of his brief, was asking himself.

*

Mr. Justice Conroy, looking round the court as he rose to leave for the luncheon recess, saw near the doorway his old friend Sir Nicholas Harding and hoped, a little pettishly, that he was finding his nephew's performance edifying. The protraction of the case for the Defence beyond what he felt was reasonable was undoubtedly trying his lordship's temper.

Maitland, crossing the court at leisure, caught sight of his uncle and deduced from his rather grim expression that he had been listening for some time, and without much liking for what he heard. But a moment later, as Garfield paused to greet him, Sir Nicholas's manner was bland and affable. Antony was smiling as he came up to the pair, and was greeted with the same suspicious amiability.

"I'm trying to persuade our friend, here . . . you're sure you won't join us, my dear fellow?"

Garfield's manner, as he repeated his excuses, had all the politeness due to a senior member of his own Inn. Antony, falling into step beside his uncle and watching his opponent retreating at a good pace, was moved to protest.

"What the devil are you up to, Uncle Nick? He might have said yes."

"In the circumstances, it didn't seem very likely." The older man's blandness persisted. "Would you have minded greatly?"

"What do you think, sir? I want to talk to you . . . to ask you—"

But his uncle was not to be hurried. "Presently," he said; and turned away, leaving Antony fuming.

Geoffrey Horton had left some minutes before, to keep an appointment, but Stringer was willing enough to forget his own intention of lunching in the Bar Mess. Sir Nicholas led the way to his favourite restaurant, selected a table carefully, and called the head waiter into consultation. Antony, for once in his life in a mood where a sandwich would have contented him, displayed a lack of interest which further annoyed his uncle, and interrupted without ceremony as soon as they were alone.

"Had you been long in court this morning, sir?"

"Long enough." His tone was not encouraging. "It did not seem that your tactics were meeting with much success."

"Well . . . no. I'm sorry about that, Derek," he added. Stringer crumbled a roll, and said with a commendable attempt at amiability:

"There wasn't anything to be done about it, so long as we decided to call them. But Thurlow's a different matter. I can't agree we should ignore—"

Sir Nicholas looked again at his nephew, who was attacking his soup with an air of concentration. "What do you think, Antony?"

"We'll leave well alone." His tone was definite. "His previous association with Fraser wouldn't really convince anybody—"

"Do you think we convinced anybody of anything this morning?"

"Well, I'm sorry about that."

Derek gave an impatient exclamation, and sat back to watch the waiter change their plates. When they were alone again Antony went on as though there had been no interruption:

"I don't want to confuse matters. I mean, we can't attack everybody." He found his uncle's eyes fixed on him reflectively. "Don't you agree, sir?"

"As a proposition it sounds . . . reasonable," agreed Sir Nicholas.

"You didn't tell me, sir."—his tone was suddenly eager. "Did you phone Sykes, as I asked?"

Sir Nicholas had his own way of dealing with importunity. "I spoke to him soon after breakfast," he said.

"Did he tell you anything?"

"A little."

"Anything I can use?" asked Antony. "Anything at all, Uncle Nick?"

"Nothing you will like . . . nothing you can use, I'm afraid. Some background detail, not enough to suggest a motive."

"What is it, sir?"

"Garfield laid stress on Harland's German 'connections.' You could prove something on the same lines now, about the man you suspect. No relationship; his maternal grandmother was widowed at an early age, and remarried. Her second husband was a German, a General of Infantry in the *Reichswehr* in the First World War."

Antony considered, and then laughed with real amusement. "Can you see me using that? The answer is 'so what?' . . . which sums the whole thing up nicely."

"I cannot think," said Sir Nicholas, shuddering, "that our friend Garfield would be so lost to all sense of decency as to make use of a phrase like that."

"Probably not. He'd think of something much more devastating." He was frowning as he spoke, and his uncle relented suddenly.

"If you want my advice," he said, "I think your instinct is right, not to complicate matters. But if you think you should attack Conrad . . . attack him."

"Easier said than done," said Antony, "on direct examination." His uncle grinned at him.

"I spoke figuratively," he explained. "However . . . it can be done. Use your head, boy; use your head!"

"I mean to." He turned again to his colleague. "Did you notice, Derek . . . was Mrs. Conrad in court this morning?"

"She was there," said Stringer. "She hasn't missed once since she gave her evidence. But I still don't agree—"

"All right, then." Only too obviously, Antony was not listening. "I'll do what I can . . . I don't see any other way. But do you suppose that damned iceberg of a woman has any feelings?"

CHAPTER 18

WEDNESDAY, the seventh day (continued)

T he crowd in the courtroom that afternoon seemed in no way diminished; Antony, who had anticipated a general falling-off of interest, reflected a little grimly that the spectators, having sat through so much of the trial, were now waiting to be in at the death.

Mr. Justice Conroy, who had indulged a faint hope that Sir Nicholas would have talked some sense into his nephew during the recess, was a trifle cast down when yet another witness was called. Maitland was clutching at straws, and in his lordship's opinion doing neither his case nor his reputation any good in the process. There was small chance of helping the prisoner, after his disastrous admissions in cross-examination; but what hope there was must surely lie in endeavouring to expose the weaknesses of the Prosecution's case (which could only be done now in the closing speech), rather than in attacking its strength.

Stringer slipped into his place while the witness was being sworn. He looked enquiringly at his leader.

"Shall I take it?"

"If I can trust you," said Antony, "to keep to our line." Derek gave him an injured look, but relaxed when he saw again the faint amusement in the other man's expression.

"I'll do it your way," he said, in a resigned tone. "But don't blame me—"

"I won't." Maitland made the promise lightly. But as he listened the feeling of uncertainty returned. Here they were, on the same old treadmill; do you remember the evening of the 16th October? . . . and what you were doing, and why? Was his decision the right one, after all? Derek was acute enough, and more detached than he could pretend to be.

"I don't remember anything particular about the early part of the evening," Thurlow was saying. "There was a sort of routine established, Sir Gervase was out most nights with the Home Guard—" He broke off, and the look he gave Stringer was almost comically helpless.

"How long had you been at Burnham Towers, Mr. Thurlow?"

"Since the previous Monday." That, at least, he remembered, and his relief was apparent.

"You were spending your leave there. How did that come about?"

"Because of Charlie Conrad. We'd taken rooms in Shipford, about twenty miles away . . . and very uncomfortable they were. But on the Sunday afternoon we happened to meet Charlie."

"Yes, I see. And Mr. Conrad, I take it, was your only acquaintance at the Towers?"

"Well, not exactly."

Stringer, intent only on setting the witness at ease, was caught by the change of tone. He resisted the impulse to exchange glances with his leader, and his voice remained bland and friendly.

"No, Mr. Thurlow?"

"I knew Mrs. Conrad slightly . . . Miss Esther Marne, she was then. And I knew Doctor Fraser."

"And on the Friday evening you all dined together, and then Sir Gervase went out?"

"Yes. That's how it was each evening we were there."

"And after that—?"

"We went for a walk, my wife and I. Afterwards, I was in the billiard-room with Hugh Torrington and Harry Wilmot."

"You knew, of course, that Doctor Fraser was in the study that evening."

"I knew that . . . of course." His tone was reserved. But before Stringer could move to his next point, the witness was inspired to add: "I doubt if I'd have gone to the Towers if I'd realised he was there; we did our best to keep out of each other's way." He paused again, and seemed to be regarding with rueful amusement the confusion into which his unwary words had led him. "I was his secretary once, but I'd left him two years before. So we'd nothing to talk about, really. Nothing at all."

"I see," said Stringer again.

"Besides," added Thurlow, surprisingly, "he went there to work, at least that's what he said. I know it was only letters—"

"How did you know that, Mr. Thurlow?"

"How . . . how?" He broke off, and looked straight at Stringer, but not as if he saw him. "Someone said something . . . we were joking about secret weapons . . . I don't really remember."

"Please try to be a little more precise, Mr. Thurlow. Why did you think Doctor Fraser was not working that evening?"

"I don't know. It was just that there came into my mind . . . something about a love letter. I've never thought about it from that day to this. It was only a joke."

"Thank you." He hesitated a moment, and then made up his mind. Better get away from the subject, if he didn't want Antony to think . . . but Antony, contemplating ruefully the unexpected frankness of the witness, was angry only with himself.

They went back to the events of the evening, but Thurlow's memory remained as unreliable as ever. He remembered that he had found Marjorie on the terrace, when he came downstairs with her coat; but he didn't remember anybody whistling, it wasn't the sort of thing he would remember; and certainly he hadn't seen Harland going down the drive. Later, when he went into the billiard-room . . .

". . . they were in the middle of a game. Hugh said, 'we'll just finish this, and then we'll have a drink,' and I sat down by the fire."

"Do you remember what time that was, Mr. Thurlow?"

"No, I don't."

"How long, for instance, before the commotion when Doctor Fraser was found?"

"Twenty minutes . . . half an hour? I really don't know." He added, irritably: "Good heavens, it's twenty years ago."

"Was the window open when you went into the billiard-room?"

"I don't . . . no, just a moment. It must have been closed, because soon after I sat down Hugh said it was stuffy, and he pulled back the curtain and opened the window, and went out on to the path."

"If I suggested it was a few minutes before ten o'clock when Colonel Torrington pulled back the curtain, would that agree with your recollection?"

"I just don't know. It seems quite likely. Anyway, Harry protested a bit, but Hugh wasn't taking any notice; he said he wanted a breather, so Harry came over to the fire and we talked until he came back."

"How long was that, Mr. Thurlow?" He became aware that Maitland had pushed a note along the table to him, and glanced down as the witness replied.

"No more than a few minutes. I didn't notice particularly, because we were talking."

"You and Mr. Wilmot?"

"Yes."

"Was that the only time the game was interrupted?"

"So far as I remember . . . yes, I'm pretty sure of that."

"And when Colonel Torrington returned—?" (He was aware that Maitland, beside him, relaxed; so the point—whatever it was—had been made to his satisfaction.)

"They started another game."

"Did you see Guy Harland pass the window?"

"No, I didn't. I had my back to it. After a while Wilmot got fidgety, so Hugh drew the curtains again, and it was soon after that—"

But the rest of his recollections, and the repetition of what he had already told, could not be said to be of any great interest. Garfield left the cross-examination to his junior, who asked a few desultory questions and let the witness go.

When Maitland got up, a few moments later, to begin his examination of Charles Conrad, he thought he had never seen a more unpromising subject. Conrad's manner was confident . . . a successful man, with every right to self-assurance. There was also, underlying his answers to the preliminary questions, a note of hostility which was perhaps only to have been expected.

"And in October, 1942, you were living, I believe, at Burnham Towers, and were employed as Production Engineer by Fairfield Chemicals Limited?"

"That's right."

"How long had you been resident there?"

"Two years, just about."

"And Guy Harland was also living at the Towers?"

"Yes."

"By your arrangement, I believe, Mr. Conrad."

"Yes . . . in a way."

"Will you tell us, please, how that came about?"

"It was when he was getting married. There weren't many places around where you could get accommodation."

"So you made the suggestion."

"I spoke to Lady Torrington first, and then I asked Guy—"

"What prompted you to do that, Mr. Conrad?" He was taking a chance here, he knew, and his air was studiously casual; but Garfield, for the moment, showed no desire to intervene.

"He was a friend of mine. I wanted to help him."

"But the suggestion did not come from Guy Harland? It was your own idea?"

"Oh, yes, quite my own idea."

"Nobody else suggested to you that it might be a suitable arrangement?"

"No, of course not."

"Guy Harland had nothing to do with the first approach to Lady Torrington?"

"Why, no, he hadn't." Conrad looked suddenly more at ease, less aggressive than he had been a moment ago. Perhaps, after all, there was some sense in the questions . . . something that wasn't connected with him, or with Esther.

"The matter might have been brought forward by Doctor Fraser," said Maitland, labouring the point.

"Oh, no. I don't think he cared for the idea much, as a matter of fact."

"And—still speaking of October, 1942, Mr. Conrad—you were at that time a colleague of Harland's, as well as his friend."

"That's right."

"What impression had you of the nature of his work?"

Conrad frowned.

"Later I knew very well that it was a project concerned with biological warfare," he said. "I can't remember now, I don't think I knew that at the time."

"Only that it was important?"

"We all knew that."

"The security precautions alone were informative, no doubt."

"Well . . . yes."

"So that other people might well have been interested in the project, besides the members of Doctor Fraser's group in the laboratory?"

"I suppose so. But that isn't to say—"

"And, of course, the other members of the group would have an equal knowledge with Guy Harland of the value of what they were doing?"

The witness's reply was lost in the vehemence of Garfield's protest. Maitland, waiting without much interest for the expected storm to subside, was telling over in his mind the points he still must make.

Conrad would be angry now . . . the point of his questions, though made by inference only, must surely be obvious enough. Without turning his head, Antony could get no glimpse of Esther Conrad; was she even in the court? But Derek would have told him—surely—if she wasn't there. He bowed to the Judge, who seemed to have finished whatever remarks he had been making, and turned back to the witness.

"We will pass, then, to the events of the evening of October 16th. Will you tell the court what you remember?"

"It was a bit confusing," said Conrad, shortly. "Even at the time, when we were all arguing about what we had been doing, I couldn't fix other people's movements in my mind . . . only as they related to my own."

"Your own movements, then."

"Well, after we'd had our coffee I went into the billiard-room with Hugh."

"At what time was that?"

"I don't remember. About ten to nine, I should think, because it wasn't long before I noticed it was nearly time for the news."

"What did you do then?"

"I went into the morning-room, because the wireless was in there. It was a thing Sir Gervase and Lady Torrington didn't seem keen about."

"And your wife was there. Did you expect to find her?" The question came casually, but the witness seemed genuinely aggrieved by it.

"How on earth do you expect me to remember a thing like that?" he demanded. "I expect I thought she might be there."

"I see. Well now, Mr. Conrad, you say you observed other people's movements 'in relation to your own.' Can you tell us anything of what Guy Harland was doing that evening?"

"I saw him when he came back to the drawing-room, after his talk with Doctor Fraser—"

"One moment, Mr. Conrad. Did you at that time see his silver cigarette case in his possession?"

The witness paused.

"I didn't see it," he said at last, grudgingly. "But he must have had it on him, because Esther said—"

"Thank you. You were telling us—"

"Oh, about that evening. Well, I didn't see Guy again until after Doctor Fraser was found. I was with Esther until ten-fifteen, and then we went out into the hall together, and she went to the study. And after that Guy came downstairs."

"Did any other member of the party come to the morning-room during the evening? To listen to the news, perhaps?"

"No." He paused there, and added with a return of belligerence, "If you're still thinking of that cigarette case—"

Garfield intervened at this point, and Maitland—turning back the clock again to the dinner hour—began patiently to encourage the witness to recapitulate the events of the evening. There is, very properly, a clear limit to what Counsel may do in direct examination; and perhaps it was something of a triumph to have achieved so quickly the witness's annoyance. Antony, twisting and re-wording the same series of questions, was conscious only of the man giving evidence. Derek Stringer, more acutely aware of the feelings of the court, could have told without looking up the precise moment when annoyance succeeded apathy among the majority of those present. Once, during a brief period of silence, he twisted round to get a glimpse of Esther Conrad; her face told him nothing. She was frowning a little as she listened, but her calm was unbroken. Startlingly good-looking, he thought her, not sharing his leader's antipathy for the lady. He thought Maitland's present line a foolish one, if only because it was foredoomed to failure. Neither of the Conrads was likely to take fright at this stage, even if they were responsible for what happened twenty years ago. And that in itself was unlikely, an argument based on an unproved—and probably unprovable—premise.

Guy Harland had by now accustomed himself to the changes in his old friend, but Charlie Conrad was still occupying his mind. A chap as full of contradictions as the next man, cheerful and casual on the surface . . . but he'd never doubted, in the old days, that he'd make his mark in some way. There was Esther too; funny he'd never realised it, but Charlie was the right man from her point of view. He wished vaguely that he knew what Maitland was after; considering what had happened yesterday it hardly seemed worth the bother . . .

Mr. Justice Conroy, for all his air of immobility, was seething with impatience. He was not without sympathy for Maitland; if you were to presume Harland's innocence, Conrad seemed the only possible alternative. Garfield, of course, was in one of his righteous moods—the Judge could recognise it in every word he spoke, in the set of his lips, the very way he moved; but whatever the Crown Counsel might think, Conroy himself was in no doubt of Maitland's sincerity, though he was equally convinced that his belief in his client was misplaced. He began mentally to rehearse the speech for the Defence . . . "it is very doubtful," Maitland would say, "on the evidence of the butler—who is surely, members of the jury, a disinterested witness—it is very doubtful whether Guy Harland was in possession of his cigarette case after he talked to Mrs. Conrad in the hall. And to whom could this lady most easily have handed it? To Charles Conrad, the man she later married. They spent the evening together, without interruption, in the morning-room at Burnham Towers. And I am sure I may remind you, without impropriety, that this same man, Charles Conrad, was instrumental in introducing Guy Harland to the household at the Towers. As my client has himself pointed out, if a scapegoat were needed, what more appropriate one could have been found? And there is the further point, admittedly a small one, that as an employee of Fairfield Chemicals Conrad was in a position to know a good deal about the work that was being done in the laboratory; though you may think that the intimate position in which he stood with Doctor Fraser's secretary was an even more hopeful source of information." That's what he'd say, the Judge thought, coming back and directing a sour look round the court; and the jury won't believe him, he added to himself, any more than I do.

But Maitland wasn't concerning himself with the possibility of being believed. He knew it was unlikely that he could achieve the result he wanted, but if this didn't work there was nothing else . . . certain defeat, which didn't matter in itself, but there was Harland to think of . . . Harland and the wife he hadn't seen for twenty years. And at that moment Antony was aware, with sudden clarity, that for all the doubts he had expressed he was no longer in any doubt about the basic truth of the accused man's story. If he had had more time to think about it, he might have found a certain wry amusement in the knowledge; the chap didn't really deserve to be believed, and certainly had made no push to help himself. But he had no time to formulate the thought; he was only aware, paradoxically, of an increased anxiety and at the same time a slackening of the tension he had been under for the last few days.

However, anxious or not, he had now done all he could. "To go over this for the last time—and I am sorry to have wearied you, Mr. Conrad—it seems we have established certain points. For instance, that Harland did not deliberately plan to insinuate himself into the household of Burnham Towers."

"I've explained several times what happened." That he was irritable was natural; if he felt any uneasiness at this prolonged questioning, the fact was admirably concealed.

"Yes, I am grateful for your patience. And it seems that knowledge of the secret nature of Doctor Fraser's project was not confined to his own group . . . was probably not confined even to members of the firm?"

"A thief would hardly have moved without some more precise knowledge—"

"I am glad you agree with me, Mr. Conrad." The witness eyed him blankly. "You have also told us that your acquaintance with the lady who is now your wife, and who at that time was Doctor Fraser's secretary, was an intimate one?"

"I . . . wonder." Conrad seemed to be considering the question, and for the first time Maitland felt he could discern some emotion beyond the anger he had from time to time allowed to appear.

"Would you agree with me that Guy Harland was the most obvious suspect when these crimes were discovered? Because he lived at Burnham Towers, and because of his close association with Doctor Fraser."

"It seems a fair statement."

"Then you will also agree, Mr. Conrad, that if someone wished to provide a solution to satisfy the authorities, he might well have elected to implicate Guy Harland?" He paused, but not long enough to invite a reply. "And to that we may add, may we not, that the person who arranged for my client to join the household at the Towers was—as you have admitted—yourself?" He made the suggestion deliberately and sat down again before Garfield, coming to his feet with an outraged swirl of his gown, could begin to express his displeasure at the impropriety.

*

The Judge's patience was not much further tried that evening; Paul Garfield detained the witness for a few minutes only, and his preliminary remarks were sufficiently scathing to keep an even more mischievous nature than his lordship's amused for that length of time. Conroy cocked a hopeful eye at the Defence Counsel, and was sorry to see that he did not appear to be attending. No fireworks, then; which seemed a pity.

But Garfield's remarks went unheeded by the person most nearly concerned. Maitland, relaxing after the sustained effort of his examination of Charlie Conrad, and aware—as Stringer had been earlier in the day— of the sheer futility of his efforts, knew only that he was utterly weary, and sick with the consciousness of failure. He had thought there was a chance, but he knew now the hope had been a foolish one. He scrambled to his feet when the Judge left the court, but the action was purely mechanical, and he sat down again and began to pile together his papers, still without much awareness of what he was doing. Beside him, Derek got up, and he heard him speaking to Geoffrey Horton in a low voice. But the words didn't register, and presently the two men moved away. The room was clearing now; he tried to fix his mind on the next move, and was again in a state of indecision. Should he go home to work on his speech for to-morrow, or would it be better to go back to chambers? He became aware that his clerk was standing in front of him, and saying something in an urgent tone. He pushed the untidy heap of papers across the table towards him, and felt as though, with the gesture, he was giving up whatever grasp he had on the conduct of the case.

"I'm sorry, Willett. Were you waiting for these? I'll go straight home, I think."

But Willett wasn't listening, he was concerned only to get his message through to his principal—who seemed, that evening, to be unaccountably stupid.

"Mr. Maitland," he said, leaning towards him with his hands on the table, and speaking as impressively as he could. "That Mrs. Conrad, sir; she's waiting to speak to you."

Antony looked up then, past the clerk's shoulder to where— incredibly—Esther Conrad stood. Willett saw, without understanding, the sudden blaze of excitement that was schooled to impassivity as Maitland got to his feet. He said, over his shoulder:

"Find Garfield, do you mind? Ask him to join me." But before he had finished speaking he was moving across the room.

She turned as he came up to her, to face him more squarely. He was smiling a little, and she thought with inconsequent surprise that she had never hated anybody before . . . not really hated them. But Antony, had he been aware of her thoughts, would have cared nothing for them. A gamble had come off . . . the fish had taken the bait; his surface thoughts might be incoherent, but underneath the tangle his mind was concentrated, to the exclusion of everything else, on the problem of making the most of this unexpected opportunity.

CHAPTER 19

THURSDAY, the eighth day

T he Judge, an old campaigner, was immediately aware next morning of a change of atmosphere in the court; there was a sort of simmering excitement among the Defence lawyers, and Garfield—though he would have sworn yesterday that this was impossible—was looking even more austere and disapproving than usual. He eyed Counsel for the Defence suspiciously when he saw him on his feet, and asked in a tone that was not far removed from the querulous: "*More* witnesses, Mr. Maitland?"

"If your lordship pleases . . . I should like permission to recall one of the Crown's witnesses, Mrs. Esther Conrad." Mr. Justice Conroy looked at him in silence, and he added persuasively: "My learned friend agrees—"

The look the Judge bent on Paul Garfield could hardly have been more reproachful. Harland (who had seen with bewilderment his Counsel sweep into court rather late, with an armful of books and an air of suppressed excitement) muttered to himself by way of comment: "*Et tu, Brute*." But added, a moment later, with an echo of the Judge's querulousness, "Nobody ever tells me anything."

Garfield, meanwhile, had risen to his feet, and favoured his learned friend for the Defence with a look that was anything but cordial.

"I do not agree with my friend's conclusions, my lord. But in the interests of justice—"

"A matter has come to our attention," said Maitland, helpfully. Conroy looked from him to his opponent in a doubtful way.

"Very well," he said at length. "In the circumstances I can have no objection. No doubt you will make the reasons for this request apparent to us, Mr. Maitland."

"I shall endeavour to do so, my lord." But as he waited, the doubts were there again to trouble him. Even in the face of Esther Conrad's statement, Garfield's attitude had remained disbelieving. "All this may be true," he had said, "and Harland still be guilty." And finally, explosively: "No reasonable person could doubt his guilt." But he had not been proof against the appeal for justice; the jury must have the facts, however incapable he felt them of interpreting the case correctly.

He came out of his reverie to find Derek tugging at the sleeve of his gown. Derek's eyes were red-rimmed with lack of sleep, but—like his leader—he was obviously too worked up to be conscious that he was tired.

"She isn't here," he said. "Do you suppose—?" Antony looked down at him a little blankly, and after a moment he got up and went towards the door.

When it became at last apparent that Esther Conrad was nowhere in or about the court, Maitland, with the frown back between his eyes, asked the Judge's permission to re-examine his own witness of the previous day. Conroy agreed more readily than might have been expected, and had a question of his own for the witness as soon as he had taken the stand and had been reminded of the continuing efficacy of his oath.

"Was Mrs. Conrad aware that she would be recalled to give evidence this morning?"

"I . . . I'm afraid I don't know, my lord."

"You can tell us, at least, if she was preparing to come to court."

"I don't know that, either." There was little remaining to the witness of yesterday's calm, nor did he seem any longer to be angry. He looked around a little wildly, and said with a note of desperation in his voice: "She went out last night, and never came back to the flat."

Conroy glanced across at the Defence Counsel, and something in Maitland's expression sharpened his interest in a point he had been making almost idly.

"Did you expect her to return?" he asked.

"Yes . . . but then I thought . . . we had a disagreement, you see, so I thought perhaps she had gone to a hotel."

"Thank you, Mr. Conrad." The Judge sat back, but before Maitland could frame his first question Stringer slipped back into his place and pushed a note along the table in front of him. He picked up the slip of paper, and was scarcely aware that, mechanically, he was making the correct apologies.

"If I may have your leave, my lord—"

"Take your time. Take your time, Mr. Maitland." Conroy's voice was definitely testy now. Antony, staring down at the note, seemed to be availing himself only too readily of the permission; but then he looked up and said to the witness without preamble:

"Did you know why your wife has not come to court this morning? Did you know that she is dead?" Dimly he was aware of the rising murmur of voices that followed the announcement; of the Judge, immobile again, but alert . . . only too alert; of Garfield, coming to his feet in a hurry. But above all he was conscious of the stunned look on Charlie Conrad's face.

"I don't believe it," he was saying. "I just don't believe it."

"I am sorry, then, to break the matter to you so baldly." Maitland was completely unaware that he was himself showing the effects of shock. He was dealing with the news as instinct directed, and had no time for any feeling of compunction. "My information is that she was found dead in Hyde Park this morning, in the bushes near the Lancaster Gate."

"What had happened?" Conrad's voice was no more than a whisper. "How did she die?"

"She was strangled," said Maitland. And turned to meet his opponent's attack.

"My lord!" Garfield's protest was clear above the pandemonium. "This does not concern the court—"

He encountered an unprofessionally furious look from Maitland, and added a shade uncertainly:

"My learned friend will remember—"

"I remember," said Maitland, "the s-statement we both heard last night. The woman who made it has been murdered—"

"I should like to know, Mr. Maitland," interrupted the Judge, "the source of your information."

"I have it from the police officer in ch-charge of the case," said Maitland. "My learned friend, Mr. Stringer, was lucky enough to encounter him when he left the court. The officer had felt, very p-properly, that the Defence, at least, would have some interest in knowing what had happened."

"Yes, I see," said the Judge, mystified. He glared at Maitland, as a matter of principle, as though daring him to give any more overt sign of the fact that he had lost his temper.

"I am t-trying very hard not to be c-controversial," said Antony, "but in the circumstances, the murder of a witness—" He turned back to Garfield, and added defiantly: "Can you blame *that* on Guy Harland?"

"I think," said Garfield, at his smoothest, "that we have enough to do in considering the indictment as it stands. This attempt to introduce extraneous matter—"

"Extraneous!" The word came with the effect of an explosion. But it had the result, fortunate for the Defence Counsel, of carrying him beyond mere loss of temper into a state of anger in which he was as cool and deadly as ever his uncle had been. "I am quite willing to continue my re-examination of the witness, my lord," he said, and looked enquiringly at the Judge.

"In the circumstances, Mr. Maitland," said Conroy, in a tone of mild remonstrance, "I do not feel—"

"It must be as your lordship pleases." The formal acquiescence did not deceive the Judge for an instant. "If you wish to dismiss the witness I must ask for an immediate ruling on a rather difficult matter. Last night Mrs. Conrad came to me with a statement; and, as I felt was proper, I asked my friend to hear what she had to say. In view of what has happened, what is to be done? May I introduce the statement into evidence, and call upon my friend for corroboration?"

Mr. Justice Conroy gave him a look of angry dislike, and glanced rather helplessly at Garfield, whose lips were clamped together in a thin line, and whose expression in general was far from encouraging. Before anything further could be said, however, the witness—whom they had all been inclined to disregard—said clearly, and almost calmly:

"I . . . am willing to continue, my lord." Maitland pounced on the concession without waiting for further permission.

"I shall not detain you long, Mr. Conrad. Did you know that Mrs. Conrad had spoken to me yesterday?"

"She told me—"

"Did she tell you the substance of her statement?"

Conrad shook his head. "Unless . . . was it about her evidence?"

"It was." He paused for a moment, eyeing the witness, and then said deliberately: "Twenty years ago, were you in love with the lady who later became your wife?"

"Yes, I . . . from the first time I met her."

"But it was four years later, in 1946, when you were married. It wasn't because you were away in the Services . . . you continued to work for Fairfield Chemicals throughout the war, did you not?"

"Yes . . . we both did."

"Then, what delayed your marriage?"

"She didn't share my feelings." After a moment he added: "Not then," but doubtfully, so that Maitland thought the question had been in his mind before.

"In 1942," he said, "you were in love with Miss Esther Marne, but she did not return your affections?"

"That's how it was."

"So if you had asked her at that time to—let us say— to help you frame Guy Harland, do you think she would have agreed?"

"I . . . didn't—"

"No, Mr. Conrad. She wasn't in love with you. Who did she care for in 1942. . . blindly, desperately, so that she would have been willing to help him, even in an act of treason?"

"She was in love with Harry Wilmot . . . damn him!" said Conrad. "I never thought he really cared much for her, and then he went abroad—" He broke off, and stood looking at Counsel, his mouth hanging open a little in an expression of surprise that might have been ludicrous had it not been for his obviously genuine grief. He added, quietly: "Lately, I've wondered . . . how far I could trust her." He leaned forward suddenly, speaking to Maitland as though they were alone together.

"You say she came to you yesterday about her evidence. You've got to tell me . . . was it because she loved me, or because she hated him?" For a moment the two men confronted each other, and then Conrad, as though despairing of an answer, turned towards the Judge with a blind gesture of appeal. "My lord, I can't—"

And Mr. Justice Conroy took hold of the situation, as smoothly as though every word and action had been rehearsed.

"You may stand down, Mr. Conrad," he said, and turned to catch the usher's eye. "For the present, nobody must be allowed to leave the court," he went on. His gaze swept round the crowded room, as though daring anyone to defy his expressed wishes, and came to rest finally on the Defence Counsel. "Now, Mr. Maitland," he said, grimly.

"I must request permission to put Mrs. Esther Conrad's statement in evidence, my lord. My clerk took a note of what she said, and my learned friend, Mr. Garfield, can confirm its accuracy."

"Well, first, Mr. Maitland, I think we must hear proof of the witness's death. Did you say the police officer was present?"

"Detective-Inspector Sykes is in the building, my lord. Perhaps he may be called?"

Sykes was fortunately not far to seek, and what he had to say did not delay the proceedings for long. The Judge ruthlessly excluded anything beyond the bare fact of death, and the cause of death; accepted as the minimum he had the right to expect the doctor's note which the detective had had the presence of mind to bring with him; announced firmly that he would expect a death certificate in the proper form to be produced at the earliest possible moment; and finally relented sufficiently to dismiss Sykes with a word of thanks for his cooperation. Antony, who should have been making the most of the breathing-space, was momentarily distracted by a mental picture of the Inspector, stumping down the long flight of stairs and shaking his head over the unpredictability and general oddness of the legal profession.

The Judge was speaking again.

"With regard to the Defence's application, Mr. Garfield, I should like your view on the admissibility of the statement in evidence."

Paul Garfield stood up, and still he seemed undecided. "My lord," he began; and then turned, and looked full at Counsel for the Defence. Maitland met his look squarely, and realised that—for the moment at least—all the hostility he had felt towards his opponent had vanished. The man was sincere; and perhaps, at last, recognised his own sincerity. Counsel for the Prosecution turned back to the Judge, and said abruptly: "I feel it should be admitted, my lord."

"Very well." It was impossible to tell from Conroy's tone or countenance what he was thinking of the developments. "I presume you have the statement, Mr. Maitland."

"Yes, my lord. I . . . I am sorry there is only one copy."

"That will suffice. You produce the statement of Mrs. Esther Conrad, made to you yesterday in the presence of Mr. Paul Garfield? Thank you. Now, perhaps you will tell the jury briefly the substance of this new evidence . . . you will, of course," he added, looking at the Foreman, "receive full copies as soon as they have been prepared."

"Mrs. Conrad told us that her evidence concerning my client's cigarette case had not been accurate. Guy Harland handed her the case, which she retained. Later she passed the case to Mr. Harry Wilmot, by arrangement . . . when she heard him whistling she opened the morning-room window, and he came up to speak to her."

He paused, and looked down at the table as though he had a note there of what he was saying. "The reason adduced for this . . . the reason Mrs. Conrad said Mr. Wilmot gave her . . . was that he wished to play a practical joke of some kind on Mr. Harland."

"I . . . see. And now, Mr. Maitland, in view of the very extraordinary circumstances—"

"If your lordship pleases, I should like to recall Mr. Harry Wilmot. I do not think the Crown will object—"

"You realise, of course, that though Mrs. Conrad's statement contains a serious accusation, it is hardly conclusive."

"The evidence must create a strong presumption that Guy Harland was deliberately implicated, my lord. If I may have your permission, I will endeavour to clarify the matter a little."

"Very well," said Conroy. And smiled, surprisingly, with an air of benignity which quite unnerved Counsel.

Afterwards, Antony realised that the short interval while Wilmot was recalled and admonished concerning his oath should have given him an opportunity to think out the best course to follow. The news of Esther Conrad's death had shocked him more than he realised. He was doing his best with each point as it came, and still with the same deadly calm, but so far had no plan of action.

When he got up to face Harry Wilmot he realised that there was to be no capitulation. The witness was pale, as seemed to be habitual with him, but quite collected. Too calm, as a matter of fact; there should have been some evidence of hostility, but none was apparent.

"Why did you ask Mrs. Conrad to get you something of Guy Harland's, Mr. Wilmot?"

"You're mistaken. I made no such request."

"You are telling me her statement was incorrect. I should like you to think carefully before you answer. The court will remember, as I do, that the statement was made voluntarily, and might have done her considerable harm."

"I have no means of knowing . . . if what she said was true. About getting possession of the case, I mean. If she did so, it wasn't for me."

"When did you first go to Germany, Mr. Wilmot?"

For the first time, the witness seemed taken aback; perhaps the change of subject bewildered him. "In 1931," he said at length. "I made a short visit during the summer."

"You had relations there?"

"My grandmother." He stopped, but—encountering a somewhat stony stare from Counsel, who looked as though he was prepared to wait all day—went on finally: "Her second husband was German."

"A General of Infantry, I understand, in the *Reichswehr*."

"He was retired, of course. He was an old man."

"How old were you in 1931?"

"I was fifteen."

"An impressionable age, Mr. Wilmot."

"Do you think so?" (No one could have said, thought Maitland, that he was getting any help from the witness.)

"And you returned to—Kurischeburg, was it not?— every year from 1931 to 1937?"

"I . . . believe I did. My grandmother's husband died that year, and she returned to England. Which ended my connection—"

"You are telling us you made no friends?"

"Of course I did—" His tone was faintly contemptuous. "Where was the harm in that?"

"A very natural circumstance. You corresponded with these . . . friends, no doubt?"

"Until the war prevented any further exchange of news."

"Come now, Mr. Wilmot. If you have read anything at all of the evidence in this case you are no longer so ingenuous as to think the outbreak of hostilities necessarily terminated all contacts. I am not suggesting that you entrusted your communications to His Majesty's mail." He was taunting the witness deliberately, and had the satisfaction of seeing a faint flush on Wilmot's cheeks. And for the first time Maitland began to see his way, dimly; to formulate a plan.

"I do not know what *could* be done—"

"In the meantime you had left school, and been through university; and obtained your present teaching position, I believe?"

"If you are speaking of the time of the 'outbreak of hostilities,'" said Wilmot, gently sarcastic, "I had been there for a year."

"Had you missed your yearly visits to Germany?"

"Not really. I had other interests."

"Your career, no doubt? I suppose you regard teaching as a vocation?"

"I . . . no!"

"Would you have preferred some other profession?"

"If I could have afforded it."

"Yes, I see. However, you were in the army very soon after the war started?"

"I volunteered."

"And from the summer of 1940 on, you were a frequent visitor at Burnham Towers?"

"I don't see—"

"Answer the question, Mr. Wilmot."

"Well . . . yes, I was." He added, sulkily: "I told you all this before."

"If I am boring you, I am sorry for it." Wilmot did not reply, but his look was expressive. "No . . . exactly! And we are all extremely interested in what you have to tell us. You were a friend of Colonel Torrington, and you knew Doctor Fraser well, and his assistant, Guy Harland?"

"Quite well."

"And the late Mrs. Conrad, who was then Miss Esther Marne?"

"I knew her, yes."

"Intimately, Mr. Wilmot?"

"No, not intimately. We were friends. I should say she spent more time with Conrad."

"But when you asked her to help in this . . . trick you were going to play—"

"I've told you. That wasn't true!"

"I think it was not the first favour you had asked of her. She had kept you informed, had she not, of the progress of Doctor Fraser's work?"

"No . . . no."

"Was it true that you were in love with her?"

"It was not."

"That is hardly relevant, perhaps. Her affection for you was all that was necessary—"

"But, I didn't—" He broke off, and Maitland said swiftly:

"What didn't you do, Mr. Wilmot?"

"Ask her for something of Guy's. Ask her to meet me."

"You had used that signal before, no doubt. Schubert's 'Serenade'?"

"If somebody whistled it that night, it was not I."

"Do you know the tune?"

"No . . . At least, well, I'm not sure." He was showing signs of agitation now, and Maitland wasn't surprised when he added, after a pause: "It must have been Conrad."

"Somebody was whistling," said Maitland, "at the time Mr. Conrad was with Colonel Torrington in the billiard-room."

"But the rest of it . . . he was with her all the evening—" He leaned forward eagerly, and struck his fist on the ledge in front of him. "Perhaps not the whistling, but he could have done the rest."

"What could he have done?"

"Gone to the study. Struck Fraser and taken the papers. And left the gun on the floor."

"But he couldn't have fetched the gun, Mr. Wilmot. You won't suggest he was carrying it on his person. And after dinner he had no opportunity—"

"He had all the evening . . . all the time he was with Esther. It was so easy, it wouldn't have taken him a minute. The drawer wasn't even locked—"

"How did you know that, Mr. Wilmot?"

"I—" He looked around him, and for the first time with something approaching desperation. "I suppose Guy must have said, afterwards—"

"Shall I tell you what happened? It's really very simple. You were on leave, were you not, and so had the whole day at your disposal while Harland was at his place of employment? Not too difficult, I think, to find an opportunity to take his gun out of the drawer that wasn't locked, and hide it in your own room. After dinner, you went upstairs with Harland. You could have fetched the gun and been outside in the shrubbery with time to spare before he set out on his walk. And after your talk with Esther Marne, the study window was not too far away; and not much danger of being seen, with the blackout curtains drawn across every window. You were very clever, Mr. Wilmot, but you made one mistake. You said to Robin Thurlow that the doctor had gone to the study to write love letters. I can sympathise with your frame of mind. The danger was over as far as you were concerned, and everything was arranged so that Guy Harland would pay for your sins. It was a relief, I'm sure, and you were a little light-headed, and the remark to Mr. Thurlow was just a joke. But what put it into your mind if you hadn't seen Doctor Fraser, with a complicated formula, perhaps, scribbled down on a sheet of pink, scented note-paper?"

"Thurlow didn't, say—"

"He didn't remember . . . then. But I'll wager he's thought about it since, if you want to put the matter to the test." (Such a move, he knew, would be both unpopular and unconvincing, but he didn't feel called upon to point that out.) Wilmot shook his head in a dazed way, and Maitland went on relentlessly: "I see you don't think much of the idea. But how did you know about the pink note-paper, Mr. Wilmot?"

"Guy told me . . . that must have been it."

"*Before* you talked to Robin Thurlow in the billiard- room. Come now, that's not just unlikely, its impossible!"

"I . . . don't know—"

"You may be interested if I tell you, Mr. Wilmot, that the existence of the pink note-paper was previously known only to the police. And—shall we say?—one other. Just as the fact that the drawer Guy Harland kept his gun in was unlocked could have been known only to him . . . and to the man who 'borrowed' the gun. That is twice you have betrayed yourself. How did you know these things innocently?"

"You're making a mistake. I haven't admitted—"

"You've told me enough, Mr. Wilmot . . . more than enough." He paused, and all his attention was concentrated on the man he was attacking. He did not know the court was silent, that Stringer was holding his breath beside him, that Garfield had half risen in an agony of indecision as to whether he ought to intervene. He saw only Harry Wilmot, and he spoke to him directly, as though they were alone. "You were a traitor," he said, "over and over again. Not only your country . . . not only your oath of allegiance: you betrayed your friend, the people who gave you hospitality, and—at the last—the woman who loved you. Did she die easily, Wilmot, when she came to meet you last night? And as a final act of treachery, when your German friends were beaten, you broke faith with the idea you had served . . . you forgot whatever dreams you had and went quietly back to the safest job you knew, where no one was likely to ask you awkward questions, or ever suppose—" He stopped short, and looked round the court as though he, in his turn, was bewildered by what was going on. As he caught the Judge's eye he said, quietly: "That's all, my lord. Need I go on?"

"You have said quite enough, Mr. Maitland," said Mr. Justice Conroy firmly. Counsel sat down suddenly, and brought up his left hand to cover his eyes. The Judge looked at him reflectively, and then turned to the witness. Wilmot tried to assume an air of bravado, but wilted a little under the directness of Conroy's gaze.

"After what has happened, I must ask you to remain within call, Mr. Wilmot." (His glance at the usher was expressive, and could have left no one in any doubt that he meant to be obeyed.) "I shall adjourn the court for ten minutes," he added. "Mr. Garfield, I should like to see you during this period." He raised his voice a little as he added: "And you, Mr. Maitland, if you please."

CHAPTER 20

THURSDAY to FRIDAY, after the verdict

" **B**ut what would you have said to Mr. Conrad," asked Jenny, that evening, "if the Judge hadn't taken over just then?" Antony thought this an unfair question, and said so. "I don't see what I could have said," he added. "She was better at hating than loving, in my estimation."

"It was surely," said Derek, "anxiety on her husband's behalf that brought her to you. After all, that's what you were aiming at."

"He was also her meal ticket," said Antony crudely. "And if you're going to remind me that she's dead, my love," he added, catching Jenny's eye, "I am perfectly well aware of it."

"Then tell me," said Jenny diplomatically, "what happened next."

"We got down to the question of admitting her statement. We couldn't have got it admitted, you know, without Garfield's goodwill. And it's lucky there's no question of an appeal."

But Jenny was impatient of technicalities. "Well, what did she say?" she demanded.

"She said that Harland gave her the cigarette case, and she kept it and gave it to Wilmot," said Derek. Antony and his uncle exchanged pitying glances, and Sir Nicholas said emphatically:

"If you are contemplating matrimony, my dear Stringer, you should realise from the outset that when a woman asks for information she expects details. Above all, she wants to know why." Derek looked harassed, and seemed to be considering some form of protest, but the older man had already turned to Jenny.

"You must understand that Mrs. Conrad was not concerned to make things easy for the Defence. What we gathered about her motives was mainly inferential. It seems obvious, however, that she was at one time— er—extremely attached to Wilmot—"

198 | SARA WOODS

"She'd gone in off the deep end over him," interrupted Antony, impatient of this circumlocution. Sir Nicholas shuddered, and glanced despairingly heavenwards. "Well, think of it . . . it was obvious, anyway. There was Conrad, an up and coming sort of chap with plenty to offer, but it took him five years or so to persuade her to marry him. In other words, she didn't take the plunge until Wilmot returned to England and she was sure there was nothing doing in that quarter. To get back to 1942, she knew he was on embarkation leave, which probably put her in a state of mind to agree to anything he wanted."

"She had already," Derek reminded him, "been keeping him informed on the progress Doctor Fraser was making."

"Yes, but she didn't admit that. She didn't admit she knew why Wilmot wanted 'something everybody knew was Guy Harland's' either . . . she said he told her it was for a joke, and I didn't press her, but obviously it was a lie. It was Wilmot, of course, who whistled the 'Serenade', as a signal for her to open the morning-room window. Neither of them seems to have had any doubt she'd come up with something . . . in view of Harland's careless habits, I suppose that was reasonable. Anyway, what she had got was his fountain-pen, which she picked up in the lab. The cigarette case was obviously better, because everybody knew he was in the habit of leaving it about, and no one would have been surprised to know he had dropped it in the study. So she took the opportunity which offered, and gave that to Wilmot instead. The advantages of having a scapegoat were obvious from his point of view."

"Well, yes, of course, but why did he—?"

"I can tell you what I think," said Antony. "It's based partly on what Sykes told me, partly on Esther Conrad's statement, and partly on a talk I had with Hugh Torrington after the court rose."

"And a good deal of guesswork," put in Sir Nicholas, unkindly.

"A good deal of guesswork," agreed Antony. "Well then, I think Harry Wilmot was one of those clever, rather introspective chaps who have a hell of a time at school; and I think he was one of those people who couldn't take it in their stride, but resented it bitterly. The same thing happened when he was called up: Torrington told me he couldn't stand any sort of ragging, though he learned to dissimulate pretty well. To go back: he spent a long vacation with his grandmother in Germany, and had the time of his life there. Witness the fact that he returned again and again—every year from 1931 to 1937. The general was an important figure in his own district, and for the first time Wilmot found himself made a fuss of, taken seriously. The next bit is pure guessing . . . no, it's more than that, because it's what must have happened."

"Deduction," said Derek, "is probably the word you want."

"If it had just been a matter of sowing his mental wild oats," said Antony, ignoring the interruption, "well, better men than he have done that. But obviously he made friends in Germany, and someone must have got in touch with him in England after the war started. And at that point, instead of screaming for the nearest policeman, he started quite seriously to consider what could be done. I don't know, of course, if there had been any previous incidents; probably not. But certainly his friendship with Hugh Torrington, and his frequent visits to Burnham Green, must have set him thinking about possibilities. Or the tip that Fraser's habits would bear investigation may have come from outside."

"What happened to-day must have been a bit of a shock to Torrington," said Geoffrey Horton. He was in a silent mood, and inclined to sound apologetic.

"Pretty bad. He's one of those chaps who can't resist a hard-luck story, always on the side of the underdog. When he was giving evidence I felt he was sorry for Harland, in spite of what he must have thought of him. I didn't realise at that stage, of course, that his friendship for Wilmot had been based on that . . . on pity for a man who always got a rough deal, if only in his own estimation."

"To be honest with you," said Geoffrey, "I thought it was Conrad you were after. I didn't agree, but at least it seemed more sensible—"

"I didn't see why Conrad should have put the plan into operation before Fraser had finished the dirty work for him. To a lesser degree that applied to Thurlow; he could have insinuated himself deliberately into the household, for all I knew, but he still had a week's leave to come, he'd have given it that long, anyway . . . and with the added advantage of having less people around after Hugh and Harry Wilmot had gone back from their leave."

"It all sounds delightfully obvious," murmured Sir Nicholas.

"The only thing I am certain of," said Antony, candidly, "is that it was a carefully thought out plan, complete to the last detail: both for getting possession of the laboratory reports, and for incriminating Harland. The one thing Wilmot couldn't control was his own movements as a member of His Majesty's Army. That's why he had to move before the series of experiments was completed—and why the plan was altered and Harland taken to Germany, I expect; because obviously it would have been easier to leave him to be quietly dealt with by our own authorities, which is what would have happened, on the evidence as it stood."

"But in the event," said Sir Nicholas, meditatively, "you think the . . . the final formula for the new culture was produced by *Herr* Gunther?"

"I think so," said Antony, again. "I don't know."

"Wilmot has a lot to answer for," said Stringer, rejoining the conversation suddenly.

"I meant every word I said to him in court," said Maitland, with a vehemence that contrasted oddly with the light tone he had been using. "The . . . the basic treachery might be forgiven him: who's to know how things look to the other man? But the rest—"

"It is ironic to think," said Sir Nicholas, "that if Wilmot had returned from the war and married Esther Conrad, Guy Harland would almost certainly have been found guilty to-day, instead of being acquitted."

"It may be ironic," said Antony, with feeling. "I find it a damned uncomfortable thought." Jenny, sensitive as always to his mood, asked quickly:

"What will happen now?"

"To Wilmot? Not my department, thank goodness. It's up to Sykes, I should think."

*

But Inspector Sykes, arriving in chambers the following afternoon just as Antony was on the point of leaving, shook his head sadly.

"It isn't legal proof, Mr. Maitland . . . it's nothing like legal proof."

"That, I am thankful to say, Inspector, doesn't worry me at all." Antony's spirits seemed to have revived since the previous evening. "Reasonable doubt was all I wanted, and on that basis—"

"You got your acquittal. But you didn't help me prove—"

"I told you," said Maitland, "how it would be. I didn't need to prove anything against Wilmot . . . only that he framed Harland. The Prosecution's case fell to the ground there, and I didn't need anything more; because the German evidence, alone, wasn't worth a row of beans. But the rest follows logically, you know."

"And how would you like to present a case to a jury that was based on logic, and nothing more?" Sykes was nettled, and showed it, and Antony smiled at him with quick sympathy.

"So now the work begins. I wish you joy, Inspector."

"Well, now," said Sykes. "That's 'appen too much to expect. But I think," he added, brightening, "that we can get him for the murder of Mrs. Conrad. You see, it was like this—"

*

Twenty minutes later, Antony left chambers. He was alone, because he had lingered for a word with Willett about next week's programme, but he had gone no more than a couple of paces before he heard someone speak his name, and turned to find himself face to face with Guy Harland.

"I was waiting for you," said Harland, obviously. "Can we talk?"

"Do you want to come up—?"

"I'd rather walk; do you mind?"

"Not a bit. We'll go down on the Embankment," Maitland decided. But Harland was in no hurry to open whatever subject was on his mind and they got quite a distance and came to a halt leaning on the wall and looking out across the river, before he spoke again.

"Somehow or other," he said, "I didn't seem to say much to you yesterday. In the way of thanks, I mean."

"You said all that was necessary." Antony turned, and gave his companion a long, clear look. "That wasn't what you brought me down here for," he declared.

"Well, I might have tried to write it," said Harland. "It's always so difficult to say things like that. But the thing is . . . I can't find Mary." The words came in a rush, but Maitland was looking out across the river again, and took his time about replying.

"I gave you her address," he said at length. "The one she left with me, that is."

"Oh, she had been living there," admitted Harland. "But she left earlier in the week, and the landlady didn't know—"

"What about the travel agency?"

"I saw them, too. She hadn't been in since Saturday. They thought it must be "flu." The words came savagely. He turned for the first time to look full at his companion. "I've got to find her, Maitland," he said.

"I'm sorry." said Antony, at a loss. "If I hear anything—"

"You might, don't you think? She might get in touch with you?" His tone was eager, but after a moment he went on more quietly: "You see, I'd given up hope . . . I never thought it was possible that I'd be free again. Then yesterday, I had to start again . . . living, trying to live." He paused and looked down at the dark water, and said almost as though he were speaking to himself: "I haven't much to offer her, God knows; but at least, thanks to you, I can offer her my name again."

*

Antony, who had his own plans for that evening, finished up by giving his former client dinner; and evolving over the liqueurs some fairly impractical schemes for tracing Mary Harland. It was therefore with mixed feelings that he received the news, conveyed to him by Jenny in the upstairs hall, that Mrs. Harland was waiting to see him; had been there, in fact, since seven o'clock.

"Why on earth didn't you tell me when I phoned?" he demanded.

"I thought, perhaps, it was business." Jenny eyed him consideringly. "Wasn't it?" she asked.

"In a way," said Antony, making for the living-room door. "I was having dinner with her husband."

"Well, she ate yours," said Jenny. "So that's all right, isn't it? I'll make some tea," she added, "you may need it," and went away to the kitchen.

Antony, who privately felt that something stronger might be indicated, pushed open the door of the living-room and went in. He crossed to his usual place, with his back to the fire, and looked down at the visitor. "You're not going to leave the poor chap high and dry, are you?" he asked, without preamble.

Mary Harland showed no signs of surprise at this rather unceremonious greeting. She eyed him for a moment, and then said with equal bluntness: "I hoped you'd tell me, Mr. Maitland, whether that's what he wants."

"Oh, lord!" said Antony, ruefully. He gave her his sudden smile, and enquired in an amused tone: "Hadn't you better see him, and find out?"

"I lost my nerve," she said, frankly. "I don't often do that, but after so long—"

He turned to look down at the fire, and gave it an encouraging kick. "Are you sure what you want, Mrs. Harland?" he asked gently. "Is that what's troubling you?"

"No." It was quietly said, but it carried utter certainty. She sat forward in her chair, and went on earnestly: "When I knew Guy might be alive, I wondered, of course. Only then I knew, whatever happened, I couldn't marry Philip. And when I had been to the court and actually seen him . . . I told you I didn't care what he'd done, and in a way that was true, I thought I could make myself forget. But now I know he really was innocent . . . and you believed him, but I didn't . . . I'm putting this awfully badly. Can you understand at all?"

"I think I understand." He left his contemplation of the fire, and gave her the sharp enquiring look she had seen on their previous meetings. "Your husband, I may tell you, is very anxious to find you."

"What is he going to do?"

"He's going back to Brightsea. There'll be difficulties, of course. I'm sure if you felt you couldn't face it—"

"I could face . . . that." It was her turn to look away now. "If only I hadn't been such a fool," she said.

Maitland looked down at her, and was not conscious of the shabby tweeds, or the fact that a dispassionate observer must that evening have seen only a tired woman with no pretensions to beauty. He thought there was something gallant about the way she held herself; and did not suppose for a moment that she had not faced the problems ahead with her usual clear-sighted courage.

"Mrs. Harland!" he said, and saw her come sharply out of her reverie, and begin to fumble for handbag and gloves. A moment later she was on her feet.

"I'm sorry," she said. "I meant to thank you, and instead I've just talked about myself."

"What do you mean to do?"

"I must see Guy, of course. I know . . . I must do that. But it's too late, isn't it, Mr. Maitland? I can't help him when he knows—" She held out her hand to him, and started to turn away; he took it, and held it, and said again sharply:

"Mrs. Harland!"

"I ought to go. I mustn't trouble you any longer."

"You can go when I've finished what I want to say," he told her. "It's in the nature of a confession."

"I don't understand."

"You gave me a message for your husband. I didn't deliver it, not in the form you intended." He paused a moment, and met her questioning look steadily. "There are very few men who would relish being told 'I think you're a traitor, but I love you just the same." He heard her catch her breath, and went on quickly. "So I told him you believed in him, and always had. Was that right?" He released her hand then, and smiled at her reassuringly. "I'm adding to your burdens, I realise that . . . but if I were you, I don't think I'd disillusion him."

*

Half an hour later, Sir Nicholas, encouraged to make a late call by seeing the living-room light from the square as he came home from the theatre, found Jenny and Antony drinking the tea that their visitor had refused. "I sent her back to her husband," Antony explained. His tone was complacent to the point of smugness.

His uncle sank into his favourite chair, and eyed the teapot with disfavour. "I suppose nothing will ever keep you from meddling," he complained. "What do you suppose the—er—harvest will be?"

"*I* don't know," said Antony. But added seriously, a moment later, "they need each other, I think."

"A gratifying thought, no doubt. To-day's good deed!" said Sir Nicholas, caustically. He accepted a cup of tea absent-mindedly from Jenny, and looked his nephew up and down. "However, I find myself unexpectedly in sympathy with Harland. He gave me the perfect comment on Paul Garfield when the case closed yesterday."

"Now, look here, Uncle Nick," protested Antony.

"It's bad enough with the newspapers—" Sir Nicholas grinned at him.

"I was not referring to that unfortunate comparison," he assured the younger man, "though no doubt it will take some living down. I happened to be close at hand when Garfield spoke to him after his acquittal; Harland seemed dazed, I thought, and no wonder. But as our friend moved away to speak to you I heard him mutter to himself: 'a man cannot make him laugh, he drinks no wine.' And I thought the comment well expressed."

Antony said, "Extremely well," but he still sounded suspicious. Jenny laughed, and said:

"Have another cup of tea, Uncle Nick."

"At this hour? I shouldn't be able to sleep," said Sir Nicholas, outraged. And looked down with horrified disgust at his empty cup.